THE CONSCIENCE OF A KING

The Medieval Saga Series
Book Six

David Field

SAPERE
BOOKS

THE CONSCIENCE
OF A KING

Published by Sapere Books.

24 Trafalgar Road, Ilkley, LS29 8HH,
United Kingdom

saperebooks.com

ISBN: 978-1-80055-935-6

I

France, 1229

They were bringing back the dead and wounded. It would have been difficult to tell which was which, were it not for the shrieks of agony as those carrying the not quite dead stumbled on the wet, uneven ground between the tents. To ten-year-old Simon de Montfort, it was an irritating distraction as he struggled with his Latin psalter in the late afternoon sun. He hoped that his father was not among the casualties, but if he was then no doubt the news would be brought to him eventually.

It had been the same, day in, day out, for almost a year. His father, also named Simon, was somewhere in the vanguard of the mighty force that was laying siege to Toulouse, which the hated Count Raymond had seized back from them the previous year. It had come into their temporary possession during the early stages of what, since Simon's first year in this life, had called itself a Crusade. The enemy against whom they notionally fought — who were called Cathars — seemed, from what Simon had seen of them, to be no more dangerous than ploughmen, stonemasons and priests, but they were alleged to be a mighty threat to the entire fabric of Christendom. This, at least, had been the opinion of a previous Pope who had styled himself 'Innocent', and who had first given the blessing of Christ to the ill-assorted assembly of warriors, religious zealots and bloodthirsty land-grabbers who made up the supposedly Christian host.

At some stage in the past Simon's father had been appointed as the recognised leader of this army, and under his leadership it had laid waste to most of the Languedoc. This was part of what they called 'le Midi': that area of France from the Loire to the southern coast that was not so firmly in the grip of the Capetian kings who ruled from Paris. In the Languedoc, royal dominance was under constant challenge from powerful barons such as Raymond of Toulouse, and King Philippe had been secretly appreciative of the drive south by forces under the notional command of the Pope. In reality, the army was led by men such as Simon's father who were under feudal bondage to the king, so that whatever land they overran would be held under his suzerainty.

While Simon had been growing up in military camps on the fringes of one siege after another, they had overrun a good deal of land in the name of Christ. The unwarlike — and largely unarmed — people who had been besieged, killed, or burned out of their villages as the Crusade moved south hadn't seemed much of a danger to Simon, to judge by the few who had been dragged back into the camp tied like hogs, and abused for the ribald amusement of the rough men at arms. Simon had learned at a very early age not to question the reason for all this loss of human life, but grew more convinced, as the years went by, that it was all about land and titles.

Not that his father seemed to be lacking in estates. He was already the feudal lord of what they called Montfort-l'Amaury, a large area of rich pasture just north of Paris that had been first granted, over a century earlier, to the Amaury de Montfort after whom Simon's brother was named. Although Simon's father had benefitted from a substantial dowry when he married Simon's mother, the union had not added to the de

Montfort estates, which remained centred around Montfort-l'Amaury.

Simon himself had been born in the castle from which his parents ruled this estate with a strong hand and a religious fervour that had allegedly spurred them to take up Pope Innocent's call to exterminate Catharism, but it seemed to Simon that their primary motivation had been the desire to acquire more land in le Midi.

Simon and his family had until recently enjoyed a luxurious, and largely undisturbed, existence behind the castle walls of Toulouse, until Count Raymond had begun to fight back. While they had been rooting out more Cathars in the Foix region — with Simon in his parentally imposed role of younger son hidden away in a tent studying religious tracts — Raymond had taken back his birthright. Now, the notional Crusader army was back out in the countryside, laying siege once again to the town that Simon Senior had so well fortified during his years of occupation.

Today had been the first day of this siege, and there had been Crusader casualties — the ones whose groans had disturbed his studies. Simon put down the book his tutor had set him to study in order to find his older brother Amaury, who at twenty-three years of age was already a seasoned warrior who commanded one wing of their father's force. He would be able to advise Simon whether or not he could look forward to a return to the warm firesides and feather-down beds inside Toulouse Castle.

Amaury was knocking back the contents of a wine gourd when Simon found him in the tent in which some of his companions in arms were having their wounds dressed by monks. Skilled in matters of healing, the monks travelled with the Crusader forces in return for their keep. Amaury had spent the entire Crusade riding alongside their father and his immediate entourage, hoping for the opportunity to win his spurs in combat. He grimaced as Simon walked up to him and asked about their father.

'He is supervising the dispatch of those who sought to break free in a sortie from the main town gate, but he sent me back with the main force before I could witness what was to happen to those who had been captured. Father ordered me back to camp without further delay. The nearest I came to glory in battle was finishing off some old man whose leg had been hacked off at the thigh. His screams were drowning out the orders from my serjeants — I hit him hard on the head with my mace, and he fell silent.'

'Was there much plunder to be had?' Simon asked sceptically.

'None that I could see, else I would have claimed it,' his brother replied with a smirk.

'And the siege remains unsuccessful?' Simon asked.

Amaury nodded as he took another swig. 'Father fortified the town too well while we dwelt within it, and Count Raymond has many men positioned on its walls.'

'Why do we pursue this futile campaign?' was Simon's next question.

'Because the Pope wills it. He fears the Cathars, not for their wealth or their military might, but because they challenge the word of God and the authority of Rome. And the Pope clearly has the keeping of God's will, and can preserve from the fires of Hell all those who do his bidding. Even King Philippe is anxious to obey the former Pope Innocent's orders. Although he pretends to be indifferent to our campaign, he will do nought to stop it ever since Innocent placed Raymond of Toulouse under excommunication. These lands that we currently harass and occupy were once Raymond's, as you know. Father hopes that they will one day be ours in perpetuity, if our new Pope, Honorius, is pleased with our progress.'

'So the Vicar of God awards lands to those who slaughter fellow Christians?' Simon asked with a disapproving shake of the head.

'He denies that they are Christians,' Amaury reminded his younger brother, 'which is why this is called a Holy Crusade.'

Unsure of where his brother's loyalties lay, and mindful of their father's sudden temper if challenged as to his religious fervour, Simon opted to remain silent on the subject. 'Where is Mother?' he asked.

Amaury put down the wine gourd, belched, then let out a raucous laugh. 'While cheering on our men as they lay siege to the town, she espied two of Count Raymond's men seeking to lead an ox to a place of safety. After ordering two of Fulk's foot soldiers to secure the beast, she had it brought back to camp and slaughtered. Then she ordered the cook to run it through its length with a lance, which she then commanded two prisoners to hold over the fire to roast the carcass. The last I saw of her, she was threatening the poor wretches that if the ox was either burned or too raw when served at table, they would be the next to roast over the same fire. What fate befell them I know not, but either way there will be roast meat for supper.'

Simon was in no hurry to eat, but he had been trained by his mother to appear on time for all formal meals, wherever they might be served, and a large tent on a battlefield was no exception. It was by far the largest tent present, and there could be no mistaking the de Montfort battle standards rammed into the ground on either side of the entrance flap.

The soldiers on either side of the entrance bowed their heads slightly in token recognition, and moved their lances upright to allow Simon to enter. He was immediately assailed by the smell of roast meat, and was startled by his father's bellowed command to approach the table.

Simon Senior was clearly well into his cups, and his wife Amicia looked on with concern as he rose to his feet and swayed alarmingly. He only remained upright by hanging onto the loaded board, on which roast oxen was the most obvious dish, with fruit and cheeses a less appetising alternative. However, there was clearly no shortage of rich claret. The smell of this sprayed from Simon Senior's breath as he commanded his oldest son, Amaury, to kneel before him, then drew his sword.

Everyone held their breath as Simon Senior looked down at his firstborn and grimaced.

'This day has been long in coming, but today, as we stood before the battlements of Toulouse, I felt the chill of death upon me. It is fitting that there is someone of noble rank to continue the work of retrieving what is ours from the thieving hand of Count Raymond and his tribe of heathens. You have proved your worth in battle, and today you shall be known to all the world for your courage and supremacy over mere soldiers. Kneel, Amaury of Montfort.'

Amaury did as requested, with a slightly fearful eye on the massive blade that his father brought down gently, but unsteadily, onto his left shoulder, narrowly missing his neck in the process. Then, by some miracle, Simon was able to lift it upright and transfer it to the right shoulder without cutting off Amaury's head.

'Rise, *Sir* Amaury de Montfort.'

Shortly afterwards, at the insistence of his wife, the older Simon was lifted by two attendants and carried to his cot.

II

The next morning Amaury was in full chainmail and pacing up and down in front of his tent, holding the bridle of his warhorse, as Simon bid him good morning. Their father had been late in rising.

'My first day as a knight, and I'm kept waiting, along with my men and the standard bearer, while the citizens of Toulouse are afforded the opportunity to reload their mangonels and sharpen their arrowheads,' said Amaury grumpily.

'Mean you to renew the siege?' Simon asked.

'What would *you* do? Sit and read your precious Bible?'

'At least I can employ it to seek God's intervention for the souls that will be lost in yet another day's meaningless slaughter,' Simon replied, just as their father rode up on his destrier and commanded Amaury to follow him. As he kicked his horse's sides with his spurred boots in order to depart the war camp, Simon Senior looked down at his younger son.

'Look after your mother when I am gone,' he instructed.

Two hours later, while nodding sleepily through his psalter Simon was roused by distant wails and shouts. He slipped out through the tent flap in time to see a crude stretcher slung between two horses being led back into camp by Amaury. His mother scurried on foot in order to keep up with it, all the while holding the hand of the fully armoured man who lay on the canvas. With a feeling of dread, Simon stepped into view and met his brother's mournful glare.

'Father is probably dead,' he was told. 'A rock from the battlements hit him square on the helm, and there is much blood seeping from it. We are taking him to Brother Ignatius, since his is the best physic, but see to your prayers of intervention for his immortal soul.'

Simon's strongest memory following the death of his father was of his mother's heartbroken wailing at the Requiem Mass a week later, while his father's body was being preserved for the long journey back to its designated burial place in Montfort. He also remembered Amaury's wild curses when advised that the defences of Toulouse had been so effectively organised that the rock that had killed their father may well have been launched by a woman.

'By God's blood they will pay for this!' he vowed as he left their mother in a weeping heap on the ground. He caught sight of a white-faced Simon and took him roughly by the shoulder. 'You must swell the ranks of those who will tear Count Raymond's heart from his chest. I shall give orders that you are to begin your battle training on the morrow.'

It seemed to be generally accepted that Amaury would assume command of their late father's forces. However, the unlikelihood that he would also be entrusted with the direction of the entire Crusade in his father's stead was confirmed when a messenger arrived from the court of King Philippe, to whom news had been sent of the death of Simon Senior. It was announced to a general meeting of all soldiers convened a week after the funeral Mass that His Majesty had assumed overall direction of the Crusade, but that day-to-day management of battle had been devolved to Sir Amaury de Montfort, who was confirmed in all of his father's lands and estates. By then, he had one more soldier in training.

The morning after the Mass, Simon had looked up from his reading as the tent flap was thrown wide open, and in strode Fulk de Sevres, the standard bearer to the de Montforts. He was a giant of a man, well over six feet in height, and with the girth of an ox. He was rarely known to smile for any reason other than seeing a man fall under his sword or battle-axe, and he was legendary for his cruel punishment of any who failed to carry out his orders to the letter. He was both feared and admired by every warrior who wore the Crusader surcoat of white with a red cross, and to even question his wisdom or authority was to risk the most terrifying of reprisals.

'On your feet, boy!' he yelled.

Simon shot up and stood there trembling as Fulk's mouth opened in the faint suggestion of a smile.

'Until today, you were entitled to my respect as the son and brother of my commanders in the field. Today you have become a recruit into the force of which I am proud to carry the standard aloft, and you must earn my respect all over again in your new role. You will forget who you are, but remember who *I* am — are we agreed on that?'

'Yes — sir,' Simon replied in a voice that he hoped did not sound to Fulk as weak as it sounded to him.

'Very well. Now, strip down to your hose.'

'I beg your pardon?'

'Do you suffer any defect in your hearing?'

'No — sir.'

'Then never — *ever* — request that I repeat an order. In the time you take to do so, you could be run through by an enemy lance, or pierced through your mail by a well-aimed shaft. Understood?'

'Understood.'

'Then why are you still dressed as if for Mass in the cathedral?'

Simon hastily slipped off his surcoat, tunic and undershirt, until he stood in only his hose, shivering in the stiff breeze that was blowing through the still open tent flap.

'Outside, and run to the armourer's tent,' Fulk ordered him. 'The important word there is "run". And I mean *quickly*!'

Simon shot through the tent flap as if fired from a bow, and ran as hard as he could to the tent inside which several blacksmiths were forging new blades, while Hugh the Armourer was sharpening old ones. He was beaten to the place by Fulk, who glared at Simon pityingly as he doubled over in search of breath.

On a command from Fulk, one of the blacksmiths put down his hammer and walked to the side of the tent, where a crude anvil lay partly hidden by guy ropes. He lifted it with a grunt, walked over and dropped it at Simon's feet. Fulk nodded and smirked at Simon.

'Pick that up and run with it to the riverbank over there. When you have done that, pick it up again and run back here. I shall be waiting — and counting. You will be required to do all of that five times, and I shall not be impressed if the time you take on the fifth occasion is any slower than on the first. Understand?'

'Yes,' Simon replied weakly.

'Before you even *think* about questioning why you are to do this, thereby incurring my mailed fist across your cheek, be advised that it is designed to build up your stamina and improve the strength of your arm. You would seem not to lack height for a boy of your age, but you lack muscle. Only when you possess that will you be able to even *lift* a sword, let alone take on an enemy with it. Now, pick up that anvil and start running.'

If Simon imagined that this would be the worst of it, he was wildly mistaken. After four arm-breaking, lung-torturing days of running backwards and forwards to the riverbank carrying an anvil — by the end of which he had begun to do it in a time that seemed to earn Fulk's grudging satisfaction — he was brought back to the riverbank, handed a blunt battle-axe, and told to begin felling trees, first with his right hand and then with his left. Two days into this, Fulk said the first thing for a week that had not been a sharply barked order.

'Your left arm would seem to be stronger than your right.'

'I wouldn't know,' Simon gasped in between cutting blows with the axe.

'That was a statement, boy, not a question. When I seek your opinion, you will know.'

The only days when Simon was spared the torture were those on which Fulk was commanded into battle by Amaury, and Simon began to guiltily hope that his tormentor would be killed in the seemingly endless siege that was being waged against Toulouse. During one of their rare evening suppers together — when Simon could barely lift either of his arms in order to carve meat from the roasts that lay on the board before him, and was obliged to instruct one of the pages who attended them to do so on his behalf — he was advised by a disgruntled Amaury that their ultimate commander in chief, King Philippe, seemed obsessed with the retaking of Toulouse rather than the extermination of the Cathars, who were in the meantime being allowed to continue unchallenged in their heretical practices in the outlying villages and towns. The Pope was, at the same time, seeking to recruit new armies to defend Jerusalem. It appeared that what had in the meantime become known as the 'Albigensian Crusade' was no higher than second in the priorities of those who had launched it in the first place.

The de Montforts were, seemingly, reduced to being a private army in the service of a king who was determined to extend the Kingdom of the Franks into what he was now boasting was a new nation called 'France'.

Into the second year of the fruitless siege, Amaury began to grow impatient and ordered small raiding parties into the surrounding countryside, to harass villages and leave their inhabitants in no doubt that God was watching their sinful observances, and would shortly be sending His soldiers to burn out their heresy. Amaury did not bother to inform the king that he was engaging in this tactic, which he justified to himself — and to Simon, when he enquired why Fulk was absent — by claiming that it kept up the morale of his men to be able to plunder and rape defenceless farming families. Simon tried to protest that this was both inhuman and an unjustified dilution of the forces that should be aimed at Toulouse. He was angrily told by his much older, and more experienced, brother that when he was a fighting man himself, perhaps his counsels would be listened to.

This made Simon more determined to work at becoming a soldier. On those occasions when Fulk dragged him from his bed at first light to continue the regime that would make a man of him, he gritted his teeth, steeled his resolve, and set out to impress the source of all his physical suffering. By the time he was fifteen he was declared ready for weapons training, beginning with the sword.

'Your first lunge is to the leg, like this.' Fulk demonstrated as he made a feint towards Simon's right leg, from which he jumped back, narrowly missing the blade that Fulk had pulled back at the last moment. 'Then you lunge to the arm, this way,' Fulk went on, 'and finally, to the head. You must be ready to parry each of these strokes in turn. On this day of days, you may ask questions, before you lift a sword for the first time.'

'How will I know which blow is to come first?' Simon asked. 'Is there some sign given by my adversary as to which part of me he will strike first?'

'No, it is in the order I said,' Fulk replied testily. 'It is always in that order — leg, arm, head.'

Simon shook his head, but was reluctant to challenge what he had just heard.

'What do you not understand?' Fulk pressed.

'I understand, but am at a loss to see why a fight that could end in death should be conducted like one of my mother's chess games, with the opening moves agreed in advance.'

'It has always been that way while I have been a fighting man,' replied Fulk.

'So,' Simon speculated, 'if my opponent is expecting my first lunge to be at his leg, why may I not take him by surprise and cut off his head?'

Fulk stared at him in astonishment, then burst out laughing. 'It would certainly come as a surprise,' he snorted, 'but it would be against the rules of chivalry, and any man engaging in such an unworthy action would be shunned.'

'But he would still be alive,' Simon countered.

Fulk handed Simon the second sword that had been lying in the grass beside him. 'I can only teach you the ways I have always known, the ways which I was taught. This is how you parry.'

For the next couple of hours, Simon grudgingly followed Fulk in the thrust-parry process that seemed so pointless, while asking himself whether he would prefer to be regarded as a dead man of honour, or a living cheat. Then it was on to his first lesson in axe-wielding, in respect of which there could be no argument that the target was anything other than the head. Finally, he took up the lance, which he would only be required to carry if on horseback, or in a line of infantry seeking to unhorse knights charging towards them.

Three months later, Fulk declared him as ready as he'd ever be and took him to Hugh's tent to be fitted with his first mail suit, chausses that chafed his calves, gauntlets and helm. Simon detested the last of these, since it restricted his vision, until the armourer deferentially pointed out that only a direct blow from an axe could dent it, whereas bare-headed he could be split in two down to his neck by a mere sword blow.

The death of the hated Raymond of Toulouse in 1222 made no difference to the stalemate over Toulouse itself, since his son, also called Raymond, succeeded him and began a campaign to retake some of the remaining towns in the Languedoc that had been in Crusader hands. One of these was Carcassonne, a walled stronghold on a hill overlooking a wide plain two days' ride east of Toulouse.

When King Philippe died in 1223, succeeded by Louis VIII, and before the new monarch could send word west as to how the Crusade should be conducted, Amaury decided that the time had come for a show of strength in which the two competing armies could meet out in the open. He was tired of sieges, and if he could lure Raymond out by marching on Carcassonne, with the town itself the obvious prize for the victor, then perhaps some progress might be made. Over the course of this long drawn-out campaign, his mother had died of grief at the loss of her husband and another son, Guy, who had perished in much the same way during a fruitless siege on the township of Castelnaudary.

Simon was invited by Amaury to join the attempt on Carcassonne to watch and learn. He was now approaching his seventeenth birthday and was already an impressive six feet in height, with an obvious muscular development that was the result of the rigorous training he had undergone at the hands of Fulk de Sevres. Before sunrise on a sharp morning in early September, he presented himself to Hugh the Armourer, who tightened the straps on his chainmail before selecting a suitable sword from the rack at the rear of the tent, swirling it around to test its flexibility and strength. He then handed it to Simon.

'This is now your sword, sir. If and when it gets blunted in battle, bring it back to me and I will sharpen it. But unless it is shattered in action — in which case you will probably die immediately afterwards anyway — it will always be your sword, and you must care for it as if it were your child.'

As the men began to gather on the ground in front of the river, Simon collected his horse from its tented stable and led it out to join them. Fulk saw him approaching and grinned.

'My lord tells me that you are not to join the rout, but must watch from the sides. I have selected an escort of my best men, who will act as your personal bodyguard while explaining to you what is happening, and why.'

'And what if we are attacked?' Simon asked.

'Then God be with you,' Fulk replied with a grimace as he walked away and called the men into line.

As the sun rose fully in the autumn sky, the walls of Carcassonne caught the reflected shimmer of the armour of those who were preparing to defend it. The Crusader host was gathered in a wood on a hill overlooking the heavily fortified township in the valley, and Simon was near the back, surrounded on all sides by tense and surly seasoned warriors. Amaury was discussing tactics with several of his seconds in command, and there seemed to be some dispute regarding the wisdom of attacking the town in a direct frontal charge.

However, it was equally obvious from the tone of his voice that Amaury was ill-disposed to yet another slow siege, and was looking for a swift and decisive victory that day.

On his command, the main body of men began to descend the slope on horseback, leaving Simon and his group of a hundred or so to move forward to the edge of the wood in order to take their places. Led by Amaury, the Crusader horde gathered speed and thundered towards the northern gate of Carcassonne, then hastily dismounted as the arrows and rocks began to descend upon them from the town walls. The Crusaders began to fire back, and their front rank prepared the battering ram that was brought up to join them. Then the northern gates opened unexpectedly, and Amaury and his front ranks charged in with triumphant yells.

'That was too easy,' muttered a man by Simon's side who, to judge by the scars all over his face, was not watching his first engagement. The noise from inside the town walls grew in pitch until the screams and oaths were audible even a mile or so away, where the observing group remained in the wood. Then a sudden flash caught the corner of Simon's eye, and he looked north, to where it had come from. To his horror he could clearly see a sizeable force of heavily armoured men pounding south towards the town gates, and as they grew closer, the battle banners of Toulouse became more visible.

He looked back towards the northern gate of Carcassonne, where a strange scene was unfolding. Amaury and his men seemed to be retreating from the town, and each man in the rear ranks was walking backwards and holding a hostage in front of him as a human shield against the heavily armed soldiers who were driving them out. Amaury's front ranks were considerably depleted as they turned and stared fearfully at the

21

newly arrived force that was thundering towards them from the north. They were caught in the middle of a pincer trap.

Without a second thought, Simon yelled to those around him. 'To me! Take the enemy flank from the side!'

'We were supposed to be guarding you against danger, my lord,' one of his escort reminded him.

'The one in danger is my brother! I cannot sit here and watch his force slaughtered. The men down there are all your friends and comrades in arms. With me!'

He turned his horse's head and dug in the spurs. The horse leaped down the slope, gathering momentum as it went, and Simon had the satisfaction of hearing other horses behind him, some of which overtook his as they threw mud and stones into the air in their effort to engage the host to the north. The enemy suddenly became aware of their approach and flanked to the right to meet them. As the distance between the two groups narrowed, Simon feared that he had led the men into an impossible charge in which they were almost hopelessly outnumbered. But he might as well die now, rather than turn his horse's head and play the coward.

Just before the inevitable first impact, Simon leaped from his horse and began laying about in all directions with his sword. His very first victim in battle was beheaded in one stroke. The remaining torso fell onto the man to his left, who was Simon's next victim as he slashed down across the man's shoulder and removed his arm.

It never occurred to him that he might be in danger himself as he hacked his way determinedly through the enemy ranks, pausing only to wipe blood from his eyes. Slowly but surely the ranks ahead of him thinned, until suddenly he found himself confronting a Crusader in what was left of a white surcoat, who yelled urgently for him to hold back his hand. Simon lowered his sword arm, and only then realised that he was on the point of exhaustion.

A ragged cheer went up as the men who had followed him down the hill met up with their colleagues. Arms were thrown around steaming blood-soaked surcoats, while chainmail creaked to celebratory dances from those who had any remaining energy. From out of this joyful throng rode Amaury, with Fulk de Sevres by his side.

'Thank God you found the courage,' Amaury said. 'Should you wish to join the pillaging, feel free to follow me back into the town, where they will pay dearly for their stubbornness and trickery. But perhaps you might wish to return to camp, to convey news of our success.'

'Hold!' Fulk commanded as Simon retrieved his horse and swung into the saddle, turning its head in order to depart. Fulk sidled his horse up to Simon's, red-faced with embarrassment. 'Forgive me, my lord, I had forgotten that you are no longer apprenticed to me. From today I shall speak to you with the respect that you have earned, since you fought bravely and well. I wished merely to advise you that I am proud to carry the battle standard of *two* de Montforts.'

III

As he rode back towards the camp, Simon was nauseated by the stench of blood on his surcoat. He had not kept count of the number he had slain, but he would be surprised to learn that it was less than seven, and he wondered if it made any difference to the condition of his soul that he had killed in defence of his own life, and that of his brother and his comrades in arms. He was met at the camp entrance by enquiring grooms, to whom he passed on the news that Carcassonne had been overrun at last, before requesting that one of them summoned Brother Benedict to his tent. As well as being a skilled physician, Benedict was ordained, and could therefore hear Simon's urgent confession. After handing over his horse, and before heading for his own tent, he slipped out of the stinking surcoat and threw it with a cry of disgust onto the pile outside the armourer's tent. It would be collected by the washerwomen.

Simon was on his second cup of wine, served by his relieved steward Armand, by the time that Benedict ducked through the tent flap. His hands were tucked into the wide sleeves of his well-worn monastic smock as he bowed respectfully, then looked more closely at the blood on Simon's chainmail.

'You wish me to dress your wounds, sir?'

'In a sense. I have no physical wounds, but I fear for the damage I have today inflicted on my soul.'

Benedict looked meaningfully at the chainmail. 'That is not your blood?'

'Indeed not. If I had lost that much blood, I would be among those being carried back into camp even as we speak.'

'Then you have killed in battle?'

'At least seven times,' Simon admitted. 'Is there a penance hard enough to preserve my soul from God's wrath?'

'You are a Crusader, sir, and all those you kill in God's name add a further good mark upon your account with Him.'

'Is human conscience so slippery that taking the life of a fellow creature is not only not a sin, but is in fact a pious act if it is done at the behest of the Pope?' Simon asked sternly. 'Does His Holiness stand between us and God, diverting the blame to himself? If so, then his soul must be the blackest in the whole of Christendom.'

Benedict bowed his head in pious supplication. 'The Holy Father is God's representative in this wicked life, as you must know from your scripture learning, sir. All holy brothers such as myself serve him and the Mother Church without question. We are taught that to take the life of a heretic is a blessed act, and I cannot hear your confession if you have committed no sin.'

'The men I killed were in the army of Raymond of Toulouse,' Simon told the monk, 'and who is to know whether or not they were heretics?'

'This I cannot answer, sir, but I am led to believe that the followers of Count Raymond are protecting the heretics, and must therefore be accounted along with them.'

'So I have committed no sin by slaughtering seven fellow human beings?' Simon asked cynically. 'But were I to have sodomised one instead, I would need to make penance, is that what you are telling me?'

'If he were a heretic, the point would be a fine one,' was all that the simple cleric could offer. Simon dismissed him with a wave of the hand, an action he immediately regretted as his arm muscles reminded him that they had endured a hard morning. He flung himself into the soft chair at the side of his cot, and was mentally reliving every slash and squelch when the tent flap flew open, and Amaury threw a bundle onto the ground in front of him. It was a young girl.

'Since you missed all the plunder,' Amaury told him with a sneer, 'I brought you back this present. Her mother should be sufficient to amuse the men who took them both, so I saved her for you. Do with her as you wish — kill her if it pleases you — but I thank you once more for saving the day.'

He was gone as swiftly as he had arrived, and Simon looked down with pity at the shivering girl as she cowered as low as possible. Since it was a hot afternoon, Simon surmised that the shaking was prompted by fear, either for herself or for the mother who had been captured along with her.

Simon stood up, crossed to the entrance, and retrieved the woollen cloak he employed on cold nights. As he strode back towards the girl, she curled herself into a protective ball, and tried to flinch away from whatever kick or lash she feared was heading her way. Instead, Simon gently slipped the cloak over her shoulders and spoke as reassuringly as he could.

'This will keep you warm. I will not harm you, have no fear of that.'

The girl wrapped the cloak tightly around herself as she looked up briefly. Simon went back to his chair and studied her more closely as he waited for her to speak. She was slightly built and could be no more than twelve or thirteen years of age. Her black hair was cut severely short to her head, and she had dark brown eyes that somehow reminded him of a raven.

Eventually she looked up, and Simon asked for her name. There was a dry gargling whisper that he couldn't decipher, then the thought came to him that she might be thirsty. He took a second goblet from his bedside table, poured some red wine into it, walked over and handed it down to her.

'Your name again?' Simon asked.

'Antoinette. Antoinette of Bouriac.'

'Well, Antionette of Bouriac, where exactly *is* Bouriac, and how did you come to be in Carcassonne?'

The girl gave him a bitter hint of a smile. 'Bouriac is a village outside Carcassonne, where my mother and father kept an *auberge* before the soldiers came. Your soldiers, or those of Count Raymond, it made no difference, and we moved into the town for our own safety. We were staying with my uncle Bertrand, who was killed along with my father while trying to defend us. The brute who brought me here ran him through with his sword before ordering that I be brought back here, trussed like a hog behind his horse.'

Her voice had risen in condemnation as she spoke, and Simon opted not to advise her that the brute in question was probably his brother. But her answer had given him an idea.

'If your mother and father owned an *auberge*, you are experienced in serving food and wine?'

'Of course.'

Simon yelled, and Armand reappeared from where he had been standing outside the tent, awaiting any further order. Since the deaths of their parents and brother, Simon and Amaury had mostly kept separate tables in their respective tents, and were served by members of their own personal households. Their food — which consisted of whatever could be foraged from the surrounding countryside — was cooked for them both in the kitchen tent close by the river, near a ready supply of water should there be a fire.

'Armand, of late I have seen nought of the girl who served my meals — what was her name again?' Simon asked.

27

'Yvette, sir.'

'And is she still in my service?'

'Regrettably not, sir. When one of your brother's bowmen deserted at Castelnaudary, she went with him, or so I am informed. If he is caught and brought back, he will of course be put to death, but do you wish the girl pardoned?'

'That is not my immediate concern,' Simon replied. 'When she fled my service, did she leave aught behind in the way of clothing?'

'Only her service bliaut, with your family crest on its breast.'

'That will suffice. Bring it to me, since from memory the girl Yvette was little larger than this poor girl at my feet.'

Armand bowed out, and Simon smiled at the girl.

'In exchange for your life and honour, would you consent to enter my service as a serving wench?'

The girl nodded, and Simon sat deep in thought for a moment.

'With a change in fortune must come a change of name. "Antoinette" is too much of a mouthful when shouting orders, and since you remind me of a small blackbird, you will henceforth be known as "Merle". My meals are frugal, and I drink no more wine than the average man, so your duties will probably prove lighter than those to which you became accustomed in the *auberge*.'

Armand re-entered the tent carrying a pale blue gown that had sewn onto it the de Montfort family crest of a silver lion rampant with a forked tail on a field of red. On Simon's instructions he laid it on the ground and waited outside while Simon rose and made a display of turning his back on the girl while she slipped on the gown.

The hasty rustling behind him ceased, and he turned back with a smile.

'See that you serve me well. Now you will be formally introduced to your new taskmaster.'

Armand re-entered on the shouted summons and Simon pointed to Merle.

'This young lady is to replace Yvette in my service. Her name is Merle, and she is but a child of — thirteen?' he asked of Merle with a raised eyebrow.

'Seventeen,' she replied indignantly.

'She is apparently a slightly built girl of seventeen, Armand. See to it that she is properly trained in all her duties, and advise the household — and anyone else who may show an unhealthy interest in her — that she is reserved for the master. If any hand is laid upon her other than mine, that hand will be cut off. Am I understood?'

'Yes, sir,' Armand assured him as he bowed out of the presence, beckoning for Merle to follow him.

The sun was sinking low over the western hills as Simon sat studying his Bible for some reassurance that, as Brother Benedict had sought to assure him, there was no sin in killing a heretic. The tent flap opened silently, and Merle appeared with a wooden board loaded with cold meats, cheeses and fruit, while Armand followed behind with a flagon of wine. When Armand withdrew with a bow, Merle placed the food on the board and poured fresh wine into Simon's goblet. Then she stood to the side in deference as he reached for his paring knife, then looked up.

'You may not have been informed, but I do not wish to be observed when eating. It is a disorder left over from my mother's day, when she would comment adversely on my manners at board. You may withdraw.'

'You seek nothing further of me?' Merle asked softly.

'I think not, since there is more than enough to feed my feeble appetite this evening. If I wish for more wine, I will summon Armand, but you may leave me.'

When she looked hesitant, Simon grinned.

'You were not referring to food and wine, were you?'

She blushed, and her eyes fell to the ground. 'No, master. You have put it abroad that I am reserved for you, and I thought that perhaps when you had eaten...' She left the sentence unfinished, and Simon felt compassion for her.

'I reserved you for myself because I wished you not to suffer from the rough brutes who constitute our camp. They seem to regard every woman as their own to abuse.'

'I am no virgin, Master,' she told him with a face as red as the wine in his goblet. 'There were many soldiers who came to our *auberge*, and it was safer not to resist their rough demands.'

'*You* may not be a virgin,' Simon replied, 'but I *am*, should you find that possible to believe. I am barely a year older than you, and I choose not to court foul diseases from the camp prostitutes, or take a captured woman by brute force. I also believe the stricture that our Lord Jesus Christ gave us, that carnal pleasure should be confined to the marriage bed. You will only be required to satisfy one of my appetites, but for your own safety say nought of this in the hearing of others, if you do not wish to be violated in the mud by every lecherous man at arms in this miserable camp.'

A tear slid slowly down her cheek as she stood there fighting for the words. Eventually they came in a torrent. 'You are the first man I have known — my own uncle not excluded — who has not seen me simply as a vessel in which to spend his filthy seed. I will serve you loyally until the day of my death, and you will never want for anything that it is in my capacity to give —

other than my body, that is.' Then she broke into wild sobs and sank to the ground.

A bemused Simon rose from his chair and lifted her to her feet. As she continued to sob uncontrollably, he held her tightly to him and began to murmur words of reassurance and comfort. Eventually she raised a tear-stained face and smiled as she tugged at his youthful beard and invited him to continue with his meal. She then went to find a quiet spot in which to give prayerful thanks to God.

IV

There were several other attempts to suppress the Cathars, all of them unsuccessful, and all of them without Simon in attendance. He had, so far as he was concerned, proved to anyone who was interested that he was capable of wielding a sword in battle. However, he was far from convinced that a special place in Hell was not reserved for those who took human life for no reason other than differences in how the word of God was to be interpreted.

Simon also spent many hours in quiet conversation with Merle, seeking from her an understanding of what it was about the beliefs in which she had been raised that made her people such a threat to the established Church. He concluded that their only offence was to live as simply as possible, without the pomp and display so beloved of the Pontiff of Rome, and their belief that every person — male or female — had their own direct relationship with God that owed nothing to the intervention of a priest.

When Amaury made enquiry, and was advised by Armand that the young serving wench called Merle spent long hours alone with Simon after his meals, he drew the natural conclusion that she had become his brother's mistress. He was at a loss to understand Simon's reluctance to take to the field of battle again after his first experience in Carcassonne. Even the subsequent retaking of Carcassonne by Raymond II of Toulouse did not seem to be of any interest to Simon. Finally, late one evening, Amaury burst into his brother's tent in a foul temper, much the worse for having consumed two flagons of the local vin de pays.

'Dismiss your woman, and listen carefully to me, brother,' he demanded.

Merle gave a shriek as she recalled her coarse handling at the hands of 'the brute', and ran from the tent, leaving a red-faced Amaury glaring down at Simon where he sat.

'It seems that you grow soft. While I and my men keep risking our very lives in an attempt to win further lands and honour for the family of which you are a member, you spend your time idly fondling a country girl. When may we expect your strong sword-arm back in our lines?'

'When I can see some purpose to it,' Simon replied calmly. 'If you were genuinely fighting to promote the word of God among the heathen — which is the true mission of any Crusade — then I would not hesitate to stand alongside you. My sword is ever available for a just cause. But so far as I have been able to deduce, the people of the Languedoc have received the word of God already, and have put it to better purpose than His Holiness and all his grovelling retinue. As for you, dear brother, you would appear to me to be fighting, not for God, but for your bruised honour and the theft of as much land as you can acquire. This is not my way, and I suspect that it was not our father's.'

'By God's blood, Simon, were you not my brother I would smite your head from your shoulders for such insult! But since you appear to hold the family honour in such low esteem, perhaps you would not be offended were I to send you as an emissary to King Louis.'

'Where is the disgrace, or insult to honour, of attending the royal Court on behalf of a Crusade leader?' Simon asked.

Amaury continued to glower at him. 'The dishonour lies in not taking to the field of battle. But, if I am to be honest with you, I see little future in battering at the walls of towns that either choose not to yield, or yield softly in the certain knowledge that the bastard Toulouse will come to their rescue when our backs are turned. Our forces grow too small to be of any effect, yet Louis has become the third Capet to ignore our requests for reinforcements. If he wishes to rule the Languedoc, then he may come here in person with his own men and secure it.'

Simon laughed. 'You wish me to journey to Paris with *that* message? His Majesty would have my head — or is that what you *really* intend as my fate?'

'Clearly not,' Amaury sought to reassure him as he took a seat. 'I wish you to convey to His Majesty that, out of the love and loyalty that I bear him as his liege subject, I make him a gift of all the lands of the Languedoc that the de Montforts have at any time in the past conquered in the name of God.'

'Most of which have been recaptured by Raymond of Toulouse?' Simon said.

'Precisely,' Amaury replied. 'I see that you possess an understanding of diplomatic intrigue. If Louis will not grant me the army to finish the task, then he may employ his own.'

'And assuming that I retain my head in the process of delivering that most prickly of messages, do you wish me to return here in order to sit daily in my tent reading my Bible?' Simon asked.

'Much though you might find that to your satisfaction,' Amaury sneered as he filled a goblet and added to his insobriety, 'I think it would be best if you began to behave like a de Montfort, and upheld our interests elsewhere. When you have finished in Paris, you should journey to our family estates in the Île, which, for ought you care, may have been seized by greedy neighbours in our absence. Once you have restored them to peace and tranquillity, I will join you there, and then you may journey to England.'

'And why to England?' Simon asked.

'Because that is where *your* estates lie,' Amaury replied. 'As of this evening, I make you a free gift of my claim to our English estates, in exchange for your relinquishing all claim and title to these lands in France that you seem so reluctant to defend.'

'And I have a choice?' Simon enquired sardonically.

'No, brother, you do not,' Amaury told him as he rose to his feet. 'Unless you wish to climb back into your chainmail on the morrow and hack off more Cathar heads.'

With that he lurched out of the tent, leaving Simon deep in thought and seeking to recall those stories passed down by their father of the lands across la Manche that had once been theirs, but which Simon Senior had lost during his younger days. As had been his custom, he been the first to rally to the battle banner of King Philippe Augustus when he sought to expel King John of England from the Dukedom of Normandy, which John had seized from his own nephew Arthur of Brittany. To add to his sins, rumour had it that John had murdered Arthur by his own hand while he held him captive at Rouen. John had also outraged Hugh de Lusignan by stealing his intended bride, Isabella of Angoulême. Simon and Hugh had joined forces to drive John out of the last of his French territories after laying siege to, and subsequently capturing, his allegedly impregnable fortress of Château Gaillard.

Not inclined towards a forgiving nature, John had reacted by blocking the inheritance of Simon's father to his estates in Leicester, of which, by birth, he was the fifth earl. Instead, the irascible John had handed the lands to a de Montfort cousin who was also the Earl of Chester. The rightful Fifth Earl of Leicester by direct descent had never sought to challenge this alienation of his birthright, but had instead concentrated on his French possessions. He had passed on this sense of priority to his sons, neither of whom had even taken the trouble to learn English.

Following the early death of King John, England had for some years been under the effective control of a regent, the doughty warrior William Marshal, in the name of John's son Henry. Henry was the third of that name to rule the lands across la Manche, and was a year younger than Simon himself. Marshal had died only recently, and the likely response of the youthful King of England and his current advisors to any de Montfort claim to the Leicester title and estates was untested. Simon might as well stick his hand into a beehive to ascertain whether or not the bees were at home.

However, this was a matter for the future. In the meantime, Simon could at long last shake off the alternating mud and dust of a military camp for something more comfortable and mentally engaging, while at the same time retaining the grudging goodwill of his much older brother, who could have cast him out without any hope of inheriting anything.

The next morning, while the men were given a day off from fighting in order to sharpen their blades, replace their arrows and groom their horses, Simon sought out a somewhat green-faced Amaury. He was being plied with something that smelt disgusting by a determined-looking monk, who was also instructing a serving boy to hold steady with the bowl into which Amaury obligingly spewed half his stomach contents. Simon stood politely to the side, awaiting audience.

'What do *you* want,' Amaury demanded testily, 'other than the opportunity to witness the folly of drinking wine into which others have probably pissed?'

'If I was listening to you, and not the wine, yesterday evening,' Simon replied without any trace of sympathy, 'I would learn from you how many I may take with me on my return to the Île. Apart from requiring a sufficient company to impress the king, I may need to evict those who may have taken root in our home estates, of which of course I have no memory, since I am told that I was carried from there on the pommel of our father's saddle before I was even one year old.'

'I was fourteen then, and I can still hear your squawks of protest when you were taken from the arms of your wet nurse,' Amaury gloated back. 'Hopefully you will cut a more imposing figure when you ride back in.'

'I will impress no-one if all who accompany me are servants,' Simon pointed out. 'My meagre household consists of no more than five. There is Armand, Hortense the cook, the two kitchen hands Emile and Helene, and your "present" to me, Merle.'

'The girl from Carcassonne?' Amaury asked.

'She will be coming with me for my comfort,' Simon replied evasively, 'but what of fighting men? Am I to present myself to the king in Paris with less of an entourage than a country squire?'

'You may take a score, and Fulk will choose them,' Amaury told him. 'He still thinks highly of you, despite your constant absence from our ranks, and he would wish to have you adequately protected. In fact, it might be best if Fulk himself joins you — he grows impatient to see his family again, and he knows the land around Paris.'

'He still has family in the Île?' Simon asked disbelievingly. 'We have been in the Languedoc these past sixteen years or more — does he fondly imagine that his family still remember him, and that they will welcome his return?'

'Whether they will or no, he wishes to go. I have it in mind to abandon this whole region within the month anyway, and follow you back east. We may not be destined to engage the enemy further, and I would rather that his strong arm be in your service until I can join you back home.'

'Would it not be better for you to make your gift of these lands in person to King Louis? Or was I correct to suspect that I will become yet another messenger who does not live much longer than the message he has to impart?'

'Save your cynicism for the English Court,' Amaury replied with a sneer. 'They have high regard for forked tongues over there, or so I am informed. Now, see to your arrangements — I wish to see you gone within the week.'

With that he turned his back, went white in the face, and urgently demanded the repositioning of the vomit bowl.

V

Five days later, at first light, the procession moved slowly off on a command from Fulk de Sevres, who rode at its head. Immediately behind him were a dozen foot soldiers at the start of the longest continual march they would ever endure, and behind them rode Simon on his favourite courser, Bernard. The centre of the line was given over to a huge wagon behind a massive plough horse, containing the few personal furnishings that Simon could fit into it, a selection of cooking implements, enough food and wine for a few days, two physician monks and various servants, among whom was Merle, constantly looking back at the only countryside she had ever known. Following the wagon were the remaining infantry who made up the rearguard.

It was slow progress, with barely ten miles covered every day along the muddy, and sometimes almost non-existent, track north-east. Whenever possible they would prevail upon a monastic house to give them sanctuary for the night, although most abbots drew the line at taking in the soldiers, who were obliged to take what shelter they could in the nearby hedgerows. But there were still many nights on which the entire company was obliged to settle down in a coppice, or on a shaded riverbank, light a fire, and cook whatever small game or fish they had managed to capture on their journey. On these occasions, Simon would insist that Merle snuggled into him as they lay covered by only a cloak or a feather quilt, both to keep her frail frame warm, and to make it clear to any soldier with dishonourable intentions that she belonged to 'the Master', and that they should treat her with caution and respect.

It was late on the afternoon of a mild autumn day when they spied a collection of church spires and the high tower of an imposing castle in the distance. Fulk halted the procession and nosed his horse back to where Simon was standing in his stirrups to ease the cramp in his thighs after seven hours in the saddle.

'In the far distance is Paris,' he told Simon. 'But I must leave you here, since my home village is just ahead. Where the river bends to the left, you can just make out the church of St Martin, where I was christened almost forty years ago now. If God be merciful, I have a wife and two children who have probably been mourning my believed death these many years. You are now in command of this tired company, and must present yourself to King Louis as best you can.'

'I will return for you in three days,' Simon assured him.

Fulk smiled politely. 'That will depend upon what I find in yonder village, sir. If all is not well, I may be the one to come in search of you.'

'Thank you for everything you have done for me, Fulk,' Simon said as the two men dismounted and embraced. 'You made me into a man, and, what is more, a man who can stand his ground if challenged. Should you find that all is well with your family — as I dearly hope you do — then you are honourably discharged from the service of the de Montforts, and if you are ever in need of a friend...'

'And should all *not* be well down there?' Fulk asked. 'May I assume that I will still be welcome in Montfort-l'Amaury? It is but a day's ride to the north-west of here, and you may almost see its ramparts from where we sit. And while you take in the view, I will take my leave.'

'Return to us soon!' Simon yelled after him as the old warhorse picked its way carefully down the stony track towards the distant river. Then he turned to address the rest of the company. 'We will bide the night down by that river, then on the morrow we'll seek audience with the king. It might be good for us all to take the opportunity to wash, in order that our presence does not offend the more delicate noses of the Court. That is, of course, always assuming that His Majesty will receive us.'

Two days later Simon bent the knee and lowered his head in obeisance to a man who looked no older than him. They were in the Palais de la Cité, and King Louis VIII looked down from his ornate throne seat in curiosity at this tall knight dressed in a livery he had never seen before, although his heralds had advised him what to expect.

'You bring tidings from the Languedoc?' Louis asked. Simon nodded his head and gritted his teeth in anticipation of incurring the royal wrath.

'I bring you the Languedoc itself, sire.'

'Your meaning?'

'My beloved brother Sir Amaury has authorised me, on his behalf, to make a gift of the whole of that area insofar as it is his to give.'

There was a hollow laugh from the shallow platform that raised the throne. 'To judge by the reports I have received — which I might add have been somewhat lacking of late — he has little left of those lands that your father was so successful in capturing in the first place.'

'It is true, sire, that the treacherous devil Raymond of Toulouse continues his father's policy of defending the heretics against the just might of the Pope's forces, which my brother has the honour of commanding. But given Your Majesty's well-deserved reputation for military prowess, he now deems it appropriate that the heir to the Kingdom of the Franks continues the battle to suppress the spread of heresy in the south-west.'

Louis looked thoughtfully up at the ceiling before replying. 'In your journey from Toulouse, did you pass through Poitou?'

'No, sire, we kept well to the south, journeying through Bourgogne, then through Auxerre into the Île.'

'So you saw nought of Aquitaine either?'

'No, sire.'

Louis sighed heavily, and gestured to the heavily wimpled young woman at his side. 'As you may know, my queen, the gracious Blanche, is of the house of Castile, and also the house of Aquitaine, through the line of the illustrious Eleanor, the grandmother of the current King of England, Henry. He and I have long contested the regions to the south-west of here, since your father rid me of John in Normandy. I could lay claim to the crown of England, were I not pledged by treaty not to venture again across the sea to seize what is arguably mine. But I would prefer to consolidate my lands here, particularly those to the south-west that seem to believe their best future lies under the suzerainty of Aragon.'

'My brother is similarly disposed,' Simon told him, 'and he and I have reached an agreement that while he will defend his titles under Your Majesty, I am to travel to England in order to claim back our earldom from those to whom it was unjustly given by that same King John.'

'It seems that we have interests in common, Lord Simon,' Louis said. 'When do you intend to venture across la Manche?'

'Whenever opportunity permits, sire.'

'See that you return to us here before you set off,' Louis instructed him. 'Should you succeed in reclaiming your English estate, it could well be the beginning of another breach in the Angevin wall.'

'I will be sure to do so, sire.'

'This is good. Now, perhaps you and your immediate retinue might wish to refresh yourselves in the banqueting hall that is just through those doors behind you. I am told that you travel with a small company of soldiers, a few priests and servants, and a young woman. Is she your wife?'

'No, my travelling companion only,' Simon told him.

Louis gave a low chuckle. 'Whatever, you and your party shall be well fed and watered before you journey out of Paris to your former estate, which you will find much changed in your absence.'

This proved to be an understatement. Aghast, Simon looked at the bony cattle that grazed listlessly on sparse, coarse grass by the river that ran through the valley leading to the distant ramparts of Montfort-l'Amaury. Here and there could be seen the ruins of what must once have been herdsmen's huts, and the wheels on the water mill were motionless as they filed past it in solemn procession. As they approached the ramparts they saw the drawbridge being hastily raised against their approach, and a line of archers standing menacingly along its southern battlements.

Simon signalled for the procession to halt, and rode on alone until he was within hailing distance of the ramparts, which themselves appeared to be in sad need of repair. He raised his voice to be heard as he demanded that the drawbridge be lowered.

'That may only be done on the authority of the Lord of Nanterre,' he was advised.

'And why might that be?' Simon demanded.

'Because this stronghold is his,' came the defiant reply.

'This stronghold rightly belongs to the de Montforts, of which I am one!' Simon bellowed back indignantly. 'Lower the drawbridge immediately — I command it!'

'You have only a handful of men and one baggage wagon,' the man shouted back. 'Unless you have a larger force than that, leave!'

Simon turned his horse angrily and rode back to where his companions sat in a circle awaiting his return. He grimaced as he jumped down from Bernard and gave them the news. Then he looked back down the road they had travelled, which was heavily wooded on both sides, with the river on the far left-hand side.

'We will make camp down this road, out of sight in the trees, then on the morrow we will decide what is best to be done. Armand, let us see if there will be rabbit for supper, shall we?'

Several hours later, as they sat around the low but intense fire that they had lit in a clearing, Merle protested as Simon carved the entire breast from a pigeon that he extracted from the embers, and handed it to her on the point of his knife.

'I am supposed to be serving *you*, my lord.'

'There will be plenty of time for that, once we are back in the fortress of my ancestors,' he replied. 'Now eat this, before you disappear completely inside that cloak of mine. You have grown no fatter since the first day I set eyes on you.'

'Little wonder, since we have hardly dined on rich food these past months,' Merle replied. 'That is not a complaint, since I have never felt so reassured, so highly regarded, even — may I make so bold as to say — so *loved* in my entire life. It is just in my nature not to take on more flesh when I eat well. Some women would delight to change constitutions with me, I have no doubt. Would you desire me if I were fatter?'

'Not in the sense that you probably meant,' Simon replied with a frown. 'Please do not think of me in carnal terms, and have no fear that I will abuse the trust that you have placed in me. Your virtue is ever safe in my hands, Merle, you may rest content in that knowledge.'

'Sometimes I do not find that knowledge so restful,' she muttered as she snuggled closer and planted a chaste kiss on his cheek. Just then they heard a hoarsely whispered challenge from one of the soldiers they had placed on guard at the fringe of the wood in which they were camped, and a large man strode purposefully towards the fire through the shadows. Simon leaped to his feet and grasped his sword hilt before releasing it with an excited exclamation.

'Fulk! You have returned to us!'

'Nothing amiss with your eyesight, at any rate,' Fulk observed as he looked down into the embers. 'Is there aught left to eat?'

'Some rabbit, and probably half a pigeon,' Simon told him. 'You must swill it down with water, I'm afraid.'

'No matter,' Fulk replied as he turned over the embers with his boot.

'How went things at home?' Simon asked cautiously.

'As badly as I had anticipated,' Fulk muttered darkly. 'The woman who used to be my wife had taken up with the blacksmith, by whom she has two daughters, one not much younger than Merle here. As for my own daughter, she is married to the miller's son, and closed the door in my face when I asked to see my grandchildren. My son was killed in a skirmish with retainers of the Lord of Nanterre who he came across in an alehouse, attempting to rob the landlord.'

'So is your wife happy with the blacksmith?' Merle asked tactfully.

'Probably not any longer,' Fulk said, 'since I ran him through the guts with a lance, and left him impaled on the front door of his forge. I am now a fugitive, it would seem.'

'You mentioned the Lord of Nanterre,' Simon reminded him. 'The reason why you find us in this wood is that he has overrun Montfort-l'Amaury in our absence.'

'He has taken *much* in our absence,' Fulk spat into the fire, 'including the life of my son Pierre. I would deem it an honour to assist you in taking back what is rightfully yours, sir.'

'The castle is defended,' Simon told him gloomily, 'and from what I could see, there are more men in there than we have out here.'

'Men who have no doubt grown fat, lazy, over-confident and sloppy in their guard duties.'

'I sense that you have something in mind,' Simon said, 'so be seated and let us consider whatever it is.'

Fulk thought for a moment, then looked behind him. 'You still have the wagon?'

'Of course.'

'And do you know whether or not Gaston of Nanterre is in residence down the road?'

'Not for certain, but I gained the impression that he was not,' Simon told him.

'Excellent,' Fulk muttered. 'I suggest that once the sun rises, we make him a delivery.'

'In what sense?' Simon asked, intrigued.

'We take the wagon, suitably loaded with your best furnishings, and insist that his lordship bought them recently, and ordered that they be delivered.'

'And you conceal your men in the wagon?' Merle asked.

Fulk shot her a withering glance before he explained. 'The men on the gate are bound to look under the covers, so

46

obviously not. However, once we are inside, I will cut the drawbridge ropes so that it cannot be re-raised, and my men will make a full charge over the moat from where they will be concealed in the trees, and hopefully led by you, sir,' he added, with a knowing look at Simon.

'You will be leading him to his death!' Merle protested, earning another disapproving look from Fulk.

'On the contrary, he will be leading *himself* back into his birthright. But, since you are obviously concerned for the success of the mission, you may also be part of it.'

Simon was about to protest, but Merle eagerly sought a more detailed explanation.

'I will obviously be driving the cart, heavily disguised as the merchant,' Fulk told her. 'But the guards will suspect nothing if there is a woman by my side. You might even wish to distract them by raising your gown above your knee for the occasion.'

Despite Simon's misgivings, Merle eagerly accepted the role. Shortly after daylight the cart was unloaded of everything that did not resemble the furnishings of the wealthy, and was hitched up to the horse and trundled out of the wood onto the main track. A few yards short of the raised drawbridge Fulk muttered the instruction to Merle, who raised her gown up to the middle of her thigh. The ruse worked to perfection, and once the wagon was over the drawbridge there came an imperious yell from down the road, as Simon in full chainmail raced towards the entrance with twenty soldiers close behind him wielding swords and axes. At the crucial moment Fulk reached behind him for the sword hidden under a bale of wall hangings and slashed the two drawbridge ropes, running through two guards who tried to prevent him.

Simon led the charge into the courtyard, into which stumbled the remainder of the modest, almost token, garrison. He slashed and thrust in the way he remembered, and had accounted for three of the defenders before he felt an agonising blow to his lower right leg that cut clean through his mail. Then it all went black.

VI

Simon came awake with a shriek of agony, to the stench of burnt flesh. The excruciating pain burst through him in waves, and he tried to move his leg to relieve it, but there were two large men at arms holding him down below the waist, each of them tearfully begging his pardon for what they had to do. Then Merle's distressed face appeared before his, as he lay stomach down, naked, on the bolster.

'Forgive us, my lord, but Brother Claude insists that it is necessary.'

'Indeed it is, my lord,' came the voice of his torturer, 'and we had hoped that you would remain insensible while we did what we had to do. But if we are to avoid the loss of the limb through poison, the wound must be burned clean. Soon will come the honey salve, but before that…'

Simon gave another shriek as the hot iron was applied once again to the gaping wound, and tears rolled down Merle's cheeks as she gripped his hand and prayed hard for God's intervention in his suffering.

'Sweet Jesus, no more, I beg you!' Simon pleaded as he smelt cooked pig again.

Claude gave a grunt of satisfaction. 'It is as good as I can make it, my lord. God will bring you comfort in your hour of suffering.'

'So long as it is *only* an hour,' Simon joked weakly, then vomited onto the bolster.

Merle wiped first the bolster, then his chin, as she offered him a glass of wine, which he was able to swallow by turning his head towards the lip of the goblet. The two soldiers who had been holding him down moved away, bowed, begged his forgiveness yet again, and backed out through the chamber door, both green of face.

'Do you wish me to apply the honey salve?' Merle asked softly.

Simon nodded through his searing pain. 'Yes, if you would be so good. But if Claude comes near me again with the hot iron, kick him where even a monk would feel pain.'

She sniggered, then on impulse she kissed his lips. 'I have never witnessed such courage, my dearest Lord Simon. I will be with you for as long as you need me, and Claude has promised a draught that will make you sleep. Hopefully your leg has been preserved, and within weeks you will be on your feet again, directing the men.'

'Unless Nanterre returns with a stronger force,' Simon muttered ominously.

'You need have no fear of that,' said another familiar voice, and Simon twisted his head far enough to recognise Fulk standing alongside the pallet on which he lay. He grimaced as he looked down at Simon's lower limbs. 'You were lucky, sir, but you forgot what I first taught you. The first blow is to the leg.'

'Even from behind?'

'*Especially* from behind. However, you were wise enough — for once — to wear your helm, else the blow you received from the hilt of the same sword would have caved your head in. But we won the day, and you are now back in Montfort-l'Amaury, albeit somewhat temporarily indisposed.'

'And what makes you so certain that Nanterre will not return to take back what he regards as his?' Simon asked, wincing as Merle began to apply the honey balm.

'One of his men was captured alive, and my men were all set to roast him when a better use occurred to me. I sent him back to his bastard lord with a message from Fulk of Sevres that if he comes within ten miles of me, I will cleave his head from his shoulders and feed it to the wild hogs that infest the woods around his estate, in settlement of the debt that he owes me for the death of my son.'

'And that will be sufficient to keep him away?' Simon asked in a tone of scepticism.

'It will if he enquires of the fate of the local blacksmith, who did nothing worse than lie with my wife. And now, if you will excuse me, I shall seek audience with the cook, who appreciates my rough and ready tongue more than you or your companion. What is more, she has promised not to make a funeral pyre of one of the scrawny beasts we brought in from your lordship's fields. Do you wish for some of it to be sent to you?'

'I will see to that,' Merle told him, and he gave her an exaggerated bow that lasted all the way to the chamber entrance. Merle frowned after him, then leaned down and kissed Simon on the forehead. 'If you will forgive me, I must apply more honey.'

For the next three weeks Simon lay helplessly on his pallet, only once attempting to roll over onto his back, then abandoning the attempt with a scream. He was entirely dependent upon the loyal, gentle Merle, who even helped him to make the necessary ablutions. She never once complained, and when he expressed his embarrassment at the forced intimacy she smiled lovingly down at him and asked who he thought had been the one to strip off his chainmail when he was first brought into the chamber.

'I would not expect this service from a *wife*,' he replied.

'There are some things that require love beyond that of a wife,' she replied with her eyes downcast and a blush on her pale cheek. He left it at that, and began to make mental plans for when he was once again able to rely on his right leg.

During the second month, he was seated awkwardly in a chair in the corner of his chamber when Merle looked back from the window through which she had been gazing out at the distant farmland.

'Lord, there is a large body of soldiers approaching from the west!'

'Help me up,' Simon demanded, then hobbled to the window. 'I am sure that Fulk has the measure of them, but if not he will be chided for his tardiness in not preparing an appropriate welcome for my brother.'

'The brute,' Merle reminded him.

'The man who brought you into my life,' Simon added, 'and the man who will no doubt regret his rough behaviour when he learns how well you have looked after me.'

An hour later, Amaury was squatting down at the side of Simon's chair and seeking reassurance that he was making a full recovery.

'I'm well on the mend,' Simon announced proudly, 'thanks to this fine young lady you threw at my feet in Carcassonne. In the fullness of time I shall require that you make a complete and genuine apology for your rude behaviour, but in the meantime, a word of advice. If Brother Claude ever comes near you with a white hot iron, run for your life.'

'At least your strange sense of humour remains intact,' Amaury said. 'When does he say you will be fit for travel?'

'Have some mercy!' Simon chided him smilingly. 'But you made the same enquiry that I received from King Louis.'

'How did he respond to my gift?' Amaury asked as Merle slipped silently from the room.

'I am still alive, as you can see. But may I take it that you saw naught of him in the Languedoc?'

'Not so much as a stray arrow. We left things as they were, and without Fulk's men I deemed it wiser to quit the territory not long after you. We obviously could not progress as fast as your smaller party, and we have been many weeks on the road.'

'Is our family estate much as you remember it?'

Amaury spat on the floor. 'It is a ruin, thanks to Nanterre and his peasants! It will be a year or more before the grazing stock is replenished, and at least that before this wreck of a castle can be made habitable. You will not remember it, of course, but thanks to our mother's gracious tastes it was the height of fashion and equipped with all the necessary comforts. Now it is as if it had been under siege for a lifetime.'

'Even if I had any memory of the place I left sitting as a babe in arms on my father's horse, I have had little opportunity to inspect the rest of the dwelling, confined as I have been to this chamber.'

'It was once mine,' Amaury reminisced. He looked cautiously behind him before adding, 'I lost my virginity to a kitchen wench in here when I was barely fourteen, and she, from memory, was little older. Mariette, her name was.' His eyes glazed over at the memory, then a thought occurred to him. 'How fare you with Merle? Has she yet grown into a woman?'

'She was a woman when you first threw her on the ground in front of me at Carcassonne,' Simon answered with a frown. 'As for the *real* import of your question, the answer thereto is none of your business. Apart from making full use of your "gift", what do you require of me now that you are back?'

'As we agreed, I wish you to travel to England to claim your inheritance there. That does not mean that I do not want you here — simply that I wish there to be no dispute over our French lands.'

'There will be no dispute,' Simon assured him. 'But you should know that King Louis also wishes me to cross la Manche, in order to sniff the wind at the Court of King Henry.'

'As his ambassador?'

'He did not appoint me as such,' Simon admitted, 'but he left me in no doubt that he would welcome news of how matters sit at the English Court. But I fear that I will be greatly disadvantaged, in that I do not speak English.'

Amaury snorted quietly. 'And think you that they all speak English at the English Court? Henry regards himself as French, and prefers our language, so most of the leading nobles of the land, even if they did not speak French as children, rapidly learned to speak it in order to retain favour. Even the royal childminder, William Marshal, was obliged to speak it in the presence of John's feeble offspring. Trust me, you will be at no disadvantage.'

'How do you know these things?' Simon asked doubtfully.

'Because we have cousins over there, do we not? One of whom still occupies estates that are rightfully ours. In your best interests I have kept up correspondence with some of them, and thanks to me your cousin Ranulf believes you to be a mighty warrior who is champing at the bit to revenge the disfavour done to our father by the late King John.'

'Does King Henry think that?' Simon asked fearfully. 'If so, then he will have me quietly done to death ere I have travelled a day's ride into his kingdom.'

'King Henry is but yet a boy, and younger than you, brother. He has no skill in battle — at least, none that has yet been put to the measure — and when he was a boy of nine our own King Louis invaded his shores and was almost pronounced King of England. It was only the death of Henry's father John that brought the English barons to their senses, and they rallied round the Earl of Pembroke — William Marshal, no less — and drove Louis out. He was not even King Louis in those days, but as part of the peace treaty drawn up in London he is pledged not to invade again. Perhaps he sees you as his legitimate way around that treaty. At all events, it is not Henry of whom you need to be wary, but the barons, and, chief among these, William Marshal's son, if he be still alive. His name is also William.'

'And what do you know of this William Marshal?'

Amaury frowned. 'He is hard to read, they say. He is rumoured to be a man of dissolute character, but he has the support of most of the leading barons of the nation. They are the ones who enjoy the effective power, since they forced Henry's father to sign a treaty not long before he died, in which he promised them that he would never act again without their blessing and approval. It would seem that Henry has been held to that promise, not that he is in any position to renege upon it, given his youth and inexperience. In order to consolidate his position, William Marshal had his son married off to Henry's younger sister Eleanor, who was a mere child of nine at the time. It is to William Marshal the Younger and his henchmen that you must plead your case, it would seem.'

'Things may well have changed ere I can travel.' Simon grimaced down at his right leg. 'I can hardly limp into the royal presence like some beggar seeking alms.'

'How long will you be biding with us?' Amaury asked.

Simon shook his head uncertainly. 'As long as you can tolerate my presence, it would seem. I have not left this chamber since I was first carried into it unconscious, and I mark my progress daily by the ease with which I can walk to that window. Were it not for Merle, I would not even have progressed this far.'

'Is she gifted in physic as well?' Amaury asked sarcastically.

'She is gifted with the most loyal and loving nature, and she attends me almost every hour of the day, seeing to my every need. And *that* need as well, I have no doubt, were I to request it of her. But she is too gracious for me to make such demands of her, in answer to the question that you dearly wish me to answer.'

'I hope you do not have it in mind to wed her,' Amaury cautioned him. 'In the matter of marriage, one must reach higher than a country wench.'

'I shall not disappoint you in my eventual marriage, should a suitable lady appear on my horizon,' Simon assured him. 'But for now my horizon is limited to what I can espy from yon window, and it is nothing but fields, woods and rivers.'

'Then you must hasten your bodily repair, while you still have King Louis' blessing for your journey to England. And I must leave you in order to see to the repair to the battlements, if we are to retain even our French estates.'

A week later, leaning heavily on Merle's arm, Simon edged gingerly down the narrow flight of stairs into the main hall, where his breathless, wincing arrival was greeted by rousing cheers from the servants who were laying the board for dinner. He remained down there for long enough to partake of a hearty meal of venison and fish — all robbed from a neighbouring estate — and to sink enough red wine to ease the pain of the return climb to his chamber. After another week or so, during which he repeated this minor triumph daily, he ventured down the flight of stairs from the far side of the main hall into the keep, where he made a speech thanking those men who had assisted in the retaking of Montfort-l'Amaury. He was cheered as he limped heavily back up two flights of stairs, with one arm draped around Merle's shoulder. As she lowered him towards his pallet, he saw a tear roll down her cheek.

'Why do you weep, when I am making such good progress?' he asked gently.

She folded him in her arms, and he could feel her body trembling as she whispered her reply. 'Precisely *because* you make such good progress, my lord. But I fear that once you are fully restored to health, you will risk your life again in some vainglorious escapade.'

'When I am fully restored to health, I have it in mind to pursue my rightful title in England. Will you miss me?'

'No, my lord,' she insisted as she laid him gently back on his pallet and pulled the covers over him, 'because I shall be going with you.'

His eyes widened and he shook his head. 'You cannot, and you must not, Merle. For aught I know, I shall be riding to my sudden death. I know not in what manner my arrival at the English Court will be welcomed — if it is welcomed at all.'

'All the more reason to have those about you who love you, and who owe you their lives. If nothing else, I can taste your food, to ensure that you are not poisoned.'

'You would do that for me?' he asked, open-mouthed.

She sat down on the side of the pallet, lifted his hand to her mouth and kissed it. 'You have shown me respect and regard such that a simple country girl could never have hoped for at the hands of a lord such as yourself. Were it necessary for me to cast myself from that chamber window in order to preserve your life, I would gladly do so. Now rest, that we may further test the strength of your leg on the morrow. I am growing tired of this place and would see if England is the green land that they speak of in travellers' tales.'

VII

Three months later, to the heartfelt cheers of every man at arms in the courtyard, Simon finally mounted his faithful Bernard, who whinnied in pleasure to feel Simon's weight once more in the saddle. After throwing the stable boy several coins as a reward for having kept him so well-groomed in the year or so that he had been unridden, Simon gingerly moved both knees in a sign for Bernard to walk slowly down the slope towards the drawbridge, which was lowered to further cheers as Simon rode through it, Fulk by his side on his own mount. As they took a gentle horseback stroll around the lake, Simon looked back towards the castle, where he could just make out a small figure in a blue gown waving to him from the window of the chamber in which he had spent so many months being tenderly nursed back to health. He waved back reassuringly, then turned to his riding companion.

'Tell me, Fulk, what do you do with fillies that are born to our brood mares? I assume that they are not kept for warfare — are they put to death?'

'No, sir, they are sold at markets. Since they are so well bred, they fetch a high price as future brood mares. And, of course, we keep some of them for the like purpose.'

'Do you account yourself a good judge of horseflesh?'

'My father was a farrier, sir, like his father before him. I had held a hundred horses by the bridle while my father shod them by the time that I was ten. Had it not been for his insistence that I became a man at arms during the uncertain times that we lived in, I might yet be a farrier by trade.'

'Thank God that you were not,' Simon replied. 'Had you been, I would not have learned the art of warfare at such worthy hands.'

Fulk went slightly red in the face. 'Even now I blush with shame at the memory of how rudely I treated you as a boy, when you were learning how to remain alive in this brutal world. I trust that I have truly been forgiven?'

'With all my heart, Fulk, since without your skill I would not be riding around my ancestral lake on this pleasant morning. Since you mention the dangers of this uncertain world, would you consent to travel with me to England when I am in sufficient health to make the journey?'

'If your brother will permit it, I should be delighted, sir. But this is a long league from your original question regarding fillies born to brood mares.'

'When I leave for England, I would take Merle with me. I appreciate that she is not to your liking, but she serves me loyally and well, and I fear for her future were she left here unprotected against your rough men at arms. Since I — and hopefully you also — will be on horseback, I would not wish her to have to walk in order to journey with us. Would you please find her a suitable filly? And then I would deem it a favour if you would teach her how to ride it.'

'It is true that I find her too — well, too "holier than thou", if you would permit me to say so,' Fulk replied. 'But I hear nothing but good reports about her from those who encounter her daily in the household, and I have observed for myself how loyally she serves you. I will gladly seek her out a suitable mount, and will teach her the art of remaining on a horse at full gallop. But, if you will forgive me for pointing out something that may not have occurred to you, sir, there is the delicate matter that we might come into bodily contact when I am assisting her in and out of the saddle — which I assume will be of the type with which we are both familiar, and not one of those normally favoured by ladies?'

'What is the point that you have almost obscured in your ramblings, Fulk?'

'Well, sir, I may, in the course of teaching her, have occasion to touch her leg, or — God forbid — her hind quarters.'

Simon burst out laughing. 'I feel sure that the lady herself will soon make it clear how far your teaching may travel up her thigh.'

'Quite so, sir, but it is yourself whose anger I would not incur.'

'Why me, pray?'

'Well, sir, it is freely spoken among the men that the first person to lay an unwanted hand on her will lose it.'

'This is good, and as I intended it to be, Fulk, but it was not meant to apply to those actions on your part that are necessary in order to teach Merle how to remain on horseback. God knows, what you inflict on her will be naught to what you inflicted on me in those days now mercifully long behind us.'

'For which once again I crave your forgiveness, sir. But it shall be as you desire.'

Two days later, Fulk confronted Simon as he stood in the courtyard, making a few hesitant sword lunges at a straw target that had been strung up for him over the cellar door.

'I need not have feared to lose a hand unwittingly placed upon a saintly backside, sir! It would seem that Merle learned to ride at an early age, and she took to it again as if she had never been out of the saddle.'

'And you have found her a suitable mount?'

Fulk looked slightly shamefaced as he replied. 'Indeed I have, sir, and if you will forgive my actions when you were first laid low, I am happy to report that Saint Merle will travel with you on a filly that was sired by your own mount. Bernard will be trotting alongside his own daughter — we have named her "Beatrice", and she is both strong and well mannered, if a little lacking in height at this stage. But no matter — by the time we depart she will be of sufficient size to take Merle, who is light in build herself.'

The last of the winter snows had thawed from the edge of the lake as Simon took a final ride around the estate with Amaury, ahead of his impending journey to England. Amaury had freely consented to Fulk making the journey with his younger brother, but was endeavouring for the fifth time to persuade Simon to take more men with him, as a sort of token bodyguard, in addition to the ageing Fulk. Simon was, once again, politely declining.

'For one thing,' he reminded his brother, 'as we have agreed already, the greater the size of my party, the slower the progress, and the greater the expense of having them fed and quartered as we make our way through the land, small though it is reputed to be. It will also send the wrong message to the English Court, and will smell more of invasion than diplomacy. But if, as you assure me, you have already written to our cousin of Chester that I shall be landing on the south coast within the month, then our arrival will be expected. I have never heard of an invasion force announcing its arrival in advance.'

'Be that as it may, brother, I have no way of knowing how Earl Ranulf will view your arrival. Should he suspect that you will be tilting for his title, he may head you off and cut you down with only a handful of men.'

'And if I take a greater force, will he not regard that as further proof of my design to reclaim my rightful title, and may he not then send an even greater force of his own? I must ease myself into my inheritance, not charge towards it like a contestant in the tiltyard.'

'Your love of tact and diplomacy will one day lose you your head,' Amaury muttered, 'but I have fulfilled my final promise to our mother that I would do everything within my power to preserve you. Once you leave the safety of Montfort-l'Amaury, you are responsible for your own life.'

Two days later, the vulnerable-looking trio set off from the main gate, with many a wave of farewell and shouted prayer for their welfare. For the first few miles they had an armed escort from Montfort, until they were safely out of the lands still in the possession of a lord of Nanterre. As the rich farmland gave way to a flat coastal landscape after they joined the track to Rouen, the men took their leave, and Simon, Fulk and Merle picked their way in silence along the stony track until a change in the air warned them that the sea was not far away.

They had put up at various inns on their way, and by dint of enquiry they had learned that vessels regularly crossed the narrow sea from Rouen to English ports such as Pevensey, carrying fruit and wine, and making the return trip with woven English cloth. It seemed they should have no difficulty in finding passages for themselves and their three horses. They soon found such a vessel at the quayside, and Simon asked its captain how much he would require by way of payment. The man looked across at the rest of the party and named his price, a remarkably low one to Simon's mind. Then Fulk strode over and sought to have it reduced even further, demonstrating a skill at haggling that he must have learned at his father's knee — although at that young age he was presumably not gripping his sword hilt, at which the mariner was glancing nervously.

'Very well, sirs, it shall be at the price you offer. A fair price, if I may say so, for just three horses, two men and a boy.'

Simon looked back in surprise at Merle, who had overheard the conversation. As they led their mounts up the gangplank, she whispered to Simon.

'There are advantages to having small breasts. Remind me not to don any of the gowns in my baggage until we reach the Court.'

The vessel made the open ocean, and all three of them clung to the gunnels, pale-faced and trying not to vomit into the heaving ocean that one minute threw them high into the air, and the next seemed determined to swallow them into its depths. According to their captain, it was a 'fair' sea, and they dreaded ever encountering an unfair one. Eventually, after several hours of discomfort and lurching guts, they said silent prayers of thanks for their delivery as the master eased the vessel into a small harbour. They led their horses back onto dry land with legs that seemed to possess a life of their own. An hour later, they were sheltering in a hedgerow against a sudden spring shower, and confessing that none of them had the slightest idea of how to get to London.

A local innkeeper put them on a road that, he assured them in his imperfect French, was the one taken by their ancestors from Normandy. The land changed imperceptibly from chalky grassland to more verdant pasture during the three days and nights that they put up in wayside inns. In each one of these, Fulk further demonstrated his eloquence in negotiating a price for their food and accommodation with a hand on his sword hilt. Each night they shared a bedchamber, and Merle would snuggle up to Simon, seemingly by way of protection against whatever Fulk might have in mind, although Simon had his doubts. In any case, he was more than content to have Merle's comforting presence so close to him.

On the morning of the fourth day, Fulk raised a hand in warning as he stood up in the saddle to get a better view of what he had spotted ahead. They halted and watched nervously as a large contingent of armed men rode towards them, occupying the entire track as they did so. They slowed their pace to a halt when they were only yards from them, and parted in the centre to reveal a finely dressed middle-aged man mounted on a massive warhorse. He smiled in welcome as he nudged his horse slowly forward.

'Do I have the privilege and pleasure of greeting my distant kinsman, Simon of Montfort?' he asked in perfect French.

'I am he,' Simon confirmed. 'Would I be correct in assuming that you are Earl Ranulf of Chester?'

'You would indeed,' the man confirmed, 'and I am here to convey you to the king, who currently holds Court at Oxford. You are currently on the London road, and must therefore turn north-west.'

'How far distant is this "Oxford"?' Fulk demanded.

Ranulf looked down his nose slightly at this impertinence, and directed his reply at Simon. 'It is two, perhaps three, days' ride from here. You will, I hope, accept my protection for the rest of your journey? King Henry has generously put his manor houses at Horsham and Reading at your disposal, and it would seem that there are only two of you.'

'And a boy,' Merle muttered.

VIII

The party's first experience of royal hospitality was a welcome relief from the pottage and black bread that had been their fare in recent country inns. On the morning of their departure from Reading, ahead of climbing into the saddle as modestly as her yellow gown permitted, Merle had washed her hair in the manor house kitchen, and placed lavender sachets under each of her armpits, as well as one strapped to the inside of each thigh. It was uncomfortable, but greatly preferable to the body odours that had caused her acute embarrassment for the past few days.

The Castle at Oxford made the one they had left at Montfort two weeks previously look like a serf's cottage. As they dismounted, several eager ostlers dressed in royal livery took their bridles from them and led their horses to a stable that seemed to them to be the size of one of the oast houses they had passed on the first few days of their travels through England. They stood in a nervous group behind two massive oak doors in the castle itself as Ranulf spoke in a low whisper to some sort of page, dressed from head to foot in rich garments, who nodded and slipped inside the doors. A few moments later, the doors swung open again, and the same richly dressed menial beckoned for them to enter as he shouted, 'The Earl of Chester, and Lord Simon of Montfort-l'Amaury, Your Majesty.'

Had it not been for the crown perched at a slight angle on his narrow head, it would not have been immediately obvious which of the men on the raised dais was the king himself. He was an amiable-looking youth with a receding chin and a drooping eyelid, so that his overall appearance resembled that of a village idiot. His eyes followed Simon and his two companions as they made their way down towards the platform, Simon slightly ahead of Fulk and Merle. Simon bowed from the waist with what he hoped was an ingratiating smile, and the youth with the crown smiled back.

'It is customary to kneel before His Majesty,' Simon was sternly advised by the steely-faced older man standing to the king's left, but Simon ignored him as he looked Henry firmly in the eye.

'Your Majesty must forgive me, but an old battle wound at present denies me the privilege of kneeling before you. In time it will heal, they tell me, and then I will kneel.'

While he had been making his excuse, Fulk had been glaring at the man who had chided Simon on their very first encounter. He had an air of authority and confidence about him, although he now had grey hairs and was slightly stooped with age. Whoever he was, Fulk decided he would dearly love to run him through for his impudence. But he held his tongue and awaited developments.

Henry held out a languid hand for Simon to kiss as he leaned forward, then slumped back on his throne as he looked Simon up and down.

'You are tall and distinguished in bearing,' Henry observed in a weak, piping voice. 'Those of my heralds who are skilled in these matters advise me that we are distantly related through the house of Plantagenet, although the connection goes back several generations. But we have a more recent connection on the field of battle, do we not?'

'You refer to the actions of our respective fathers, Your Majesty?' Simon said in a manner suggestive that these matters were perhaps best forgotten.

'I see that your family is as well endowed with an understanding of history as mine,' Henry sneered sarcastically. Then the man who had incurred Fulk's displeasure decided to elaborate.

'His late Majesty King John of England, who I had the honour of serving on the field of battle in Poitou, was driven from his ancestral entitlements in Normandy by a wicked conspiracy of petty barons that included your own father.'

'Since you have probably never before met,' Henry told Simon, 'this gentleman is Hubert de Burgh, Justiciar of England. He is one of my closest advisers, and also one of my most loyal barons.'

'And how fares your warlike father?' de Burgh asked, as if Henry had not spoken.

'He died some years ago in the service of the Pope,' Simon replied acidly.

'Holy orders?' de Burgh suggested with a sneer.

'His own orders,' Simon replied in an even voice, suppressing his rising anger. 'He led the Pope's forces against the heretics of the Languedoc.'

'And are the lands of Poitou, Gascony and Aquitaine now at peace?' Henry asked. 'As you may know, I have a rightful claim over all of them, through my descent from my grandmother of blessed memory, Queen Eleanor. I would wish that my people live in peaceful prosperity.'

'So would I, Your Majesty,' Simon replied tactfully, 'and so they would, were it not for the wicked actions of their southern neighbour Count Raymond of Toulouse. He protects a heretical faction known as Cathars, who in turn defy the authority of the Mother Church of Rome.'

'So why are you here in England, rather than avenging the death of your father in the southern regions of your own nation?' de Burgh demanded. Simon had prepared for this moment, and looked Henry firmly in the eye as he deliberately avoided de Burgh's stern frown.

'I am here to pledge my allegiance to Your Majesty as the Sixth Earl of Leicester.'

There was an audible intake of breath among those standing around the walls, while Henry gave Simon the benefit of a sardonic smirk.

'As you may be aware, the rightful Earl of Leicester is some paces behind you, and was entrusted with your safe-keeping as you journeyed to Court.'

'I am, of course, aware that your father, in his displeasure following his return from Normandy, alienated the de Montfort claim to the earldom, but I am here to make a humble request that it be restored to me, as the rightful heir.'

'You have an older brother, do you not?' Henry asked. 'And a brother between you and he?' He had obviously been well instructed in the family history ahead of this meeting.

'My brother Guy was also killed in the service of His Holiness,' Simon explained. 'As for my older brother Amaury, he and I have reached an agreement that he will succeed to all our French estates in his sole right, while I will seek to restore the family claim in Leicester.'

'And what does Ranulf of Chester have to say on that score?' Hubert de Burgh chimed in, with a taunting stare over Simon's shoulder. Ranulf moved forward and bent the knee before the throne.

'I will, as ever, abide by the will of Your Gracious Majesty,' he announced.

'Do *all* you French ladies wear your hair so short?' asked the young girl seated on Henry's right. She spoke in tortured French that left no doubt that her preferred tongue was

English. She was looking directly at Merle with a hard stare that was almost a challenge.

'Those of us in the south, yes,' Merle replied maliciously in a heavy Languedoc accent. 'It helps keep down the lice that are such a curse to those with long hair.'

Fulk choked back a snigger, and there was an embarrassed silence while everyone stared uncomfortably at the long light auburn tresses that flowed down from under the noble girl's wimple. It was to be hoped that her uncertain French had failed her.

'You must forgive my sister Eleanor's directness,' said Henry, although he was clearly suppressing some amusement at the exchange. 'She is, as you will see, young in years, although happily wed to the gentleman on her right, William Marshal the Younger, Earl Marshal of England and the Second Earl of Pembroke.'

Simon looked where indicated, and could not believe that the pretty child of no more than fourteen years of age could possibly be married to the surly oaf who stood to the right of her throne chair. His greasy black hair hung in ungroomed hanks down to drooping shoulders that acted as a frame for a filthy doublet of indeterminate colour that bulged out where his swollen gut threatened to burst its stitching. His legs were hidden under a surcoat that looked as if it had just returned from a boar hunt in a bog, and his spurred boots were cracked and stained with God knew what. The girl, by comparison, had taken great care over her grooming that morning, and was a blooming picture of red-cheeked health as she smiled warmly back at Simon. Her eyes were the colour of ripe hazelnuts.

Fulk was making the same visual inspection of the dishevelled lout who was the son of the famous William Marshal, the man who'd preserved the throne for the nine-year-old Henry when his father John had died. His first impression was that while the father had been away campaigning somewhere, his mother must have been rolling in a hut with the local butcher. Merle, for her part, had fallen silent, but the two women had clearly not enjoyed their first encounter.

'Who are these people with whom you travel?' Henry enquired in order to break the uncomfortable silence.

Simon gestured at Fulk. 'This gentleman is Fulk de Sevres, standard bearer to the de Montforts.'

'Were you at the siege of Château Gaillard?' de Burgh asked accusingly.

Fulk half bowed in a slightly mocking fashion. 'I had that honour, certainly, but I was then a mere man at arms. As the result of my actions that day, I was fortunate enough to be raised in rank.'

De Burgh's face coloured in anger, but before he could say anything undiplomatic, Henry interposed with his next question.

'And the young lady with the short hair that so took my sister's interest? Is she your wife?'

'No, Your Majesty,' Simon replied. 'She is — how may I put it? — she is, on this occasion, my travelling companion.'

'Indeed,' Henry replied with a conspiratorial wink, 'I have heard much of your charming and convenient French arrangements in these matters. You are all welcome at Court, although whether or not you will be welcome in Leicester is another matter altogether.'

'It is my understanding,' chimed in Ranulf of Chester, 'that the Court travels next to Northampton, which is one day's hard ride from my Leicester estates. Perhaps if our honoured visitors might be permitted to join in the progress to

Northampton, I might then conduct Lord Simon on a tour of the beautiful countryside that he has yet to set eyes on.'

'An excellent notion!' Henry replied with a clap of his hands that reminded Simon of a swan beginning its take-off from the lake back home. 'See to it that our welcome visitors are suitably accommodated, and Lord Simon shall be my guest at board during today's dinner.'

'Hubert de Burgh looked as if he wanted you *roasted* for dinner, rather than being there as an honoured guest,' Fulk muttered as they unloaded their panniers from the horses in the stables.

'You must learn some courtly manners, if we are to be in royal company until we reach this place called Northampton,' Simon said, 'and was it *really* necessary to rub his face in the fact that you were in the front rank when John's favourite castle was finally overrun?'

'I do not like the man,' Fulk grumbled, 'and he clearly enjoys great influence over that wet pudding of a king.'

'Hush!' Simon cautioned him with a backward look at the grooms who were further down the stables. 'And as for you, Merle, you were most insolent to the Princess Eleanor.'

Merle pouted. 'She is a spoiled child, and clearly has learned nothing in the way of polite manners from her marriage to that two-legged bullock. However, she had a fond eye for you, I could not help noticing.'

'I am ignorant of courtly manners, as you remind me,' Fulk said, 'but would I be correct in detecting a suggestion of jealousy in that last comment?'

'Nothing of the sort!' Merle protested, although her reddened cheeks gave the lie to her words. Then, to take the conversation in another direction, she speculated on where she might be accommodated in the castle. 'King Henry clearly took me to be your woman,' she muttered distastefully, 'so perhaps I will be granted a chamber next to yours. Or perhaps the same chamber. At all events, I hope that I will have the opportunity to wash.'

'I think we *all* hope that,' Fulk joked, then leaped backwards to avoid the kick that Merle launched at him.

IX

'You must understand,' Henry told Simon in his most conciliatory tone as they sat together at the high table later that day, 'that the England to which you are now a most welcome visitor is not the nation that it was. In my father's day, it was necessary to make substantial concessions to the overweening barons who threatened his throne at a time when he was weakened by the loss of his estates across the Channel. I was but a boy of nine when he died, and I was obliged to rely on the protection of the Earl of Pembroke, the William Marshal whose son you met earlier today.'

'Was his father not also one of the barons of whom you just spoke?' Simon asked.

Henry nodded. 'He does not rejoice to see you accompanied by the man who helped to best his father in Normandy.'

'Fulk is a most loyal soldier,' Simon assured him, 'and you have my word that he will do nothing warlike if I do not command him to do so. It is like having a wolfhound on a leash.'

'And the woman?' Henry asked. 'Does *she* do all that you command?'

'I must beg Your Majesty not to think the worst of her,' Simon insisted. 'She came into my service in the most unfortunate of circumstances, and she has proved totally loyal and obliging in all the tasks that have been set her. But she is not my woman.'

'There *was* some doubt in my mind on that score,' Henry nodded, 'which is why I had a chamber adjoining yours allocated for her comfort. Should she have been your ... your "lady of convenience", then an adjoining chamber would best serve your joint interests. But if, as it transpires, she is not, then there is nothing lost.'

'Your Majesty is most gracious, and also most hospitable.'

'Is it true that you have never set eyes on the Leicester estates that you claim as yours by right of descent?'

'I had never even set foot in England until some days past, Your Majesty, so I have never seen Leicestershire. Nor, I believe, had my father, the fifth earl.'

'It was most unfortunate,' Henry continued, 'as I mentioned previously, that my father was so hasty in forfeiting the estate to Ranulf of Chester, who I am advised is your cousin of sorts. But he needed the support of loyal men around him during the period in which he was being so sorely pressed by other barons. For myself, I would gladly restore you to your birthright, but you must understand that my hands are tied in such matters.'

'By Hubert de Burgh?' Simon ventured.

Henry nodded. 'He among others, yes. You must prove your worth to him, in order that he might advise me to restore your title.'

'And the beautiful Princess Eleanor?' Simon whispered, glancing at the girl seated on the other side of the king. 'Was her hand in marriage also the price of continued peace in your realm?'

Henry frowned for the first time. 'Have a care that you do not push the boundaries of hospitality too far, Lord Simon. But it is true that Marshal's son was seeking a bride, and I considered it fitting that the ties between the Crown and the might of Pembroke be further strengthened. She is most comely, is she not?'

'She is also somewhat young in age to be sharing a marriage bed with a mature man of full vigour.'

'You mean a fat oaf who treats her like a cheap whore,' Henry muttered under his breath as he spat out a piece of roast mutton onto his trencher and reached for his wine goblet. 'Between the two of us, she is constantly complaining of his rough ways and strange tastes in the bedchamber, but were I to raise the matter I have no doubt that de Burgh would take his part. However, on another matter, we may be of assistance to each other in ways that might relieve the pressure on our royal house, while easing your path towards the Leicester estate.'

'I should be grateful to learn how that might be,' Simon said quietly as he looked across the Great Hall. Fulk was seated next to the Earl of Norfolk and his lady, seemingly engaged in cheerful banter, to judge by the broad smile on his face. Merle was somewhere out of his line of sight, seated with the ladies of Princess Eleanor's entourage.

Henry leaned in closer and cleared his mouth of what he had been chewing as he revealed his thoughts. 'As I mentioned during our first conversation, I would seek to reinforce my claim to lands in Poitou and Gascony. Should I be successful, I would place de Burgh in overall command, with some fancy title or other. There are other barons loyal to me who would rejoice in his absence from the realm, and during that time I might strengthen my grip on the throne of England, leaving the troublesome de Burgh to return in the fullness of time to discover that the boy has become a man at last. Do I make myself clear?'

'Perfectly, Your Majesty. And you seek my assistance in the recovery of your French estates?'

'Exactly. Should you prove instrumental in that regard, helping to restore the prestige of the House of Anjou across the sea, then what could be more fitting than your restoration to your ancient entitlement?'

Simon smiled. This was all proceeding beyond his wildest expectations. 'If we are *ad idem* in this matter, then it would seem that my sojourn in your country will be much shorter than I had anticipated, Your Majesty.'

'You must call me "Henry" when we are not in the hearing of the Court,' the king replied as he placed his hand over Simon's. 'But do you not wish first to lay eyes on your reward? And would it not serve to obscure our scheme all the better for you to play the part of the landless wanderer seeking his birthright? At all events, take the road to Leicester in the company of the Earl of Chester. He is an old man who needs the comfort of believing that he is still of some service to the realm.'

Later that afternoon, Simon was changing his doublet for one that had already been immaculately restored by the castle washerwomen, when the adjoining door opened, and a disgruntled-looking Merle stood in its opening.

'I merely wished to see if there is anything you need, before I lie down for a brief rest, my lord. These heavy English banquets are too much for my narrow stomach, I fear. And as for the irritating company…'

'What made you of the princess's ladies?' Simon asked with a wry smile.

'They speak of nothing but intrigues of the groin. Were I to believe but half of their empty prattle, I would be convinced that every noble in England is engaged in sampling every woman who is amenable — and that would seem to be *most* of them. No wonder that a certain indelicate affliction is known in our country as "The English disease".'

Simon chuckled. 'If it is of any consolation, we may soon be returning home on a mission from the king.'

'And what of your quest for your English estate?'

'It is all one and the same. If you would be so obliging, could you find where Fulk has been accommodated, and request that he attend me?'

'It may well be a trap, sir,' Fulk told Simon later. He was perched on the window seat, still red in the face from the wine he had sampled at dinner. 'From what I have been able to deduce, these English knaves speak with tongues so forked that one could lift a trencher with them. I was dining with the Earl of Norfolk and his lady, and it was one long tale of which knight stabbed his neighbour in the throat over a game of cards, or which lord put the flame to the home village of a man who had displeased him by being late in bringing in the harvest. They fight like dogs over a carcass, and they have the morals of rutting stags.'

'It seems that you share Merle's saintly disapproval of the way matters are conducted in this land that we are visiting,' Simon said. 'But surely there is no harm in returning home earlier than we had planned, carrying the king's commission to suppress Poitou and Gascony in the name of England?'

'You are forgetting, perhaps, that we are French,' Fulk reminded him. 'King Louis himself entrusted you with the task of spying out the land, did he not? And now you are proposing that we go behind his back and conquer lands in the south-west over which he himself would dearly love to maintain a claim? And how precisely do you suggest that you, I and the virtuous Merle take on the combined might of twenty thousand men at arms?'

'I assume that Henry will place us at the head of an army,' Simon replied. 'And the Louis to whom I gave that undertaking is the one who died but recently, leaving his son of the same name as King of the Franks, but with no knowledge of my promise. However, this is all somewhat in the future, I believe. We must first visit Leicester, as we had originally intended, in order that our new understanding with King Henry remains unknown to all but us.'

'What do you make of that fossil Ranulf of Chester?' Fulk asked as he shifted off the ledge in order to depart.

'He seems pleasant enough,' Simon replied, 'but Henry spoke in terms that suggest that his fighting days are over. Although it would seem that in his day he was a formidable ally of the late King John, in the days when rebel barons wrung concessions from him that have left the Crown weaker than it was.'

'By all means let us progress to Leicester,' Fulk suggested, 'but be wary of what you are promised by Henry. He has much about him that reminds me of a boar fighting off the hounds.'

X

They remained at Oxford for three more days, during which they tested their capacity for food and wine to an extent that they would have disbelieved only a month previously. Fulk continued to learn what he could of military matters, while Merle continued to complain of the incessant conversation among the royal ladies that rarely rose above the waist. Simon began to assess for himself how deeply the king was constricted in his actions by the stern will of Hubert de Burgh and William Marshal's grubby son, without whose blessing it seemed that Henry could not make the simplest of arrangements. Fortunately, it seemed that de Burgh had no objection to Simon and his companions journeying north with the royal progress, ahead of diverting to Leicester.

There was much of the same for two days in Northampton, where the accommodation was so limited that while Simon was afforded his own chamber, Merle was sharply advised that she would be required to take her retirement in the large communal chamber allocated to Princess Eleanor's maids. When she tearfully complained to Simon, he offered her the choice between more of the twittering that she found so intolerable, or a night snuggled next to him in circumstances that would be guaranteed to perpetuate the belief that she was indeed his 'lady of convenience'. She chose the latter, and the next day was able to report, with what appeared to be a smirk of satisfaction, that she had now become an object of envy among the wimpled gossips whom she so despised. She also seemed pleased to learn that Fulk had been obliged to spend two nights sleeping in a hastily converted stable along with some of Ranulf's men.

On the third day, Ranulf was waiting for them at first light as they collected their horses, dressed for a long day's ride through the heart of England's midland pastures, streams, woodland and hedgerows. The same men who had shared Fulk's sparse accommodation, and who had originally diverted them from the London road towards Oxford, rode ahead in the vanguard, while Fulk and Merle allowed their horses to trot alongside their rearguard colleagues. In the centre, Simon and Ranulf conversed amiably while the latter pointed out various features on their route, explaining how the English had organised their agriculture along the strip lines that they kept passing, where there were many serfs with backs bent to the hoe. As the sun began to sink below a distant church tower to the west, and a wide, shallow vale opened up before them to reveal a substantial stonework tower in its centre, Ranulf gave a sigh of satisfaction.

'Welcome to Leicester, Simon. Or perhaps I should say "welcome home", since King Henry has let it be known that he would regard it as a great favour were I to make you a free gift of your allegedly stolen inheritance. However, I am not yet that weak and foolish. For the moment, cast your eyes over what may perhaps be yours one day.'

Although he had long imagined this day, Simon did not experience the thrill that he had anticipated. It was true that the valley that lay before him was both fertile and pleasing to the eye, but he had no sense of 'coming home', as Ranulf had suggested.

'You will find no loving countess awaiting my return with open arms,' Ranulf explained in a tired voice, 'nor will children come running through the outer bailey to welcome me home.

My ailing wife prefers to spend her declining months in Chester, and we have no progeny. I have seen nearly fifty years, and I have no great desire to see many more. We will discuss this further at supper.'

Fulk and Merle urged their horses forward to draw level with Bernard as they trotted into the courtyard that fronted the stables.

'Another night wrapped in scratchy straw, by my guess,' Fulk muttered as he gazed gloomily at what seemed to be a bare tower, much smaller even than the inadequate buildings they had vacated in Northampton before sunrise that day, 'or may I claim to be your other mistress, and share a bolster with the two of you?'

Merle made a disgusted noise through her nose. 'While I am honoured to be thought of as body comforter to the long-lost Earl of Leicester, I refuse to assume the same relationship with his horsemaster.'

'That would seem to be decided, then,' Simon smirked at Fulk. 'Or perhaps the cook will take pity on you, and allow you to sleep in her hearth.'

'Provided that she extinguishes the fire first,' Fulk grimaced in reply, 'I may well explore that possibility. I still have straw up my arse from last night.'

'At least it is not between your ears,' Merle said as she dismounted.

When the party were sitting together for supper, Ranulf told them a little more about the estate. 'The fowl are from our own waterside,' he explained as he carved off a piece of breast with his paring knife, 'and tomorrow we must all stroll down by the lake. It is one of my favourite walks, and from there you can obtain a true perception of the overall size of the estate. What is your first impression of it?'

'It reminds me in many ways of my own home estate in the Île-de-France,' Simon replied, 'although you seem to possess better soil, to judge by the fatness of the beasts I saw grazing as we rode in. But in truth, most of my life thus far has been spent in military camps, as first my father, then my older brother, sought to overcome Raymond of Toulouse and suppress the Cathars, so I have little by which to judge your estate.'

'It could be *your* estate, were you prepared to hold it from me,' Ranulf said quietly. Simon turned with raised eyebrows, and Ranulf explained. 'I am led to understand that your system of landholding is the same as ours, since it came over here with William of Normandy. Every noble holds land from his fief lord, and I currently hold both Chester and Leicester from King Henry, as heir and successor to his father King John, who first gave me my estates. There is no reason why you may not hold Leicester under me, as your sovereign lord, pledged to come to my banner should I have need of military service from you.'

'And why would you offer me this?' Simon asked suspiciously.

'As you may have deduced,' Ranulf replied, 'my heart lies in my original lands in Cheshire. That is where I have made my final home, and where my wife prefers to stay, since she does not enjoy good health while surrounded by this somewhat marshy river ground here in Leicestershire. I only obtained this estate during one of King John's many fits of anger, and it was meant as a punishment to your father. It means little to me compared with Chester, and the income from the land is not so plentiful that I would wish to reside here. But I dare not offend King Henry by publicly renouncing what his father granted me, and Hubert de Burgh considers me to be loyal to him, which is at present the safest face to show him. More wine?'

Simon nodded, mentally reeling at the possibilities that were opening up. Ranulf filled both Simon's goblet and his own before continuing.

'Your man at arms, Fulk, has left my own men in no doubt that you are a fearsome warrior, and a born leader of men. He has also impressed them himself, with his tales of a life spent in chainmail, whereas most of my so-called soldiers are really converted farmers. I have no doubt that they would respond well to whatever skill with weapons Fulk can imbue them with. With you at their head, Leicester would have a formidable fighting force that I would wish to have under the banner of Chester when the day comes that Henry finally stands his ground against de Burgh, who has long exceeded his welcome as the puppeteer pulling Henry's strings.

'I may tell you, in the strictest confidence of course, that there is a growing body of resistance at Court to the continued influence of both de Burgh and Marshal's disgusting boar of a son. The day is not far away when nobles such as myself will be called to rid ourselves of those unhealthy hands on the throne of England. I am too old and tired to take to the field of conflict myself, but with you bounden to me in military service in return for your Leicester estates, I can anticipate that day of reckoning without feeling the chill of death swirling around me. The offer is there, and will remain open for as long as you wish. You could not style yourself "Earl of Leicester", of course, but must be content with "Lord Simon de Montfort of Leicester". But when Henry is fully restored to his own, so might you be.'

Simon later rose from the table somewhat unsteadily and made his way to the chamber allocated to him. Shortly afterwards he was joined by Merle, who was smiling in appreciation of the pleasant time she had spent at a lower table learning her first words of English from Edith, an elderly retainer who was the estate washerwoman.

'I think I might like it here,' she enthused.

'We may be here longer than I first thought,' Simon told her as he lay down and indicated for her to snuggle up to him. 'On the morrow, you, Fulk and I have much to discuss.'

XI

'You change your mind more regularly than your hose,' Fulk said disbelievingly as the three of them stood contemplating the lake around which the wildfowl were pecking a living from the reedy banks. 'Yesterday you were all but mounting your horse to head back to France in the service of King Henry, but today you intend to remain and assist in the removal of Hubert de Burgh.'

'There are worse places we could reside,' Merle said as she watched a mother hen leading her chicks to the water's edge.

'This I do not doubt, after my experience of last night,' Fulk said as he picked up a stone and attempted to skim it across the water, sending several birds scuttling for the cover of an overhanging willow tree. 'I simply seek some firm plan of action upon which I can set my sights.'

'I came here to claim this estate,' Simon reminded them, 'and God in his infinite wisdom has allowed it to fall into the hands of an older man who wishes to be rid of it. What could be simpler? The only price to be paid, as I understand it, is that when the trumpet sounds, we must be ready to rise up against a man who you seem to detest anyway, thereby earning the eternal gratitude of a king who will then confirm me to all the world in an estate that I have been enjoying anyway.'

'In English, this is called a "lake",' Merle told them distractedly. 'Like our own word "lac". This English language is simple to learn, and I would learn more of it, so I am content to remain here.'

'But we would *not* be remaining here, if Lord Simon has his way,' Fulk pointed out. 'We would be obliged to move with the

Court, which, so far as I can make out, never remains in the one place for more than a few days, but is constantly journeying from one draughty castle to another until the food runs out. And you both forget that the price of taking the estate on the terms that Ranulf offers is that I have to convert a sad collection of former ploughboys into a fighting force.'

'That is the price you pay for being an experienced fighting man,' Simon countered. 'Wherever you — or for that matter, we — go, that will always be your trade. And I have cause to remember how well you taught me in my time.'

Fulk had no answer to that but a grunt as he picked up more stones and began skimming them, one by one, across the lake, until Merle protested.

'You are frightening these beautiful creatures and their babies. They are so restful to watch.'

'And so delicious to eat,' Fulk reminded her. 'For all you know, you consumed their grandmother at dinner yesterday.'

Merle shot him a venomous look and began to walk quickly ahead of them, calling to the startled chicks as if summoning her children into the cottage for their midday meal. As Fulk and Simon hung back, Simon looked sideways at his companion.

'Did the cook find you somewhere to lay your head?' he asked.

Fulk lowered his voice. 'And somewhere to lay something else as well. She is a lady of good proportion and also a lustful disposition, it would seem. I requested somewhere warm within her empire in which I might rest for the night, and she offered me a place on her own pallet in the scullery. The price, therefore, was not unreasonable. I would confidently predict the beginning of a firm relationship there, provided that *I* keep firm, if you follow my drift.'

Simon laughed lightly. 'I can see that you will require little further persuasion to remain here, but I would have your more impartial opinion of which way I should go.'

Fulk thought deeply for a moment, then looked back at Simon. 'Whichever way you choose, your ultimate quarry, as you have said more than once, is the title of "Earl of Leicester". We have been here slightly less than one day, and you have already been offered it in due course if you bend the knee — when your wound will permit — to the man who is currently our host. He will no doubt be returning to this place called Chester without much further delay, leaving you to manage the estate, me to organise a body of fighting men, and Merle to learn this barbarous tongue they call English. The only alternative offer you have received is to return to the Languedoc, heavily outnumbered, in the name of the King of England, in order to seize land that King Louis of France no doubt seeks for himself, thereby rendering it uncertain whether you would ever be welcome back in the land of your birth. To my mind, that is not a choice — there is an obvious way forward, and I speak as one who is familiar with assessing odds, not as someone who would spend many more happy nights between a cook's thighs.'

'You have summed it up neatly, Fulk, and I thank you. But will you be prepared to raise a body of fighting men, as Ranulf requires?'

'I would rather do that than attempt to learn English,' Fulk said. 'We will leave that onerous duty to Saint Merle.'

'Will you not require a knowledge of English in order to instruct your men?'

'It would seem not,' Fulk replied. 'For many years now the people of England have, I am told, been required to speak French for their very survival. And, as Merle has learned, many of their words are similar to ours, since they have been adapted from them. Besides which, how many words did I need to use in order to teach you how to survive on the field of battle? As you will have observed for yourself, we fight, not with words, but with swords, axes and lances. The language of battle is death or survival, and requires no words. When a man is charging at you with a drawn sword, do you engage him in polite conversation?'

'So you will be able to produce the fighting force that Earl Ranulf requires?'

'Probably, given that our curses and theirs appear to be in the same language,' Fulk said. 'Give me but a few months and I will have them ready to take on anyone you care to name.'

Later that day, Simon sought audience with Earl Ranulf, and advised him that he would like to take up his generous offer.

'There is nothing of generosity in it,' Ranulf assured him. 'We are both the richer for this pledge, but first it must be approved by King Henry.'

'How so, since it is your land to grant?'

'It is ultimately the king's land, is it not?' Ranulf reminded him. 'I may not alienate so much as a blade of grass that I hold from the king without his approval.'

'And think you that he will approve?'

'Why not, since it was his idea?'

Simon frowned in puzzlement. 'But while we were at Oxford, he seemed to express the wish for me to return to France in order to assist in the retaking of Poitou and Gascony.'

'So he did, and so he wishes, in the fullness of time. But he does not wish Hubert de Burgh to know the more immediate reason for your elevation, which is —' here Ranulf lowered his voice and looked apprehensively at the chamber door —

'which is that you be ready with a fighting force under my banner when the time comes to challenge the Regency that has existed for too long.'

'How can he be certain of my loyalty, after such a brief acquaintance?'

Ranulf looked Simon squarely in the eye. 'It is not *your* loyalty in which he places his trust, but *mine*. Be in no doubt that should you betray his trust and mine, we will both meet our deaths. For myself it would be no great tragedy, but you are still a young man, barely older than Henry himself, and you have a golden future ahead of you, if I judge matters aright.'

'So we will be deceiving only Hubert de Burgh?'

'If it is possible to deceive him,' Ranulf nodded. 'He is himself the most devious of conspirators, and lately it is as if he knows that his day is fast approaching. He gathers his own men at arms around his stronghold in the Welsh Marches, as if preparing for some great military progress, and has instructed Marshal's son to lose no time in fathering an heir to his estates, almost as if de Burgh expects his public office as Justiciar to be taken from him. Any heir of William Marshal will, of course, be royal progeny, and perhaps Hubert seeks to further strengthen his grip on the Crown by this means, since Marshal is under his baleful influence.'

Simon shuddered at the thought of the child-bride he had briefly glimpsed in Oxford being cruelly used like some brood mare at the behest of a man who saw her impregnation simply as a means of strengthening his own position at Court. He needed no further persuasion to accede to Ranulf's wishes.

'When do you intend on putting your proposal to King Henry?' he asked.

'Not just me, Simon — *us*. And I suggest that we lose no time in so doing. The Court is currently in Nottingham, which was one of his father's favourite castles, and one in which he made several improvements to comfort. If matters proceed according to custom, Henry will remain at Nottingham for several weeks before completing the progress to York. It is less than a day's ride from here, and we should plan to leave the day after tomorrow. I would also caution that you travel without your two French companions. Neither of them earned much favour at Oxford, I regret to say. Your woman insulted the Princess Eleanor, and as for the worthy Fulk, Hubert de Burgh seems to regard him with the greatest of suspicion.'

Simon broke the news to Fulk and Merle later that day, and neither of them expressed any disappointment at learning that they would not be required to once again don their best courtly manners. Merle, for her part, was learning much about English, and the day-to-day management of a large country estate, from Edith the washerwoman, while Fulk expressed an eagerness to begin his work with the men at arms, while retaining the good offices of the cook. However, he warned Simon more than once to trust no-one in the 'nest of serpents' that he considered the English Court to be.

XII

Late in the afternoon two days later, Simon smiled as the warm summer sun emblazoned his best surcoat with light. He listened to the happy gurgling of the River Trent as they crossed it via the old stone bridge and made their way through the southern fields of this pleasant settlement, with its fine Norman castle perched arrogantly on the sandstone outcrop to the west of the small town.

They arrived to be advised that King Henry was taking supper in King John's Tower, but that he would be pleased to receive Simon in his private dining chamber, while Ranulf was consigned to the general nobles' board on the floor below. As soon as Simon was announced, Henry beckoned him over to the table he was sharing with Princess Eleanor and her husband, Hubert de Burgh and various other dignitaries whose precise identities Simon did not know. The pages were instructed to set a place for Simon between Henry and de Burgh, and Princess Eleanor smiled up at him affectionately as he bowed before taking his seat.

They were already into their second course, and Simon was invited to help himself to venison and wood pigeon, while a serving girl placed a goblet before him and poured him some wine. Henry was in a jovial mood, it would seem, and he lost no time in engaging Simon in conversation.

'How found you the lands in Leicestershire?'

'Excellent, Your Majesty. The land would seem to be very fertile, the beasts are fat, the woods and lake are plentifully stocked, and Earl Ranulf is a generous host.'

'Do you plan to remain there?' Marshal asked bluntly.

'That remains to be seen,' Simon replied diplomatically. 'I believe that Earl Ranulf has some wish that I manage the land for him, thus freeing him to bide more on his estate at Chester.'

'You are content to reside there despite having no title?' de Burgh demanded suspiciously.

'I will certainly give it lengthy consideration,' Simon replied guardedly, sensing that this was not the moment to disclose why he had travelled north.

'That scurvy ruffian who was with you at Oxford,' Marshal reminded him from the other side of Eleanor, and through a mouthful of meat, 'does he remain in Leicester?'

'If you refer to Fulk de Sevres,' Simon replied coldly, 'indeed he does, since he has much to learn of the ways of English warfare from Earl Ranulf's men at arms.'

'He will have learned enough of that at the walls of Château Guillard,' Marshal muttered darkly. 'Why should we allow him to remain in this country to learn more of our battle stratagems?'

'What of the girl?' Princess Eleanor asked. 'The one with the short dark hair? Did she travel north with you?'

'No, my lady,' Simon replied. 'She has remained in Leicester also, in order to learn more of your English ways.'

'Such as how to properly groom long hair?' came Eleanor's sarcastic reply, and Henry retrieved the conversation as best he could.

'Tell us of your *French* ways, my lord. Is it true that in your country there are low-born minstrels who write ballads and perform them to high-born ladies whose affections they can only dream of securing?'

'Troubadours, Henry,' his sister reminded him. 'They are called "troubadours", but *do* please tell us more about them, Simon.'

'In truth, I know less about them than you seem to, my lady,' Simon explained. 'It is true that during my time in the south I heard tell of them, but they are more to be found in Aquitaine, I believe. Certainly I encountered none around Toulouse or Carcassonne.'

'If you had, you would probably have had them done to death,' Marshal grunted as he rose from the table and broke wind noisily. He then made his excuses and walked from the chamber after only the most perfunctory of bows to King Henry. Eleanor shook her head in embarrassment, and Simon caught de Burgh following Marshal's departure with an undisguised glare of disdain.

'You and Earl Ranulf are invited to an audience with me before dinner on the morrow,' Henry told Simon as the remains of the third meat course were deftly removed from the board by one group of pages, while another line of them entered with the fruits and sweetmeats. 'I would know more of your intentions towards my land in Leicestershire, which we may perhaps contrive to visit for a hunt ere we depart for York. What do you say, Hubert?'

'That may well depend upon the weather, Henry,' de Burgh counselled him. 'If the ground be boggy, as it usually is once the River Soar overflows with the summer rains, then a spirited chase on horseback may not be the safest diversion for the King of England.'

'And *is* the ground boggy, Simon?' Henry asked.

Simon thought for a moment, uncertain whether or not Henry was seeking some excuse to visit the estate. 'I was walking by the lake only two days ago, Your Majesty. As you may recall, it is fed by the river further upstream, and to judge by the state of the land around the lake, there will be no risk of bogs forming unless we have a week of incessant rain.'

'There you are, Hubert,' Henry said. 'The latest news on the state of the land, from one who examined it only recently.'

'I simply seek to protect Your Majesty from peril,' de Burgh assured him. 'Seen or *unseen*,' he added, with a sideways glare at Simon.

'You can appreciate why I champ at the bit to be rid of de Burgh's cloying restrictions on my actions,' Henry said to Simon the following morning. He and Ranulf had been admitted into the presence in the richly furnished ground floor chamber of King John's Tower. 'I cannot contemplate even a simple hunt without his approval, it would seem. He does not make so bold as to forbid me from doing anything, of course — he is too sleek in his manner for that. Instead he merely insinuates what he thinks would be best, safe in the knowledge that he has the largest standing army in the kingdom with which to enforce his wishes, should it come to aught.'

'He would say that he only has your best interests at heart, and you have much to be grateful to him for, or so I am led to believe,' Simon replied diplomatically.

Henry nodded. 'This is what he would have the nation believe, and were I still nine years old it would be true enough. But I shall be twenty-two this coming October, and it does little for my dignity at Court that I must seek de Burgh's approval for my every action. We all know why we are gathered here this morning, and what is proposed meets with my joyful approval, but we may not even begin the formalities until de Burgh is with us, like an irritating fly that will not vacate a pile of horse excrement.'

'Hardly a flattering analogy for *either* of you, Henry,' Simon replied, just as a page announced the entrance of the irritating fly in question. De Burgh scowled as he acknowledged the presence of Simon and Ranulf with the curtest of bows. He looked even less pleased when he realised, as he turned, that he was being followed into the presence by another man, dressed in ecclesiastical robes.

'Simon,' Henry purred, 'may I introduce Peter des Roches, who in addition to being Bishop of Winchester, is also a fellow countryman of yours, having begun life in Touraine. He was my official guardian following my father's death, and still maintains a close interest in my welfare, as does my justiciar here. Now, please announce your business,' Henry invited them, as if he knew nothing of what they had in mind.

Ranulf bent the knee and looked up hopefully. 'Your Majesty, I seek your leave, as my liege lord, to sub-feu my lands of Leicester to Lord Simon.'

'And why do you wish this?' de Burgh demanded.

Ranulf continued to look at Henry, as if the question had come from him. 'I grow old in years, and for reasons of health would wish to keep to my estates in Chester. Mindful of the need to manage the lands so graciously bestowed upon me by your illustrious father, the late...'

'Spare us the nonsense, Earl Ranulf,' de Burgh cut in sharply, 'and answer my question.'

'I was in the process of attempting to do precisely that,' Ranulf replied coolly. 'And my answer is that I do not wish to see such rich land, graciously gifted to me by the King of England, reduced to an unproductive swamp for lack of husbandry on my part.'

'No one could mistake you for a farmer,' de Burgh replied. 'You presumably have peasants on the land who do that for you, and I hardly think that Lord Simon is a gifted estate manager.'

'You have not said anything yet, Lord Simon,' Henry intervened. 'Were I minded to grant Earl Ranulf's request, what assurance do we have that the land will be any more productive than it is at present?'

'I do not promise that the land will be more productive under my hand,' Simon replied, 'but it would seem that there is a danger of it becoming *less* productive if Earl Ranulf retreats to his Cheshire estates.'

'You are a soldier, are you not?' de Burgh reminded him. 'What know you of farming?'

'I have only ever engaged twice in feats of arms,' Simon told him, 'and on the second of those occasions, I received a wound that has still not healed properly after three years, and does not allow me even to kneel in the royal presence. While waiting for that healing moment, I took considerable interest in the management of my brother's estate in France.'

De Burgh had no immediate answer to that, and changed his line of argument. 'Henry, it is not good for the realm to have large estates held between so many different hands — particularly not *French* hands,' he added with a sweeping glance that took in both Simon and Peter des Roches. 'I counsel against what Earl Ranulf is requesting.'

'But you do not outright *forbid* it?' Ranulf defied him.

De Burgh suddenly seemed less sure of his ground. 'It is not for me to forbid or permit an action that His Majesty may be contemplating. I am simply here to advise him in his best interests.'

'That would seem to be settled, then,' Henry replied. 'It is fitting that we have the bishop with us, since the process requires the swearing of an oath of fealty. Lord Simon, you clearly cannot be required to kneel, but it is customary for you to display some outward show of obeisance to your liege lord while he takes your pledge. Perhaps if I were to instruct the page to bring that low stool over, you might sit upon it in lieu of kneeling?'

Two minutes later the process was completed, and Simon was now infeft of the Leicester estates of which he fully intended one day to be the earl. He thanked Henry and Ranulf warmly and sought leave to withdraw from the presence. Ranulf made the same request, and Henry warmly granted leave for them both to withdraw from the Court and return to their estate. They soon reached the anonymity of the courtyard below the Tower, where their conversation was drowned out by the clatter of horses' hooves as the grooms brought out the mounts for their daily exercise, and domestic menials scurried to and fro with baskets of bread, fish and cheeses. Ranulf placed an arm across Simon's shoulder while they walked slowly down the esplanade.

'A diplomat as well as a soldier,' he said. 'You almost had *me* convinced that your fighting experience has been limited, and yet Fulk never tires of telling my men at arms — who are, of course, now *your* men at arms — that in your very first engagement you slew seven men single-handedly.'

'I was fighting to preserve the life of my older brother,' Simon replied. 'There was then a lengthy passage of time before I had occasion to re-occupy lands of ours in France that had been seized in our absence, and I was unskilled enough to allow myself to be struck down from behind.'

'But if you are sufficiently fired by the cause, you fight like a demon, it would seem. Let us hope that you have that fire in your belly when the time comes to fly your battle pennants against Hubert de Burgh.'

'I am still uncertain of how he came to be in such a position of power,' Simon replied with a frown, 'and for that matter how King John came to die so young, leaving his heir Henry at de Burgh's mercy. There are clearly forces at work at the Court of England of which I know next to nothing.'

'It is as well that you know the full history,' Ranulf told him as he lowered his voice even further, 'and now is as meet a time as any. The previous king, John, behaved in his later years almost as if he *wished* to forfeit his crown. He taxed the barons unmercifully in order to finance wars in France in which he demonstrated that he was not fit to herd cattle, let alone lead an army of men. He contrived to lose what was left of his estates in France to Philippe, and then his son Louis, and in the process so incensed Louis that when the barons rose up in rebellion, Louis was easily persuaded to invade England. It was then that leading nobles such as myself and William Marshal rallied to John's banner and fought off the French threat, for which we were rewarded with the vast estates that we still possess. Prior to that, we had been obliged to defend John against an uprising by his own barons, discontented with his policies, and we persuaded him to sign a peace Charter which both sides have ignored ever since. The barons refused to back down from their aggression, and then John died of a disease of the guts on a march north, leaving only a boy of nine to succeed him.'

'Henry?' Simon asked.

Ranulf nodded. 'There was clearly an urgent need for a Regent to rule in Henry's name until he came of age, and the barons were divided even on that. But when William Marshal's forces gained the upper hand, he bullied the defeated barons into appointing him Regent. I was a willing party to that, since Marshal had the superior force, and had displayed constant loyalty to the Crown. However, it was I who persuaded the guardianship of the young Henry to be given to Peter des Roches, who you met this morning, and who had been Henry's tutor. This was resented by another leading baron, Hubert de Burgh, who was bought off by being granted the justiciarship for life. He sought to undermine William Marshal by befriending his son, and persuading Henry to consent to the son marrying the Princess Eleanor, who by all accounts he treats so badly.

'Then William Marshal Senior died, and since then it has been a grim contest between de Burgh and des Roches for dominance at Court. The end result has been that poor King Henry is like a man with *both* arms tied behind his back — hence his need for loyal men such as myself who will hopefully allow him, one day, to make his own decisions and rule the land that is his birthright.'

'What of this Charter that you mentioned?' Simon asked. 'What were its terms, and is it still being ignored?'

Ranulf gave a hollow laugh as they reached the stables, and the grooms led out their horses for them to mount. 'It is as if it had never been signed,' he told Simon. 'I was there that day at Runnymede, close by the castle at Windsor, and we all truly believed that its terms would be honoured. That men would be free of punishment without cause, taxation without consultation, forfeiture of land through royal spite, the way in which your father lost the Earldom of Leicester. I am embarrassed by the way in which I came into the title, and it would ease my conscience, as I approach the day of my judgment, to be able to hand it back to you without reservation. I think that Henry shares my discomfort, but as you witnessed during this morning's performance, Henry can do nothing of which de Burgh disapproves, while des Roches silently waits for de Burgh to overplay his hand.'

Simon had much to occupy his thoughts as they lost no time in returning to Leicester, where Fulk had a group of men running around the lake carrying logs above their heads in what was no doubt his first exercise in toughening them up. Merle emerged from an outhouse to welcome them back, a contented smile on her face and something white and glutinous all over her hands.

'I'm learning to make something called "cheese",' she told Simon. 'It is what we call "fromage", and it will be a delightful orange colour when we are finished, like the ones we saw at supper on our first night here. How went things at Court?'

'Middling well, so far as I can tell,' Simon replied. 'You may certainly continue learning all the English you can — in addition, of course, to making cheese. But we have much to discuss. When Fulk returns with the men, tell him to meet me by the lake once the sun is up tomorrow.'

'And if it rains?' she asked.

'This is England, young lady. It always rains — particularly at Court, it would seem. We must all prepare to take shelter, and we begin to build that shelter on the morrow. When you are not making cheese, you must make your own preparations for a stormy existence here in Leicestershire, so please accompany Fulk on the morrow, rain or shine.'

XIII

For the next two years Simon and his companions enjoyed a pastoral existence, with Simon leading the life of a traditional English lord of the manor, Fulk slowly and determinedly amassing a small army of fighting men, and Merle finally persuading Simon that since he had no wife, she should act the part of the lady of the manor, controlling the domestic household and completing her mastery of English.

'After all,' she argued, 'I grew up learning how to manage a country *auberge*, and this is simply a larger version of the same thing. Also, since I speak passable English, I am well placed to direct the household servants, while they in their turn can advise me on how a large family house should be properly run along English lines.'

It was Merle who persuaded Simon, against his better judgment, to adopt the Saxon tradition of a communal hall on the ground floor of the tower, in which everyone ate their meals, and in which certain privileged domestic staff were allowed to sleep on the straw once the hall was closed for the night. However, even Merle drew the line at allowing Fulk's men at arms to join the company, and they were required to eat and sleep in a converted barn next to the stable block. When Simon queried this seeming discrimination, Merle grimaced and explained.

'I have not so far complained about being in the company of groups of soldiers, since you are a man of warfare, and my lord, while Fulk is a friend of sorts. But it brings back disturbing memories of my days in the *auberge* back home, when such groups would strut through our front door, brandishing their weapons. That meant only one thing for me, if we were to avoid having our humble house demolished or set to the flames.'

Simon reached out for her, and held her to him as she trembled at the memories she was invoking. 'It shall be as you request,' he reassured her, 'since the household arrangements are under your management. In truth, we barely have room for an extra thirty or so men in the hall anyway.'

The estate that Simon had been left to manage was certainly no great castle with imposing siege-proof walls, a moat with portcullis, and battlements from which invading forces might be repelled with fusillades of arrows or barrels of boiling pitch. It was, in reality, a stone tower on various levels, with a few outbuildings for stables, tool storage and accommodation for menials such as table servers and scullions. Fulk never ceased to cast a critical eye over the lack of defences, and to warn Simon that they were all completely exposed to any enemy action.

'Since, so far as I am aware,' Simon replied, 'I have no enemies, why should that concern us?'

'Because,' Fulk reminded him, 'you have chosen to pursue your fortune at the English Court, where, or so you report, *everyone* has enemies. The day will come when we shall be obliged to defend ourselves against some powerful noble you have offended, and I would not wish to do so from inside the walls of an overgrown farmhouse.'

Eventually, Simon gave in to Fulk's entreaties, and gave orders for a new fortified residence to be constructed behind a massive earth barricade, along traditional lines. The material for the earthwork came from a ditch, fifteen feet across, that was dug around the existing property, which became a muddy pit after the spring rains set in, and by late summer had begun to resemble a more traditional moat. The stone for the outer wall was quarried locally, under the supervision of a master stonemason from the nearby village of Hinckley, together with his team of journeymen and apprentices, and at first the manual labour came from local men who were not otherwise engaged in tilling their crops or tending their beasts.

But such creations did not come free of charge, and it was not long before the modest estate income that came from tenant rents or their equivalent in livestock for the table threatened to bring the entire enterprise to a standstill. Simon began to incur debts with local suppliers, which were paid off when the rents came in, but were hastily incurred again once it was necessary to pay the stonemasons and their labourers for their services.

It was Fulk who suggested that they might save considerable expense by employing his own developing fighting men as labourers. Not only would this reduce the overall expense of the improvements, but it would keep them physically fit and prevent them fighting among themselves due to an excess of energy. This gave Simon another, more personal, idea. He was deeply conscious of the fact that the serious leg injury he had incurred during the retaking of Montfort-l'Amaury had kept him from any vigorous exercise of his own. On cold mornings, he experienced a difficulty in mobility that was alarming for a man who regarded himself — and was thought of by others — as a warrior leader. He had been acutely embarrassed by his inability to kneel in order to swear fealty to Ranulf of Chester, and he was anxious to appear more agile and youthful the next time he met with King Henry.

For this reason, he had been ignoring invitations to attend the permanent Courts that Henry maintained at Westminster and Windsor, instead employing his time manhandling rocks around the muddy terrain, and watching, spellbound, as the master mason glued them into a rapidly rising outer wall using a mixture of local gypsum and river mud.

Simon was thus engaged, barefoot and stripped of all but his under-hose, when there came a warning shout from Fulk, who was in the main courtyard with a select handful of his men, instructing them in the noble art of hacking off heads with a battle-axe. Simon was at the rear of the rapidly rising main defence wall, sweating profusely as he and another of Fulk's men laid a huge sandstone block carefully onto a spread of mortar trowelled onto the lower blocks by a journeyman. He looked to where Fulk was pointing, and saw a cloud of dust, inside which was a group of horsemen. Fulk yelled across to him with a knowing smirk.

'They are not in full armour, and are only lightly armed, so we may withstand this attack, particularly since they would appear to have brought a woman with them.'

Simon stood up fully and arched his tired back muscles as he watched the party approaching, and realised with horror that the man in the centre of the front row was King Henry, with Hugh de Burgh on his left, and William Marshal to his right. The handful of men at arms who formed their bodyguard were all in the royal livery of lions couchant, and they all slackened their pace in order to pick their way carefully over the earth bridge across what had become a moat of sorts.

Fulk stood in the centre of the courtyard, his trainee warriors grouped around him, as Henry rode out slightly ahead of his escort and looked down at him from his sweating grey stallion.

'Your face is familiar, I think. Since you do not kneel, I assume that you do not remember me as well as I remember you from our brief encounter at Oxford. I am King Henry of England, and I seek your master Lord Simon.'

As Fulk's men dropped hastily to their knees, Fulk looked back up haughtily at the king, then smiled faintly as he nodded past him to where Simon was fast approaching on foot, wiping mud from his hands onto his badly stained hose, and with sweat gleaming from the hairs on his chest.

'Here I am, Your Majesty. Had I been advised of your intended arrival, I would have been better clad.'

'I have no objection to the state of your dress,' came a light voice from the second rank of the arriving company, and Simon found himself looking into the appraising warm brown eyes of Princess Eleanor, who stared meaningfully at his groin before looking away with a contented smile. It fell silent for a moment, then Henry picked up the conversation.

'You may remember, Lord Simon, that when we were in Nottingham two years ago, I invited myself to a hunt on your estate. I am now fulfilling that promise.'

'Your Majesty,' Simon all but stuttered, 'had I been aware of your generous intention, I would have ensured that the home coppice was suitably supplied with deer. As it is, with regret, the only deer I can offer in this humble house is of the roast variety, should you agree to grace us with your presence at dinner.'

'You *would* have been aware of my wish to visit, had you not ignored my several summonses to Court,' Henry said politely, 'but I see that you have chosen to foreswear the life of a warrior in order to master the art of stonemasonry. We may be able to find suitable employment for you at Windsor, once you have completed your apprenticeship.'

There were polite sniggers of amusement from the entourage on horseback, then as several stable hands rushed forward Henry dismounted and handed his horse's bridle over to one of them. This was the signal for everyone to dismount, Eleanor assisted from her side-saddle by her heavily perspiring husband. As the company made its way towards the main tower, Merle appeared in the doorway in a flour-covered apron. Her face froze in disbelief as she took in the sight before her, then she turned tail and scuttled back inside, yelling out orders at the top of her voice in broken English. There was a ladylike titter from Princess Eleanor, and an apology from Simon to Henry, who merely smiled.

'You have clearly found another use for the woman who accompanied you from France, Simon, but it is in connection with France that I require your counsel, and why I sought unsuccessfully to have you attend us in London. However, naught is lost if you have a passable supply of wine while your woman organises the hasty roasting of venison. At all events, let us seek shelter from this sun while you acquire some more clothes, before my sister swoons.'

An hour later, Simon had made the necessary arrangements. He had instructed Merle that even if it involved taking some of Fulk's men and shooting a deer on a neighbour's estate, she should ensure that venison was served for dinner, along with anything else passably edible that might be found in the kitchen. 'And do not be rude to the Princess Eleanor,' he added.

Merle grinned back mischievously. 'I have already had satisfaction in that regard,' she told him. 'When the royal party came inside, she enquired of me where the nearest garderobe might be found. I was able to advise her that the only one inside the tower was adjoining your privy chamber, where you were probably changing, and where her presence might excite comment. Instead, she might make use of the communal hole under the canvas at the rear of the building, and I would detail two of Fulk's men to mount guard to ensure her privacy. The look on her face was worth a king's ransom.'

'This is no time for your impish humour, Merle,' Simon replied sternly. 'See to it that there is venison while I keep Henry amused.'

As they sat round the long rustic table, where they were served with an indifferent local fermentation by an equally local serving girl who was obliged to suffer William Marshal's groping hand on her bottom behind his wife's back, Henry came to the point.

'Simon, what know you of the temperament of the current King Louis of France?'

'I only ever had audience, and that briefly, with his father, Your Majesty. His father, as you will have cause to remember, was a doughty warrior, but my brother advises me in his irregular dispatches that the current Louis is but a pale shadow of his father, and somewhat beset by rebellions among his nobles, some of whom are of course English.'

'You are in regular contact with Lord Amaury?' de Burgh asked accusingly.

'Why not, since he is my brother?' Simon replied.

Henry grunted. 'That may be of some value to us in our plans. Where are your brother's estates, exactly?'

'In the region they call the "Île-de-France", Your Majesty. It is to the south of Normandy, and it is the seat of the French Court. Its centre is Paris itself.'

'And may your brother be numbered among those who seek to rebel against King Louis?' de Burgh asked.

'Not that he advises me,' Simon replied, unhappy at where the conversation might be heading, 'but of course that is not something that one would include in a despatch, in case it fell into the wrong hands.'

'What know you of the Duke of Brittany?' Henry asked.

'Nothing other than his name,' Simon replied, 'and even that escapes me at this exact moment.'

'Peter de Dreux,' de Burgh reminded him, 'and he invites His Majesty to invade, along with other disaffected nobles who must be numbered among your brother's neighbours.'

'You intend to tilt for the Crown of France?' Simon asked with a sinking feeling in the pit of his stomach.

'There could not be a better time,' de Burgh insisted, 'since it would seem that once we cross the water, there will be many who would wish to be associated with our cause.'

'Including, you believe, my own brother?' Simon asked.

'Perhaps,' Henry intervened, 'but I am not here to seek your assistance in subverting your brother from any oath he may have sworn to Louis. I wish you to guide us through the lands that lead to Paris, with which you assure us you are well acquainted.'

Simon thought quickly. He could not hope to escape this call to arms merely on the grounds that he would be obliged to take on his own brother, since the Plantagenet kings had a long tradition of doing precisely that, and Henry's father had been the worst of them in that regard. Suddenly, he thought of a better excuse.

'Your Majesty forgets that my former life was spent further south, in the Languedoc, and that for most of the time that I spent at Montfort-l'Amaury I was an invalid nursing a serious battle wound. I know parts of England better than I remember the Île-de-France, and would, I fear, prove to be but a poor guide.'

'Some might misconstrue that excuse as cowardice,' William Marshal piped in.

Simon shot him a furious glare and his hand flew involuntarily towards his sword hilt before he remembered himself and apologised to Henry, while Marshal's face regained its colour.

'No-one considers you a coward, Simon,' Henry assured him. 'Not even William here,' he added with a scowl at his brother-in-law. 'But even if you assure us that you would not be a useful guide, could we not rely upon your bringing onto the field of battle that fine body of men who were engaging in arms training as we arrived?'

'I regret that they are few in number,' Simon explained, both embarrassed and horrified that Henry might be in such need of an army that he would even consider the handful of partly trained men that he had seen earlier in the courtyard. 'I am managing this estate on behalf of Earl Ranulf, and his is the main force. I take it that he has already pledged his support, in which case the few men I could bring out would be a mere drop in a larger body of water.'

Henry seemed, for the moment at least, satisfied with that explanation. After a very late dinner of barely roasted venison, washed down with watery grape juice, the royal party seemed content to depart back to Nottingham, which they would not reach until after dark. As Simon waved them farewell, Fulk sidled up to him.

'I trust you did not pledge my feeble army to the king's battle pennant?'

'No, which is perhaps as well for them. If Henry pursues his life's ambition to win back Plantagenet lands in France, he will be much the poorer, in both men and finances. And talking of the poor and needy, where in God's name did you source that wine that was served at dinner? It was as thin as one of de

Burgh's smiles, and tasted as if it had been strained through my hose — *after* I had drunk it.'

By a strange irony, Simon's regular correspondence with his older brother Amaury enabled him to keep abreast of Henry's progress through France far more reliably than any Court gossip might have done, and the news was not encouraging from an English point of view. Whatever prowess Hubert de Burgh might once have possessed as a warrior — which did not seem to have been great — he clearly had no concept of military strategy. He had advised Henry, during the early months of the English campaign in France, to move swiftly south-west once they had made safe landing at Calais.

Amaury, in one letter after another, expressed his disbelief that the large English force could have ignored the prize of Normandy, so intent had it been on losing no time before heading to Chinon. Amaury described how several of his near neighbours were on the point of surrendering to Henry and offering their lands and armed forces to him, had Henry, in his haste, even bothered to stop and enquire regarding their loyalties.

Those nobles who remained loyal to the Capetian monarch — including Amaury himself — held their breath as one might when confronted by a wild boar which would hopefully turn in another direction rather than charge. Within a few weeks the danger had passed them by, and Henry's forces were stomping around Poitou making a lot of noise, reviving many claims, and taking hostages who were swiftly released anyway.

Then it was on to Gascony, with the same outcome. No-one seemed to be in the mood, locally, to dispute Henry's title to Gascony, any more than they had to Poitou. By the time that Henry was advised by de Burgh that it was time to return home, he had formed firm friendships with several Poitevin and Gascon barons, who were invited to join the victorious cavalcade back the way it had come two years previously, having achieved precisely nothing other than a two-year peace treaty with Louis IX that would not have been necessary had Henry not crossed the Channel in the first place. It had, however, made deep inroads into the Treasury coffers, and de Burgh's enemies had been plotting in his absence.

Word had reached England ahead of Henry's return that he was accompanied by a coterie of highly favoured Poitevin barons. This was anathema to Anglicised barons already settled in England, who in their absence had been deprived of their original lands in Poitou by the very men who were now heading for England under Henry's patronage. Their impotent fury was whipped up by Hubert de Burgh's main rival as the power behind the throne, Peter des Roches, Bishop of Winchester. Henry landed back in England to face a very angry Court, and open accusations of treason and financial mismanagement on the part of de Burgh. De Burgh might have withstood this open challenge to his influence over Henry had not his protégé, the royal brother-in-law William Marshal, stepped over the unspoken threshold in his over-familiarity with the royal dynasty, allegedly at the urging of de Burgh.

While Henry was prepared to turn a blind eye to Marshal's sexual proclivities, even though the victim was his own sister Eleanor, he was livid when news was brought to him that William had persuaded Henry's younger brother Richard, Earl of Cornwall, to marry his sister Isabel, the dowager Countess of Hertford, who had only recently been widowed, and who had six children by her first marriage. This brought the royal family even more tightly under the Marshal influence, and this was one step too far for Henry, who retaliated by having Hubert de Burgh confined to the Tower of London.

Even de Burgh's obvious lack of freedom did not silence rumours of his having taken his revenge, for his clumsiness, on William Marshal, who died shortly afterwards, allegedly from poison. This left Princess Eleanor a widow at sixteen, and she immediately took a holy vow of chastity in an attempt to avoid being used once again as a bargaining counter on the royal matrimonial negotiation table. William Marshal's estates fell to his younger brother Richard, who was to prove resentful of the process by which he had inherited, for which he blamed Henry.

All this information came to Simon and his household second-hand, through the mouths of itinerant peddlers, mendicant friars and 'untied' farm labourers seeking employment. But far more direct in nature was the summons that Simon received early in 1236, during his sixth year of repairs, extensions and restorations to his Leicestershire lands. It was a summons to the Court at Westminster, and it was to celebrate the forthcoming wedding of Henry himself, to Eleanor of Provence, the heiress to not only her father's Provencal lands, but also to those of her mother, Beatrice of Savoy, which controlled access to the Alpine passes that led from Southern France into Italy.

It was potentially a brilliant alliance, whatever might be the attractions of the lady herself, and Henry would take it as a massive slight were Simon to ignore the summons. There was in any case another urgent reason why he needed to keep on the right side of Henry, since Ranulf of Chester had died childless during Henry's time in France, and his estates had been divided up between his four sisters. It was unclear which of them had acquired the relatively humble Leicestershire landholding around Hinckley, but since the ultimate feudal lord was the king himself, his would be the final word. He might even be persuaded to feu it directly to Simon, thereby eliminating the need for any intervening oath of fealty; if so, then it made sense for it to be accompanied by the title "Earl of Leicester" that had so far eluded him.

XIV

'It seems to be the season for weddings,' Merle observed quietly as she laid out Simon's best surcoat on his bed, ahead of his departure. 'It is the talk of the household that Fulk has agreed to marry Matilda the cook — at *her* insistence, mind you. I would never have expected that old warhorse to bow down on the command of a woman, but I suppose that there's no accounting for matters of the heart — or is it the "hearth"? And now off you go to Court, on a royal summons, to see that weedy Henry married to a powerful princess with an attractive dowry, even though she is not yet thirteen years old, so I hear.'

'She will bring him much land across the Channel in due course,' Simon reminded her.

'And is *that* any good reason for marrying?' Merle challenged him as she straightened up and slowly edged towards him. 'Should marriage in the sight of God not be for love, for life-long companionship, and for the begetting of beautiful children?'

Simon looked down at her from his impressive six feet two inches in height. 'You spent too long in the south, Merle. You have obviously become infected with romantic notions of courtly love, and impossible expectations of what is only, after all, a blending of bodies for the mutual benefit of the parties, both financial and carnal.'

'I pity you, if that is how you see your future,' Merle replied as her face expressed her disappointment. 'You plan one day to marry simply for the lands it will bring you?'

'And why should I not? As you yourself remind me, the future royal bride is barely into womanhood. Think you that

Henry finds her body to his liking? It is clearly her future inheritance that has him lusting after her, and she will make him one of the greatest feudal lords in Europe in due course.'

'But will she make him happy?' Merle asked as she looked up at Simon with a pleading look on her face. 'Do not make the same mistake yourself, Simon. Do not seek happiness in a marriage that is based solely on the desire for land and title — you are too good for that. Your sweet nature deserves someone who will entwine her body around yours in a loving embrace, and yield joyfully to your every carnal wish.'

When Simon's face creased in puzzlement, Merle gave in to her emotions and threw her arms around him, clasping him tightly as the words tumbled out over the shoulder of his leather jerkin.

'Someone like me, Simon! I have followed you this far, and I would follow you to the ends of the earth. I would give you sons who would increase your military strength, daughters who would marry well and bring in new estates. But I would also give you a love, and a carnal submission, that you have never even dreamed of! Before you marry for material advancement, remember your adoring Merle!'

Then came the tears and the shaking, and Simon pushed her gently away from him before looking down at her, red in the face with embarrassment and confusion.

'Dearest Merle, I know only too well your heart's deepest desire, but it could never be. I never had a sister, but had I done so, I could no more have lain carnally with her than I could with you. I too love you with all my heart, but as a brother, not as a marriage partner. You must accept that, if we are to reside together here on the estate.'

There was an uncomfortable silence before Merle stepped back, then turned and leaned forward to brush a crease out of the surcoat that lay on the bolster, her face set rigidly in self-restraint.

'You must forgive me if I forgot my place, my lord. I will, of course, continue to serve as the mistress of your house, if not the lady of your bed. But should you ever require the experience of mingling flesh with someone who craves every inch of your body, rather than lying coldly alongside someone you have married for their inheritance, then you need only ask. And so I bid you Godspeed to the Court, and a safe return to our midst.'

With that she swept out, head down, leaving Simon greatly disturbed in conscience.

His lingering reflections were, however, rapidly overtaken by the new sights and sounds that greeted his very first foray into London. As he guided his horse gently through the increasing throng in the northern approaches, he was obliged to negotiate around merchants' carts, beggars seeking alms, street prostitutes loudly offering him services, horses, pedestrians, men at arms lounging in doorways, inn signs creaking in the stiff breeze, and above all the smell of humanity at work and play. The collective noise was almost overpowering, and the smell most certainly was, so it was with a profound sense of relief that he finally spotted the tall towers of Westminster ahead of him down the straight, narrow thoroughfare.

He dismounted in the courtyard and gave his name to the liveried usher with the list, once his horse had been led away. The usher frowned as he fumbled through the leaves, then found Simon's name on what appeared to have been the fourth page.

'The Cheapside Building, over there behind the chapel,' he instructed Simon with a curt nod, before transferring his attentions to the latest arrival. Simon found himself in what was little more elevated than a barracks, with pallets laid out on either side of the room, a fire burning fitfully in a hearth halfway down one side, and the muted conversations of a dozen or so men dressed as if for the hunt, with their Court finery hung on pegs to the sides of their pallets. Some of them appeared to have brought personal attendants with them, who were busily engaged in cleaning boots or brushing down the surcoats hanging from the low ceiling.

'And who might you be?' a gruff elderly man asked him.

Simon gave him his name, and the man smiled.

'We are close neighbours, my friend. I am Eustache de la Zouche, and my estates lie between yours and Nottingham. When this nonsense is over, you and your lady must visit — we have far too many boars on our land.'

'Of what "nonsense" do you speak?' Simon asked.

Eustache looked carefully around him, then lowered his voice. 'The royal coronation that we are commanded to attend. The marriage took place at Canterbury some days since, and we are summoned to witness the crowning of a Savoyard child as Queen of England. We are forced to occupy this cow barn because there are so many of us, and none — yourself included, I'll warrant — dared disobey the summons. By all accounts Henry has already showered the infant with so many rich gifts that it may be necessary to tax the realm yet again to pay for all this excess. And we are supposed to be grateful — we, who were never consulted in the first place.'

'Why should King Henry require our permission in his choice of a bride?'

'Not that, you fool. I speak of the taxation. It was the downfall of his father, and may yet bring Henry to his knees. John promised that there would be full consultation with the barons before they were called upon to pay more taxes, but he never did that. Now it seems that his puny offspring intends to dishonour the treaty in just the same way.'

'What treaty?' Simon asked.

Eustache stared back at him in disbelief. 'Have you spent your entire life in Antioch, on one of those fruitless Crusades, that you have never heard of the Great Charter of Runnymede?'

'On a Crusade, certainly,' Simon replied, 'but this one was in the Languedoc, against the Cathar heretics.'

Eustache guffawed loudly. 'God's teeth, you are one of those who speaks French because you are actually from France?'

Simon nodded, and Eustache was clearly glad of the excuse to fulminate further against what he obviously regarded as a great injustice.

'A few years before his death, King John agreed with the leading barons that he would abandon the arrogant ways of his forebears, and consult with them before seeking more revenue from taxation. He also promised that none of them would be impeached, or have their lands forfeit, without good cause. Finally, he undertook to consult his *Curia Regis* before undertaking any venture that might have serious implications for the welfare of the nation. John ignored all of those promises, and lost his life while fleeing from the consequences. It must have been the will of God, they say, since the sea swallowed up most of his wealth, while he died of a massive flux a few days later. And yet his son, after confirming the Charter less than ten years ago, took it upon himself to invade France with only the guidance of that idiot de Burgh, who now languishes in the Tower, when any one of us could have advised him against it at the time. Now he seeks to impose upon the nation a child-bride who will, it is to be hoped, bear his progeny.'

Simon was taking this all in, in case what he was hearing might be used to his advantage in the matter of his craved title. 'And what say the barons now?' he asked.

Eustache lowered his voice even further, and his eyes flicked urgently from one side of the room to the other as he replied. 'They are on the point of rebellion, dear neighbour, and you may wish to consider how you will be counted when the call comes.'

Simon spent a most uncomfortable night surrounded by the snores of his fellow invitees and ate indifferent offerings of supper and breakfast at the crude table in the centre of their lodging, served by what looked like the scrapings of the palace kitchen staff. He then joined the other reluctant attendees at the lavish coronation ceremony for the foreign princess who more closely resembled a convent novitiate taking her final vows than an eager girl receiving the Crown of England. Once or twice Simon caught the eye of one of the leading clergyman conducting the ceremony, and his face seemed somehow familiar. It was not until he was approaching Barnet on the road home that he finally remembered — he was Peter des Roches, Bishop of Winchester, and the new power behind the throne. The man who could perhaps nudge Henry into granting Simon his rightful title of Earl of Leicester. But what would he have to give in return?

XV

'Do you *really* have to go?' Merle pouted as she wiped her hands on the kitchen cloth she had unconsciously carried into the hall with her on the summons from Fulk, who was hoping that she could talk some sense into Simon. 'You've been back here less than two weeks — what could the king possibly wish to speak with you about so soon, and only shortly after his wedding? Should he not be enjoying married life, instead of summoning you to his side?'

'The King of England has no shortage of matters of State to occupy his attention, and the new queen looks more like his daughter than an eager bride,' Simon assured her.

'I had forgotten that you have no carnal interest in young ladies,' Merle replied acidly as she threw the cloth down on the table, and looked to Fulk for assistance.

Fulk frowned. 'It is to be hoped that the intelligence we have from France has not yet reached the English Court, which is why I asked Merle to join us. I hoped that she could dissuade you from walking into a hornet's nest. It is unlikely that des Roches has *not* heard the news, given his extensive French family connections.'

The news to which he was referring was certainly portentous, although it was uncertain whether or not it would work in Simon's favour. It was also almost two years old, and it was perhaps too much to hope that it had not reached Henry's ears long before they had received the belated information from Simon's brother, in one of his rare despatches.

Amaury had been appointed Constable of France, a high position at the French Court of Louis that was the equivalent of that of Earl Marshal of England that had fallen, on William Marshal's death, to his brother Richard, who was rumoured to be blaming William's death on an act of poisoning carried out on Henry's orders. Amaury had been granted the high honour partly because of his loyalty towards Louis when the English army had marched dangerously close to the Île-de-France on its way to Poitou, and partly because the previous holder of the office had been his uncle on his mother's side.

One did not require the sensitively honed mind of a diplomat to work out that here in the heart of England was a minor noble with a direct line of communication with one of the most powerful soldiers in France; one who could pass on to England's traditional enemy a good deal of valuable information regarding its military intentions, the potential strength of its army, the current state of its war chest, and other things besides. But if Simon's loyalties remained English, he could be employed as a vital channel of information regarding precisely the same matters in France.

The problem lay in the uncertainty of Henry's intentions. The summons to attend at Windsor, where Henry and his new queen were enjoying their first few months of wedded bliss, could be for good or for evil. It was good if Henry could be persuaded that Simon was of even greater potential value to England than he had previously been; if so, then perhaps the king could be nudged into the final act of elevating Simon formally into the Sixth Earldom of Leicester. If, on the other hand, Simon was suspected of being a spy for Louis across the Channel, then he could anticipate viewing the world from a draughty window in the Tower of London, as a near neighbour of the recently disgraced Hubert de Burgh.

Fulk and Merle were united in their opposition to Simon obeying the summons to Windsor that had come by royal emissary only two days previously. But, as Simon continued to remind them, skulking in Leicestershire would achieve nothing other than incurring the royal wrath for the very public slight involved. It was being broadcast around the nation that despite his status as Earl Marshal of England, Richard Marshal had fallen foul of Henry's fitful temper — one of his legacies from his father — because he had declined the invitation to attend the Court at Gloucester and explain why, on the death of his brother, he had paid off his debts by alienating the dowry of his former sister-in-law Princess Eleanor. She was now entirely dependent upon her royal brother for her keeping, a state of affairs that was likely to last for the remainder of her days, given her vow of perpetual chastity.

'I am playing the odds,' Simon told them. 'If I do not attend Court, it will be voiced abroad that I am indeed a spy for Louis of France. I will also be insulting King Henry. If, on the other hand, I attend as summoned, I will appear as a man whose conscience is clear. I may even be able to force the royal hand regarding my hereditary title, given my usefulness to Henry through my family connection.'

Fulk shook his head sadly. 'I fear that there is no persuading you, but those are not odds that I would risk. Then again, I was never one given to games of chance.'

'And what will happen to us, if you are taken?' Merle urged, close to tears. 'You are bound — if only as a man of honour — to protect those who serve you loyally.'

'I am also bound, as a man of honour,' Simon reminded them, 'to pursue and claim my father's birthright.'

'That is not "honour",' Fulk argued. 'That is "pride", and it is a sin.'

'Sin or no,' Simon replied, 'it is my nature, and I leave the day after tomorrow. Merle, could you instruct your friend

Edith to have my best surcoat cleaned in readiness? The de Montfort arms, with the silver lion bearing the forked tail.'

This was the surcoat that glowed in the setting sun five days later as he handed his horse to the groom and looked around the courtyard of the lower ward of Windsor Castle. He was aware of one of the stable hands running off towards a building set into the south wall on a shouted command from the groom who had taken his horse. Within minutes, a familiar figure dressed in ecclesiastical robes emerged from it and walked towards him with a smile, and a hand raised in a silent blessing.

'Welcome to Windsor, Simon,' Peter des Roches greeted him in immaculate French. 'I asked that I be advised of your arrival, although we were not aware of which day, or indeed of the time of day. Henry is hearing Mass in the Lady Chapel back there, and I have left a priest to complete the *missa est*. They should all be back out in a few moments.'

'It is an unusual time of day for Mass,' Simon observed.

'Not for Henry,' des Roches replied. 'He is most punctilious in his observances, and considerably more pious than his father ever was. Some days he celebrates four Masses. He is a great admirer of the former King Edward the Confessor, and has proved himself to be a great benefactor to the Church, expending much towards the furtherance of the work of God. You must never lose sight of his piety if you and he are to remain friends.'

'While I am delighted to be of service to His Majesty,' Simon replied diplomatically, 'and while I bask in the realisation that he acknowledges my loyalty, I would not presume so far as to describe our relationship as one of friendship.'

Des Roches placed a ringed hand on Simon's shoulder and steered him gently towards the chapel door. 'In these treacherous times, loyalty earns its own friendship. And yet you travel alone, it would seem — what of your two companions? Are they not "friends" of yours, albeit in different ways? Why do they not accompany you?'

'The summons was to me alone,' Simon explained, 'and they each show their loyalty to me back in Leicester.'

'The man at arms — the man from Sevres — does he yet have an army that could take to the field?'

'Hardly an army — two score men at most.'

'And are they available, and ready to prove their mettle in Henry's service?'

'They are available, certainly, but not yet tested in battle, so far as I am aware. They were originally retainers of Earl Ranulf, and I know not whether they saw battle service under him.'

'Sadly, the earl is no longer with us,' des Roches reminded him, 'and yet there must be a sizeable force in Chester that now lacks any leadership. Would your man be capable of turning them into an army?'

'Have no doubt on that score,' Simon assured him as they halted a few yards from the chapel door. 'He was the one who trained me, and although he is now somewhat more advanced in years, and will shortly be encumbered with a wife, he is the finest man at arms trainer one could wish for.'

'As an ordained man of God, I obviously know nothing of the encumbrances that come with marriage. But what of yourself, Simon? Why does your woman not travel with you?'

'You refer, I imagine, to Merle. True it is that she has been my travelling companion since we left France some years ago now, but she was left behind in order to manage the Leicester estates, of which she has proved herself more than capable. But she is not my wife.'

'But she is your woman, nonetheless?' de Roches probed.

Simon bristled slightly. 'She is not my — my "concubine", I believe you would call her in the language of the Church. She is more like a sister.'

Des Roches smiled conspiratorially. 'Even sisters can make demands upon the heart that are difficult to escape, as Henry is even now discovering to his cost. You have heard, perhaps, that the Princess Eleanor has been robbed of her lands by her former brother-in-law, the new Earl Marshal, Richard?'

'I had indeed heard something of that nature.'

'As a result, she is now in residence with Henry wherever he goes, like a second wife, just at a time when he would be best left free of domestic concerns in order to have a clear head regarding how to best deal with certain threatened insurrections. That is why he has summoned you, I believe. But he may tell you that himself, for here he comes.'

A small, sombre-looking group made up of two males and three females stepped from the shadows of the chapel doorway into the last rays of the afternoon sun. Henry of England was leading the way, his bride on his arm and walking quickly to keep up with him. On her other side was the Princess Eleanor, together with a lady who Simon had never met. As for the other man with Henry, his style of dress put Simon in mind of the excesses of attire that he had seen during his brief time at the French Court.

Simon stepped from des Roches' side and bowed.

'Your wound still prevents your kneeling, Lord Simon?' Henry asked pleasantly as he held out his hand to be kissed. 'No matter — there is hopefully a long line of those who would bow the knee to me.'

'When my wound permits, yours shall be the first — and only — presence in which I will kneel,' Simon replied diplomatically, earning himself a warm smile from Henry and

Eleanor, a quizzical look from the new queen, and what appeared to be a frown from the other lady. The face of the remaining man in the party remained inscrutable.

Henry turned to each of his companions in turn with an ingratiating smile as he introduced them one by one.

'You will of course recall the radiant loveliness of my gracious queen from the coronation ceremony that you attended, and you have already twice met my sister Eleanor, sadly now a widow living a life of royal grace and favour. The other lady is the Countess Isabel, wife of my brother Richard, Earl of Cornwall. She is also the sister of another Richard, the Third Earl of Pembroke, who dissembles to attend Court upon our several summonses, and has much to explain concerning the dowry that my sister Eleanor brought to her marriage to his late brother William, who you may also recall.'

There was a polite cough from the remaining member of the party, and Henry hastened to complete the introductions.

'Last — but certainly by no means the least in my affections — allow me to introduce Peter de Rivaux, a Poitevin who serves me as steward of my household. He is said by the Bishop of Winchester here to be his nephew, although he is also rumoured to be his son.'

The ensuing silence was embarrassing, and Simon bowed ahead of taking his leave. Henry held up a hand to delay him.

'You cannot leave us yet, Simon, unless des Roches has already advised you of where you will be lodging. No, you shake your head. I thought not. Well, in view of your family's loyalty to the King of the Franks, you could be forgiven for believing that you were being consigned to the Tower. Which indeed you are.'

Simon's jaw began to drop in disbelief, and Henry burst out laughing.

'But it is not the Tower of London, have no fear. It is yon tower there.' He nodded towards a tower complex in the corner that appeared to have been constructed only recently, to judge by the whiteness of the mortar.

'It is called the Curfew Tower, and it is one of my recent additions to this fine castle, intended to accommodate welcome guests at Court such as yourself. Across the ward here is the Great Hall, where we shall expect you at supper. The royal residence can be found through yon archway, in the upper ward, to which we now make our way as we bid you a good afternoon.'

With that he began to walk away, leaving his small retinue to follow behind him politely. Princess Eleanor treated Simon to a warm smile and a slight bow as she glided past him on the arm of Peter de Rivaux, leaving the Countess of Cornwall to give him another curious appraisal as she scurried after the remainder of her party towards where the lower ward passed through an archway to become the upper ward.

Once he was in his allocated chambers on the first floor of the Curfew Tower, Simon unpacked his few spare items of clothing, laying them out carefully across the table. He was resting on his pallet when the groom who had been assigned to his service answered the light tap on the door. There was a brief conversation with what sounded like a woman, and Simon rose in curiosity as a tall, elegant lady dressed in a rich blue gown with matching wimple entered the chamber and bowed.

'I am Adele de Lusignan, and I serve the Princess Eleanor.'

'You are Poitevin?' Simon asked, intrigued.

Adele nodded. 'I am the natural daughter of Hugh de Lusignan. The "bastard" daughter, as those more cruelly minded would entitle me. When he married the king's widowed mother, Isabella of Angoulême, she would not have me at Court, and arranged for me to enter the king's service here in England. King Henry, in his turn, gave orders that I become a lady to the Princess Eleanor, who I have served these five years. She has sent me to bid you attend her.'

'Here and now?' Simon asked.

'Now certainly, my lord. As for *where*, her chambers are on the next level above these, and may be accessed most conveniently by way of the back stairs.'

'Does she not have her chambers in the upper ward, like the rest of the royal family?' Simon asked.

Adele nodded patiently. 'Indeed she does, but since King Henry's marriage she has preferred the privacy of the Curfew Tower, since it is well away from the merriment of the early days of His Majesty's marriage. Marriage was not my lady's happiest state.'

'So I am led to believe. But why does she seek audience with me at this moment, rather than a quiet side conversation at supper?'

'She does not confide that information to me, my lord. I am simply instructed to bid you attend her.'

'Go and tell your mistress that I will be no more than a few minutes, and will then accede to her wish.'

Adele bowed gracefully out of the chamber, and Simon set the groom to brushing down his second-best doublet — a green one in velvet — before he checked his hose and boots for obvious signs of travel and excess wear. He then strode up the back stairs two at a time, feeling guiltily like an assassin or a secret paramour, and not sure which of the two roles made him feel the more guilty. He knocked on the chamber door, and was admitted by a liveried page, to find Princess Eleanor seated in a padded window alcove with her needlepoint on her lap. She smiled as Simon entered and bowed, and gestured for him to join her by the window, which he did, noting with some relief that Adele had withdrawn to the corner of the chamber with her own needlepoint, so that there could be no idle gossip regarding the nature of the meeting.

'Welcome, my Lord Simon,' Eleanor said. 'How is your health — apart from your battle wound, that is?'

'Excellent, thank you, my lady.'

Eleanor took a lingering look at his broad shoulders, only a few inches from her delicate white ones. 'No doubt all that stonemasonry has kept you fit.'

'Indeed it has. But presumably you do not wish to discuss the finer points of building defensive walls with me.'

'No indeed. I wish to urge that you say nothing unguarded in the presence of the Countess of Cornwall, the broody-faced woman that you met outside the chapel.'

'She was lately your sister-in-law, was she not?'

Eleanor pulled a face and shuddered slightly. 'Pray do not remind me of those dark days when I was married to her bastard of a brother. I was barely nine years old when he took me as his wife, and I would rather have been thrown to a pack of my brother's hunting dogs.'

'My lady?' Simon interrupted, embarrassed by the sudden confidence.

Eleanor seemed to remember herself, and flashed him a small smile of apology. 'That is no matter, and is best consigned to history. She is still my sister-in-law, of course, since she is now married to my brother Richard, but I do not believe that she will have changed her ways with her change of status.'

'Her ways, my lady?'

Eleanor snorted. 'When I was married to William Marshal, she was the wife of the Earl of Hertford, and she had a whole brood of children. Since we had none, my husband always had a great affection for them — particularly, I am ashamed to admit, his nephews — and she and her family were forever visiting us at Pembroke, and wherever else we might be residing when not actually at Court.'

'And why is it important for me to know this?' Simon asked, apprehensive that Eleanor might let slip something that she later regretted.

'Because, my lord, she never let an opportunity pass her by when she might give false report of me to my husband, her brother. I was accused of besporting myself with a groom of his chamber, who was dismissed on the spot — although, thank God, the blameless man was not put to death. It was also alleged, by the vengeful Isabel, that I was extravagant in the matter of clothing, that I had too many ladies in attendance, that I worshipped false Gods, that I drank much wine while William was away in the king's service, and much more besides. She clearly seeks my downfall.'

'Why should she dislike you so, and how might that bear upon what we are likely to be discussing over supper?'

'As for the first, she is not — as I am — blessed with a fairness of feature. Her face, as you will have noted, is somewhat swarthy, like that of the rest of her family, and she is inclined to plumpness, particularly in the region of her buttocks. She is cursed with the bearing of all her family, and with their lowly humour that approaches viciousness. In short, she resents what others describe as my beauty.'

'Any woman would, my lady,' Simon suggested.

Eleanor blushed and placed a cool hand on Simon's before continuing. 'Thank you, my lord. As for your second question,

Isabel is devoted to her brother Richard, the new Earl of Pembroke, and is indebted to her family for securing her the hand of the king's brother. In return for this, she will privily advise Richard of anything she hears at Court that might affect his fortunes.'

'And you believe that Henry will wish to discuss with me — a mere knight — matters that could have a bearing on one of the mightiest noble families in the realm?'

'You heard him yourself, as we stood outside the chapel, declaiming that Richard Marshal had much to explain regarding those lands that he has stolen, which were my dowry when I married his malodorous brother.'

'Yes, but surely...' Simon began, but he was silenced by Eleanor's raised hand.

'There is much more. Richard clearly regards himself as beyond the bidding of a king. He has taken himself off to Ireland, where he has many estates, and is believed to be raising an army there. Peter des Roches will shortly be following him over with a royal force, and will harass him, but in knowledge of that — almost certainly confided to him in secret by the treacherous Isabel — he has also sought an alliance with Llewellyn of Wales, in order that his forces might rise up together with his own Pembroke retainers to march east on London.'

'And you believe that Henry will seek my support in Wales?'

'Why not, since you are a knight, and by all accounts a most brave and fearsome one in battle?'

'Those claims are exaggerated by my man Fulk, who seeks thereby to inspire his men.'

'You are truly capable of inspiring much in people,' Eleanor replied demurely, her eyes fixed on her needlepoint. 'You cause quite a flutter among my ladies by your very appearance at

Court. Be that as it may, I have warned you, and I wish that you keep this conversation between ourselves.'

'Of course, my lady,' Simon assured her as he rose, bowed, and backed down the chamber towards the door.

Eleanor looked up from her lap just before the door was opened by a page. 'Be sure to call upon me again, Lord Simon. Perhaps as a commander in my brother's army.'

XVI

Simon had no real appetite as they all sat at supper in the Great Hall. Henry, for his part, seemed content to keep the conversation focused on matters of religion, and to seek reassurance from everyone around the intimate table that the new castle extensions were the last word in stonemasonry. Eventually he leaned forward slightly and looked down the table, to where Simon was seated on the far side of Peter de Rivaux.

'Lord Simon, do you hear much from your brother since he became Constable of France?'

'In truth I never heard much from him *before* that, Your Majesty. And now even less. It would seem that his new duties fully occupy his time.'

'As indeed they must,' Henry conceded. 'But you and he are still friendly?'

'Insofar as one can ascertain from the occasional dispatch, yes,' Simon told him.

'This is good, since I have a mission for you that will require every bit of that goodwill.'

'Presumably I am not being ordered to invade France?' Simon joked nervously.

'No — and yes,' Henry said enigmatically as he carved more beef with his paring knife. 'My new bride has certain family members who are dear to her heart, and I would wish them to reside with us here at the English Court. It will be necessary to secure their safe passage across the lands of Louis of the Franks, and I cannot think of anyone better suited to lead a small armed force down into Savoy to secure that safe passage than the man who is the brother of the one most likely to prevent that.'

'You wish me to travel to Savoy with an armed escort, Your Majesty?'

'Is that not what I just said?' Henry replied testily. 'As for the details, I shall give you the sealed order on the morrow, when I take my daily ride along the river. Please ensure that you are there to receive it.'

The following morning, Simon was idly watching the mist rising off the upper reaches of the mighty Thames when he heard the snapping of twigs in the coppice behind him. He drew his sword and turned, then immediately lowered it as he recognised Henry blundering through the undergrowth and walking towards him with two heavily armed retainers, one of them holding his horse by its bridle.

'I would make a poor assassin, I fear,' Henry joked as he closed the distance between them and looked across the water. 'This is my favourite time of day. I have already heard two Masses, and my soul is secure for a few more hours. As for my kingdom, that is why I asked you to meet with me here, rather than have my real plans for you overheard by prying ears.'

'You do not wish me to travel to Savoy after all?' Simon asked.

'Indeed I do, in time,' began Henry. 'But not immediately. Here is my signed order, but it is not for you to cross the Channel.'

'Then what?'

'I wish you to take your standard bearer — your trainer of fighting men — to Chester, and there assess the readiness of the garrison to repel any attack. If they are not yet ready, then you must make them so.'

'I am not the Earl of Chester,' Simon reminded him.

'Neither are you the Earl of Leicester — yet,' Henry goaded him. 'Whether or not you become so in the fullness of time will depend upon your loyalty to me. Beginning with your journey to Chester — your authority to review the garrison is what is in this order.' He handed the small scroll to Simon, who tucked it into his belt without examining it further.

'Why do you fear that Chester may come under attack?' Simon asked, not wishing to reveal how he already knew.

Henry grimaced. 'It is rumoured that Llewellyn of Wales has offered his assistance to Pembroke, and that they are set to march east — Chester is our northern stronghold along the Welsh Marches.'

'I thought that Earl Pembroke was in Ireland,' Simon observed almost casually, and Henry shot him an accusing glare.

'Who told you that?'

'I cannot mind now,' Simon lied, 'but it was some time ago.'

'Your information was correct,' Henry conceded, 'but des Roches will shortly be crossing the sea to challenge Marshal's usurpation of my lands over there. It would seem that Richard Marshal learned of our plans, although they were well guarded, and his response has been to form an alliance with Llewellyn, who has ever been our enemy in Wales. Hence the need to ensure that all is well in Chester. Here, take this gold to see you on your way.' To Simon's extreme embarrassment, Henry reached into his tunic belt and extracted a heavy bag that jingled promisingly as he held it out.

Simon shook his head. 'I do not require payment to show my loyalty to you, Henry.'

Henry snorted. 'Your pride may one day be your undoing, Simon. It is well known that your improvements in Leicester have left you in considerable debt. I wish you to proceed to

Chester with all speed, along with your tame battle-master. I do not wish you reduced to sleeping in hedgerows on the journey. Once you have assessed what has to be done, return and report to me. We begin our coronation progress in two days — within two months we shall again be in Nottingham, which is two days' ride from Chester.'

'You are most generous, Henry,' Simon muttered shamefacedly as he took the bag of coins. 'I shall lose no time in reporting back to you in Nottingham.'

'See that you do. And now you had best begin your return to Leicester. Speak to no-one other than your man regarding what you are about. Particularly not the Princess Eleanor — she has a mischievous taste for intrigue.'

Simon bowed and rode back to the castle to collect his possessions before riding hard for Leicester. He wondered what Henry meant about Eleanor's taste for intrigue, and pondered whether or not Richard Marshal had been kept informed of matters at Court by someone other than Isabel of Cornwall.

Back home, Simon was in time for the wedding celebrations of Fulk and Matilda the cook, following the service earlier that day conducted by the parish priest from nearby Hinckley. He appeared to be as drunk as the rest of them as Simon entered the Hall, virtually unseen. Unseen except by Merle, who waved him over with a wide smile and planted a warm kiss on his lips.

'There is more in my room across the way, should you be interested,' she offered.

Simon looked down at her with mock severity. 'I fear that the wine has loosened your lips, and would loosen your clothing, were I of a mind to take you up on your foolish proposal. But this night we shall both remain chaste.'

Merle's face fell as she turned her back on him and ordered that an extra place be set at the banquet table, where Simon was soon joined by the bride and groom. Fulk did not seem to be as much in his cups as the rest of the company, but to judge by the way that he was holding up his new bride, she had enjoyed more than enough of the latest wine harvest. As she sat down heavily and began to giggle, Fulk looked up at Simon.

'How did you fare at Court?'

'Middling well, I believe, but we must ride to Chester. In view of your recent transformation into a family man, I will delay departing for two days, but then you must be ready.'

Fulk was still complaining about being dragged away from Leicester on only the fourth day of his marriage as they looked across the flat plain at the river, and beyond that the imposing castle on the hill. They crossed the Dee by the old stone bridge and urged their tired mounts up the steep slope until they came to the gateway entrance. There was only one man on guard, and he was lying propped up against the right-hand wall to the side of the gateway, which lay wide open. As they drew closer, the rhythmic heaving of his chest betrayed the fact that he was asleep. Fulk gave a loud bellow and leaped from his horse to where the man lay, kicking him hard in the kneecap. The man flew awake with a curse and made a half-hearted attempt to draw his sword before Fulk pinned his hand to the ground with his riding boot, drew his own sword and pointed it at the guard's throat as he yelled at him.

'I could have been anyone! I could have led an entire army through that gate while you slept! By God's teeth, if this is what passes for the defence of Chester Castle, then I thank my guardian angel that I live in Leicester! On your feet!'

'No-one speaks to one of my men like that — except me!' came a commanding shout from the gateway, where a tall, bare-headed man in half chainmail stood brandishing a sword threateningly.

Fulk looked back at him with a sneer. 'If this apology for a fighting man is one of yours, then you should perhaps be herding sheep for a living.'

'And who are you, to be telling me my job?' the man demanded as the colour rose in his face.

'I am Fulk de Sevres, standard bearer to the de Montforts.'

'And who are *they*?' his inquisitor demanded.

'I am Lord Simon de Montfort,' Simon told him in measured tones from the safety of his saddle. 'This man acts with my authority, and I carry the written authority of King Henry.'

'You certainly look more the part than *he* does,' the man responded. Then he spat towards Fulk, who jumped backwards as his face darkened alarmingly.

'We are here to review your men, and assess your readiness for battle,' Fulk announced.

The man sneered back. 'I am most certainly ready to do battle with *you*, goat-herd. Look to your defence!'

He raised his drawn sword to shoulder height, and despite Simon's yells of protest, the two men stalked slowly towards each other. As they came within striking distance, the local man launched a cut towards Fulk's leg, which he parried with a downward thrust of his own blade. Then it was a curving aim to the shoulder, which Fulk caught, then twisted. As the two swords clanked harmlessly to the ground, Fulk kneed his opponent in the stomach, sending him backwards. He bounced off the wall where his supposed gate-guard still sat, gawping at the contest.

As the man came back at Fulk with a dagger drawn from his belt, Fulk slipped round the thrust, then brought both of his mailed fists down onto the man's exposed neck. He dropped like a stone, giving Fulk the opportunity to retrieve his sword from the ground and stand over his fallen adversary.

'Now then,' Fulk spat down at him, 'you have a choice. Either you consent to our inspection of what passes for your forces, or I ram this sword into your poxy throat. I will count to three...'

What followed might have been amusing, had the matter not been so serious. The man who had come within an inch of being impaled on Fulk's sword got up from the ground and regarded his victor with fear and respect. He then held out his hand and introduced himself. 'Geoffrey, Earl of Flint and Constable of Chester. You are fortunate that I speak French,' he grumbled as he dusted the sandy soil off his mail.

'And you are unfortunate, in that you were foolish enough to challenge me in my own tongue,' Fulk said. 'But I suspect that I will not be so fortunate with your men.'

'You are correct,' Geoffrey confirmed with a grimace. 'None of them speak French, and many of them cannot even speak their own native English properly.'

'How is it that you speak French, here on the Welsh border?' Simon asked.

'It has been the language of my family since our ancestors fought with the first King William, generations ago. My own father was with the late King John as he began the retreat across Norfolk that led to the loss of the royal baggage. But you, I suspect, have but recently come from France, since you have not allowed your French to become bastardised the English way. However, when you speak to my men, you will need me by your side, to convert your words into their barbarous version of English. Even if you spoke their language, you would not understand, the way they render it in their half Welsh tongue.'

'I speak *some* English,' Fulk explained, 'since my wife is from Leicester. And I might add that we are but recently married, and every day that I am obliged to teach your men how to become proper soldiers is another day away from her side. Let us waste no time in kicking them into line.'

Geoffrey smiled sympathetically. 'I have been attempting to do just that for the past five years. But the last has been the worst. Since Earl Ranulf died, there has been no man here at Chester to support my efforts, and the women to whom the lands have fallen cannot be persuaded to spend money on a fighting force. They cannot understand the need to protect what they have by strength of arms, and I fear that the Welsh will one day realise their ambition of defeating the English.'

'It is not just the Welsh you must fear,' Simon told him. 'King Henry believes that Llewellyn of Wales will shortly join forces with Richard Marshal and march east to London. He believes Chester to be Henry's main stronghold here in the north against such a possibility.'

'Then the sooner you convince my men that their lives depend upon taking their duties seriously, the better,' Geoffrey frowned as he looked back at Fulk. 'I will call them out into the inner keep, and then you, my new friend, can begin to instruct them. You give me the command in French, and I will turn your words into English. We are agreed?'

'We are,' Fulk agreed, 'but always bear in mind that I speak *some* English, and will know if you are telling them true.'

They made their way under the gateway arch into the inner keep, and on a shouted command from Geoffrey the men began to shamble out from what were presumably their living quarters. Not a single man had a full kit of armour, and only half of them appeared to have brought a weapon with them.

They shuffled uneasily in a resentful-looking group as they blinked the sleep from their eyes.

'Tell them to stand in line like proper soldiers,' Fulk instructed Geoffrey, who duly obliged.

The sixty or so men in front of them did as commanded, as slowly as possible, some of them muttering oaths.

Fulk was clearly annoyed. 'Tell them they are a sorry pile of horse waste,' he commanded.

'You are a little slow to obey commands,' Geoffrey told them.

'Tell them that they couldn't stop a pig down a side alley, let alone withstand a siege by *real* soldiers.'

'You have much to learn from this man,' Geoffrey translated. 'Soon he will be assuming responsibility for your training, then God help you.'

Fulk looked around the inner keep, whose walls were all but crumbling. Large rocks had long since been detached from the tops of the walls, and lay in ruins inside the keep. Fulk pointed to various piles of them and shouted, 'Every man is to pick up one of those stones and run to the top of the Tower with it, then run back down, still carrying it. The last three men to come back down will then do it again three times. I shall be at the top of the Tower, ensuring that you all reach it.'

Geoffrey translated, and there were groans of protest from some of the men.

Fulk finally lost patience, and bellowed at them in the only English Simon had ever heard him utter. 'I will give you much pain! And more pain if you do not do as I order. Now *go!*'

Simon was shaking with laughter as each man hastily ran to a keep wall, picked up a rock and ran to the Tower.

Fulk came over, still red in the face. 'How was my English?'

'Your wife has a somewhat limited supply of words,' Simon chuckled.

'She is a cook, not a courtier.'

'I, too, have begun to learn English,' Simon said, 'but I fear that it is not as suitable as yours for commanding obedience from poor soldiers.'

'Then you must make it so, sir,' Fulk replied, 'because once I have got them fit, I shall hand them over to you for their weapons training.'

'You do not fear that I shall teach them unchivalrous ways?'

'It has kept you alive these many years. And, as you will have observed, I too was able to learn from you when showing Geoffrey which of us was the better fighter.'

Two weeks later, Fulk grudgingly declared the men fit enough to recommence weapons training. It was woefully obvious to Simon from their very first session that many of the men had never been called upon to wield, in anger or fear, their swords and axes. He expressed his concerns to Fulk as they sat morosely carving from a badly roasted mutton carcass that constituted their midday meal.

'The cooking is little better,' Fulk observed as he spat another mouthful of gristle onto the rushes at his feet. 'Not only do I sorely miss the better cooking in Leicester, but I also miss the cook. I must return without delay, now that you have the training of the men.'

'But I must soon journey across to Nottingham, to report this sad state of affairs to the king,' Simon told him. 'What are we to do?'

Fulk fell silent for a moment, then his eyes brightened. 'I would propose this, sir. In return for a favour from you, I will travel to Leicester and bring Hugh Markham back here with me. He is the best of my Leicester men, and infinitely better than this sorry bunch that passes for the Chester garrison. He may take over the weapons training, thereby leaving you free to travel to Nottingham.'

'An excellent plan,' Simon said, 'but what is the favour you seek in return?'

'I also wish to bring a new cook back with me,' Fulk said. 'And Merle too, should you wish.'

'No, Merle must continue to see to the household in Leicester. But before you leave her there, make sure that at least two of your men are detailed to see to her safety and honour. Then by all means return here with your cook, and supervise what Hugh will attempt to teach the men here. I shall leave for Nottingham on your return.'

A month later, Simon found Henry where he had last located him in Nottingham, in the King John Tower. It was mid-morning, and he had ridden through the night along the uncertain track from Derby. He was dust-smeared and smelt of horse as he was admitted to the presence, and without thinking he went down on one knee. There was a sharp reproof from his thigh, and he winced, but remained where he was and looked up. His eyes first encountered those of Princess Eleanor, which appeared to be full of sympathy and concern for his suffering, but when he transferred his gaze to Henry, he saw only fear.

'Well?' Henry demanded. 'How found you things in Chester?'

'They could not withstand a siege from a flock of sheep in their present state, Your Majesty,' Simon reported. 'However, my man Fulk is still back there with them, and has been joined by his second in command. By the end of the year they may begin to resemble a small army.'

'How small, say you?'

'A hundred at most, Your Majesty. With my men from Leicester joined to their ranks, perhaps a hundred and fifty.'

'It is nowhere near enough,' Henry complained. 'How have things become so lamentable in Chester, say you?'

'They have fallen into idle ways in the absence of their earl,' Simon replied. 'The estate has fallen to his sisters, and they lack any understanding of warfare, obviously.'

'Some women have been known to bear arms,' Eleanor observed.

'We cannot put women into the field,' Henry complained, 'although the latest dispatch from des Roches assures us that Marshal has been driven back, so perhaps he has put some of his camp whores into chainmail. Be that as it may, it is likely that he will seek the safety of the Welsh coast, and ride from Pembroke to join Prince Llewellyn in the north of his kingdom. We can then expect the main assault to be on Chester.'

'How many men is he likely to command?' Simon asked.

'Who can tell, at this time?' Henry replied abstractedly. 'His own force was once some two thousand strong, but may be heavily depleted due to des Roches' actions. However, back in Pembroke he can raise half that again, while Llewellyn has twice that number. So let us say five thousand.'

Simon's heart sank as he raised himself painfully to his feet and accepted the goblet of wine handed to him by a page, on a silent gesture from Princess Eleanor. 'We have much less than a thousand, unless of course you have retained a standing army.'

Henry snorted. 'There has been no standing army since my father's day. Mainly because when my father needed them most, they turned against him. A large body of fighting men is a dangerous commodity to have sitting around in idleness, when it can be given traitorous thoughts.'

'But a vital commodity when the nation is threatened,' Simon reminded him. 'So you rely on the leading earls to bring out their men to your battle standard when the occasion demands? As we have learned from the sad state of affairs in Chester, when there is no earl, there is no army to command.'

Henry smiled unpleasantly. 'Not a moment ago, there was, kneeling at my feet, a man who would be an earl. Consider this your great opportunity to earn the earldom that you crave, Lord Simon. Bring me an army, and I shall place an earl at its head.'

'I shall do my very best, Your Majesty,' Simon replied, 'not in order to become an earl, but because of the loyalty I owe to you.'

Henry nodded. 'We shall remain in Nottingham for another month, then we may be found in York. Return to us when you have your army.'

Simon bowed from the presence and limped outside, cursing his absent-mindedness in kneeling. He also cursed his impetuosity in offering to raise an army, and sat on a rock in the gardens, racking his brains.

He was an hour into his dejected, and much delayed, return to Leicester, when he reached a crossroads, at which a sign hung listlessly in a sagging attempt to guide travellers on their way. One of its arms pointed to a place called 'Ashby de la Zouch', and Simon's mind flashed back to his cramped accommodation in Westminster, and the bluff, overweight knight who had warned him of Henry's unpopularity. He turned his horse in the direction indicated, and by nightfall was seeking admission to a large castle that seemed out of proportion to the modest woodland by which it was surrounded. He was admitted to the Great Hall, and was wondering how best to explain the reason for his visit when his host bustled in, accompanied by his steward.

'You have accepted my invitation, at long last,' Eustache said. 'But you took your time about it — and why do you travel alone?'

'This is not a social visit from a near neighbour,' Simon explained, 'but a recruitment drive for a new royal army.'

'And what did King John do with the *last* one?' Eustache retorted. 'Turned it against his own people, that's what. If Henry has sent you to raise an army to bolster his family's tyranny, then your journey was in vain. Wine?'

Simon accepted the pewter mug with thanks as he hastily gathered his arguments. 'Would you prefer to be ruled by the Plantagenets or the Marshals?'

'Dear God,' Eustache grimaced, 'what a dreadful choice!'

'You may not have that choice for much longer,' Simon told him. 'Richard Marshal is due to cross the sea back to Wales, where he is believed to be joining forces with Llewellyn of Wales to claim the throne of England.'

'Now you have my interest,' Eustache said. 'God forbid that the Welsh take over the nation. We have been fighting with them since Adam was a boy, and they are a miserable mob. If you wish me to dust off my chainmail to fight the Welsh, you only have to ask.'

'How many men can you raise?' Simon asked eagerly.

Eustache thought deeply for a moment before replying. 'If you refer to actual fighting men who know where to find the pointed end of a sword, then no more than fifty. If you are content to take ploughboys and woodsmen who could be persuaded onto the field of battle, then you could probably count on twice that number. But who will turn their ploughshares into swords, and who will instruct them?'

Simon pointed at his own chest, and Eustache let out a sigh of relief.

'Thank the living Christ for that! I am too old for such nonsense. When do you need them?'

'Yesterday,' Simon replied jauntily as his spirits rose. 'As for their training, they will need to journey to Chester, where I have men engaged in such a task even as we stand here drinking your excellent wine.'

'You are clearly a man of considerable taste,' Eustache said. 'It comes from the valley of the Loire — by the wagonload, I am pleased to advise you. Please join me for supper. Humour my wife, who will regale you with tales of her distant youth, remain upright at board despite the copious amounts of God's own nectar that will be served, and on the morrow I will take you on a guided tour of knights of my acquaintance who hate the Welsh even more than I.'

XVII

The following day, a somewhat fuzzy-headed Simon found himself in Derby, where a further two hundred men were promised to the cause. Then he travelled across to Lincoln, where almost three hundred were pledged. Northampton yielded the same again, and finally Eustache proposed a two-day journey across to Kenilworth.

'It is a royal castle, of course,' Eustache explained, 'but if you do indeed carry the royal commission to raise an army, then it will be high time that they get up and earn their privileged livelihood. I also recommend that you travel to Bristol with the same purpose, but since my ample behind grows sore in the saddle, you may journey on alone.'

'Since my journey to Kenilworth will, you assure me, take two days, may I offer you the limited hospitality of my Leicester house before you return home?' Simon asked.

Eustache laughed throatily. 'I was wondering if we would ever get around to that. Lead on, sir squire.'

As they clattered into the courtyard at Leicester, it was obvious that much had been going on during Simon's extended absence. There was a refurbished hall, what looked like an extension to the stables, and a purpose-built barrack house for the men at arms. They rushed out and stood to attention as a groom alerted them to the fact that the Master had returned. As they climbed wearily from their saddles there was a flurry of action in the doorway to the hall, and Merle rushed over and flung her arms around Simon.

'I have missed you *so* much, Simon! Where have you been all this time? Fulk took Matilda away some weeks ago now, and I have been left to do the cooking in her absence. And just *look* at the state of your garments! Once they are off, hand them to Edith, and I shall see to their washing personally, since Edith grows feeble of late. Oh, and welcome back!'

Merle ran back towards the hall, yelling instructions and calling for people by name, while Eustache stood watching her hasty departure.

'I wish my own wife were as welcoming upon *my* return. It's normally "What do you want this time?", or "You grow fatter every time I see you." And such a comely woman! You are well blessed, my good sir, but I wonder why you tarry away so long when you have a welcome like that awaiting your return.'

'She is not my wife, Eustache,' Simon told him.

Eustache guffawed. 'Even better, you rogue! Thank God I am not your confessor.'

The reference to a confessor struck at Simon's conscience like a dagger thrust. It had been many weeks since he had attended Mass, and so far as he could recall it had been during his enforced stay in Chester. The next morning, after bidding a fond farewell to Eustache, and assuring him that King Henry would be advised of his loyalty and assistance, Simon made his way to the parish church in nearby Hinckley. The parish priest made light work of his confession, penanced him with a hundred paternosters, and left him to bow at the altar before he knelt, offered the resulting pain in his leg to God, and prayed for His guidance through what he had left to do.

'This is your home, not an *auberge* where you may rest briefly before racing off again. Even less is it a laundry of convenience,' Merle chided him as he announced that once his clothing had been repaired and washed, he must begin the laborious task of collecting together all the men he had been promised. He would then lead them, first to Chester, then to

York, or perhaps Westminster if the Court had concluded its coronation progress.

'Dearest Merle,' Simon said, looking down at her, 'it certainly *feels* like coming home, when I see your sweet face as I ride over the bridge. You must consider marriage, since it seems to have done Fulk no harm, and you would make the most gracious, loving and loyal wife for even the highest noble in the realm.'

'My lord,' she said, 'you have known for some time that there is only one man in the whole of Christendom for me, but that he is forbidden to me. Just hold me briefly in your arms, and perhaps bestow me a kiss upon me, and know that your devoted Merle will ever be here, awaiting your return.'

Simon held out his arms and she slid into them with a contented sigh. Then he leaned down and kissed her fully on the lips, only breaking off when he tasted salt, and looked up to see the tears rolling down her face.

It took him a month to collect his army, beginning in Bristol, and working his way back through Kenilworth before picking up the balance of the Leicester men who were not allocated to Merle's personal security. He then led them all uphill and down dale via Northampton, Lincoln, Ashby and Derby until he rode across the Dee Bridge at the head of over two thousand men. They wore a variety of liveries, and they looked like a pilgrimage of the destitute as they shuffled in threadbare boots and dust-besmirched hose, carrying the remnants of what twenty years ago might have been serviceable weapons. They gave a loud cheer as they saw Chester Castle approaching, which was echoed by hoarse challenges from its ramparts until Fulk rode out through the entrance gate and hailed the man at their head.

'God be praised, you have brought me an army!' he enthused.

Simon shook his head. 'I have brought you two thousand men, that is all. Whether or not they become an army will be a matter for you and I, Geoffrey of Flint and Hugh Markham. What is more, they must be accommodated and fed, which is why I must lose no time in journeying on to York, where hopefully the royal Court may still be found. We have the men — now King Henry must provide us with the money to arm, train, feed and house them.'

Simon remained in Chester for long enough to bathe, have his clothing washed, hear Mass in St. John's Cathedral, sleep for two days without a break, and feed his long muscular frame, from which his surcoat was beginning to droop like a badly hung tapestry. Matilda eagerly sought news of how matters were faring back in Leicester, and chided Simon gently for not bringing Merle back to Chester with him.

Simon and Fulk arranged a provisional programme for the training of the men, who were to be placed into battle wings according to their experience and apparent ability. Fulk had convinced himself that archers would be the most valuable should Chester come under siege, and he was particularly excited to learn that so many of the new recruits were Midland woodsmen, who in his experience made the most skilled bowmen. The castle steward was set the daunting task of arranging for the new arrivals to be billeted around the small town, and he reminded Simon more than once of the expense this would entail. Then finally, with Fulk's good wishes ringing in his ears, Simon set off across the Pennine tracks for York.

He arrived late in the evening of the fourth day, battling an early blizzard on his way down the mountainous track that he seemed to be sharing with pilgrims and mendicant friars. He had missed supper, but when his arrival at the castle was announced, Peter de Rivaux, in his capacity as steward of the household, guided Simon to a private chamber in Clifford's Tower. There a fire had been lit against the late autumn chill, a feather bolster bed had been supplied in one corner, and a substantial repast of cold meats and cheeses was served to him by liveried pages who seemed to regard him with some reverence.

He was relaxing with his second cup of a passable wine when there was a discreet disturbance in the doorway, and an usher in the royal livery was admitted for long enough to announce that Simon was required in the hallway outside. Simon walked out, and was immediately met by Adele de Lusignan. She placed her hand to her lips in a sign for silence, and escorted him a few yards down the hallway, where in a high window alcove he was confronted by Princess Eleanor, smiling broadly.

'Welcome back to Court, Lord Simon. My brother did not wish your news to be overheard by those at board, but he asked that I bid you welcome nevertheless, and summon you to his Presence Chamber on the morrow. I trust you are well?'

'Very well thank you, my lady. And I bring heartening news.'

'Hush!' Eleanor commanded him, as she placed a cool finger on his lips. 'They will all be leaving the Great Hall shortly. Since this Tower also houses the Earl and Countess of Cornwall, they will be passing by, and must not overhear anything of advantage.'

'Does Henry not trust even his own brother?' Simon whispered.

Just then, the muted sound of conversation became audible, growing louder as it approached. It was a woman's voice, and it seemed that she was giving instructions to some servant or other. As she appeared around the corner and walked towards their alcove, Eleanor grabbed both of Simon's hands in hers, and leaned towards him an adoring look in her eyes. Then she looked past him, feigned guilty surprise and murmured, 'Good night, Isabel.'

The lady stopped long enough for Simon to turn and bow formally to Countess Isabel of Cornwall. She stared at him briefly before a knowing smirk crossed her face and she continued her progress down the hallway. Eleanor giggled loudly once she was out of earshot.

'*That* will give the old bat something to gossip about, but at least she will not know the true purpose of our conversation. I doubt that Henry will permit me to attend tomorrow's audience, so hopefully he will keep me advised of its outcome. Whether or not we shall see each other again here in York is a matter for the Fates to determine, but I always walk in the gardens after dinner.'

With that she was gone in a cloud of rich perfume, and Simon was left wondering if they had a definite appointment for the following afternoon. Whether they did or not, he would take a turn in the gardens.

'Only two thousand?' asked a grumpy Henry the following morning.

'It was all I was able to recruit in the time available, Your Majesty,' explained Simon. 'Even then, they will need to be trained, fed, clothed and housed. As you reminded me not long ago, I am already heavily in debt, and since the force is raised as a royal army, I was hoping...'

'Yes, yes, of course,' Henry cut him off testily. 'There was a time when nobles bore the cost of their own retainers as part of feudal service to their king, but since Runnymede they seem to have forgotten that. No matter. You have my authority to have all necessary debts remitted to Westminster.'

'Thank you, Your … Henry,' Simon corrected himself, and was relieved to see the royal countenance lighten somewhat. 'On the subject of maintenance, how are they to be liveried?'

'Since they are defending Chester, why not the Chester livery? The local seamstresses will be most familiar with that anyway, and if Richard and Llewellyn believe that we have that many fighting men in Chester alone, they will perhaps reconsider any ambition to come further east. Do we know where Marshal's forces are now?'

'Last heard of disembarking at Pembroke,' Henry told him. 'If they march north and join up with Llewellyn immediately, the best advice is that they will lay siege to Chester within a month.'

Simon went pale. 'I cannot possibly have the men ready by then, Henry! Some of them have never fought before, most of them have grown fat and lazy, and none of them are as fit as one might wish.'

'Your problem, Simon. You have brought me the men — now teach them how to fight. If Chester falls, I will be brought once again to a humiliating negotiation table, and I will be far from forgiving to those who allowed my enemies to prevail. Perhaps you had better leave without delay — I will give your apologies to my sister.'

Not sure whether Isabel of Cornwall had taken an early opportunity to report his fleeting and somewhat suspicious-looking meeting with Eleanor the previous evening, Simon bowed from the presence, feeling very uneasy. It might not be a good idea to join the royal table at dinner the following day, even had he been invited, and he hoped that Eleanor would not feel slighted if he did not 'accidentally' meet with her in the gardens. But then again, he asked himself why that should concern him as he passed into the outer keep with his panniers over his shoulder, and requested that his horse be made ready.

XVIII

Fulk swore when Simon returned to Chester with the news. 'At least you're back here to teach them the art of dirty warfare, and Geoffrey has set his brother-in-law the task of training bowmen. So if we stay behind the walls and pray, we might just survive.'

'It almost certainly won't be that simple,' Simon assured him. 'You have far more experience of sieges than I do, and even I remember that it is sometimes necessary to venture outside the walls in an effort to release the grip. How many horses do we have?'

'Very few,' Fulk replied with a grimace. 'But more importantly, half the men you brought in wouldn't know one end of a horse from another, unless it either bit them at one end, or shit on them from the other. Any foray will be on foot.'

'What's the final tally from your initial training?'

'About three hundred who, at a pinch, could be counted on to wave a sword about for long enough to get themselves cut in two, a few dozen handy axemen who'll probably be mown down by enemy destriers, roughly a thousand who're just about capable of standing their ground with a lance, and the rest — hopefully — are bowmen.'

'What of the Welsh?'

'According to what the local men here tell me, the Welsh are also skilled bowmen, so once the battle begins, we can expect the sun to disappear from view, and to be deafened by the noise of a thousand shafts whistling through the air.'

'That's *something* at least,' Simon observed. 'We can expect Marshal's men to be tired and jaded after their recent fighting in Ireland, and we might get the upper hand on the open ground.'

'You didn't hear me, did you?' Fulk snarled. 'We'll be lucky if we can put four hundred men on the ground, and from what I've been told, Marshal has two thousand.'

'*Had* two thousand, when he set off for Ireland,' Simon corrected him. 'There may be measurably less than that by now.'

'That's *still* four against one,' Fulk reminded him. '*You* may be able to take them on seven at a time, but the rest of us are less gifted. Perhaps we should begin training the men how to pray.'

Simon did not need to be taught how to pray. Every day in his narrow chamber inside the castle, he lowered himself gingerly onto his knees in front of the small altar he had constructed and asked God for the wisdom to guide his men with minimum loss of life, and perhaps some miracle to prevent Chester being overrun. Fulk and his seconds in command took a more pragmatic approach, and the castle keep echoed from dawn to dusk with the sound of men being drilled, commands being shouted, and weapons clashing together in mock combat. The long sweep of land immediately in front of the south wall — now almost restored to its original height from the early fitness regime that had seen each rock lifted, remounted and mortared into place — became an archery butt. Thousands of shafts a day thunked into straw targets several hundred feet away from their determined trainee bowmen.

Then came the dreaded day when a dense, dark line filled the western horizon, and a massive horde of armed men slowly advanced on Chester. Outlying villagers drove their beasts into the keep, where confused cows bellowed their protest at the lack of grazing, and skittery sheep bleated around in circles. The population of the castle trebled over the course of several hours as the terrified country folk fled in the face of the oncoming wave. There were nervous stories that the Welsh never took live prisoners, or that they roasted their conquered townspeople alive on communal bonfires.

Simon and Fulk watched for several hours as the black line slowly crawled towards them, growing more visible by the minute. After the second hour, it became audible on the westerly wind that seemed to be sweeping the enemy towards them. They could hear the singing of the Welshmen, and the chinking of chainmail from the seeming thousands of mounted warriors.

'There must be five thousand at least,' Simon muttered.

Fulk swore, then added his gloomy philosophy. 'Five thousand or ten thousand, it's only the man who comes at *you* that you need worry about.'

'I don't suppose they'll be in the mood to parley,' Simon observed grimly.

'I certainly wouldn't, with odds like that,' Fulk confirmed. 'Anyway, if you'll excuse me, I'll go back down to the keep and prepare the men for a bravely fought death.'

Simon remained where he was, as his mind drifted back to his boyhood and early youth in the Languedoc, and the daily return of the dead and dying. Every one of them had a wife and family somewhere, or would at least have parents to mourn his undignified passing. Warfare was a filthy sin against God, and here he was, committing thousands to their deaths so that he might reclaim his father's English title, even though he was a Frenchman. Perhaps he could stop this insanity before it began.

He ordered the southern postern to be opened to allow what looked like a small group of priests on donkeys to slip inside the safety of the castle walls at the last minute. At least they'd be of some use, praying for the souls of the dead. Then just before the gate was closed, he nudged his horse out onto the earth ramp on the other side, and slowly descended to the town side of the river bridge that the invading force would need to cross, a one-man symbol of defiance.

There he sat, deep in prayer for the safe passage of his soul, as the enemy line advanced. He could make out the facial features of each man in the front rank, bowmen for the most part, and the set look of their faces suggested that they knew their business. Behind them were rows of mounted knights, every one of whom was capable of hacking Simon into convenient lumps to be thrown into the river.

There were several shouts of command from somewhere to the rear of the invading force, and a man rode out in full armour, his livery of a red lion rampant denoting him as a Marshal. Simon rammed his de Montfort standard into the ground with a determined thrust, and said a prayer for the man who'd once carried it proudly into battle, and the widow he would be leaving behind — if by some miracle the invaders spared her life because of her value as a cook. The man in armour allowed his horse to walk in front of the southern bridge parapet, as he surveyed Simon with a scornful look down the nose bridge of his shining helm.

'Do you intend to defend this bridge all on your own?' the man demanded. 'Are you the leader of the defenders, sent to parley, or the village idiot?'

'I am Lord Simon de Montfort, defending Chester in the name of King Henry.'

'"De Montfort"? *Another* Frenchman?'

'I am originally from France, certainly, but now I serve King Henry.'

'Is there *anyone* English left at the English court?' the man demanded. 'The last time I was there, it was full of Bretons, Gascons, Poitevins and the like. But that was before that bastard Henry had my brother done to death. I am Richard Marshal, Earl Marshal of England, and just about the only Englishman left with any title.'

'As Earl Marshal of England, you should be *defending* the nation and its king, not inciting the Welsh into rebellion,' Simon pointed out.

'I do not need you to tell me how I should be serving the nation,' Marshal snarled back at him. Even his horse seemed to take offence at Simon's remark, and began side-stepping so hard that its rider was obliged to rein it in. 'Is it true that Henry plans to bring his new wife's family over from Savoy, thereby meekly handing over other portions of this once proud realm to foreign hangers-on?'

'He does not confide that much in me,' Simon lied, marvelling at the man's knowledge of Henry's plans.

'No, he just sends you out here to die needlessly, along with your puny army. No matter — one less French bastard to suck up the nation's wealth. If you are seeking surrender terms, let's hear them. My horse grows impatient — but then he has been trained to the reek of enemy blood.'

'I do not offer surrender,' Simon yelled back defiantly. 'What I *do* seek is that you have some regard for the human lives that you plan to end this day.'

'Henry Plantagenet should have thought of that himself, before ignoring the promises made by his father, and dishonouring the treaty he himself confirmed. You have safe passage back inside your cottage walls, then we attack.'

The two men glowered at each other for a moment, and then opened their mouths in synchronised astonishment as a commanding voice boomed out from the open castle gate.

'In the name of God Almighty, and with the authority of His Holiness the Pope, I forbid this slaughter to proceed.'

There in the gateway stood what looked like God's representative on earth.

The high-ranking clergyman walked sedately down the slope towards them, as Simon's men peered over the parapet of the south wall. The man who had called a halt to proceedings wore a bright red and green chasuble, and his jewelled mitre glittered in the sun. He was followed by a tall priest holding a giant gold cross high in the air, while the priest alongside him was swinging an incense bottle from side to side with a stern expression on his face.

'I am Cardinal Oddone di Monferrato, and I am Pope Gregory's *legatus* here in England. I carry his authority to excommunicate, for life, any man who employs a weapon in anger this day. There can be no lifting of such a burden, and anyone who incurs it will suffer the tortures of Hell for all eternity.'

Simon looked back at Richard Marshal. 'What is the current state of *your* soul?' he asked.

Marshal grimaced. 'Worse than yours, I have no doubt. I have no wish to be excommunicated.'

'No more do I,' Simon admitted. 'Nor do I wish to witness the wanton slaughter that only you and I can prevent. I will stand my men down, if you do likewise.'

'Do we have a choice?' Marshal asked before turning his horse's head and walking it back to his lines, where he yelled out a series of commands that were echoed through the ranks by his captains. The muttered oaths of the mounted knights were rapidly drowned out by the wild curses of the Welsh bowmen in the front lines, as they threw down their weapons in rage and sat on the ground, glaring up at the walls of the castle in which they had hoped to settle some old scores.

Marshal walked his mount back to Simon. 'You are now honour-bound to grant me safe passage inside your fortress, where — to be fully open with you — I am in urgent need of the garderobe.'

Simon extended an arm back to the still open castle gateway. 'Best follow me inside, then.'

An hour later, the two men sat facing each other across a table in the Great Hall, at the head of which sat the papal legate who had been instrumental in preventing the bloodshed. He had raised his hand in a blessing over both their heads, and now got down to business.

'It is the great desire of both His Holiness and King Henry to see this nation in a state of perpetual peace, and for the grievances between the king and barons to be resolved. To this end, His Majesty commands that you, Earl Marshal, attend him at Windsor one week hence, alone. He gives his word that no harm will befall you, and His Holiness has threatened King Henry with perpetual excommunication should he renege on that word.'

'Does Henry also undertake to redress our grievances?' Marshal demanded.

The legate smiled in the manner of all diplomats. 'He undertakes to listen to them, anyway. He has no wish for the nation to remain divided in this way.'

'Tell King Henry that I will accede to his request, but that if our long-standing grievances are not redressed, the nation will be not one jot closer to peace,' Marshal insisted. He rose to his feet before looking back down the table at the papal legate. 'I need to return to Pembroke ere I journey to Windsor. Tell His Majesty that I may be delayed longer than a week, but that I shall answer his summons.' With that he walked swiftly from the chamber, leaving Simon alone with the legate, who had gestured for him to remain.

Once the chamber door had closed behind Marshal, the legate's face lapsed into a broad smile. 'The Princess Eleanor sends her regards.'

'And her brother?'

'King Henry sent *me*, rather than his regards. Perhaps in the circumstances that was more efficacious, since you are still alive, but it was the princess who persuaded Henry of the need to preserve you from almost total defeat, and possible death. Henry was promised that Marshal would be brought to the negotiation table in return. I have accomplished both my missions, it would seem.'

'Why do you tell me this?' Simon asked suspiciously.

'Because it is important that you be left in no doubt that the nation's welfare still hangs by a thread. His Holiness is greatly concerned that there remains a prospect of civil war in a nation from which he had hoped to recruit Crusaders for the continued security of Jerusalem, hence my presence in England. But Henry proves resistant to any progress towards peace, insisting that Marshal be obliged to surrender on his terms. As you had cause to appreciate from the size of the force that threatened this town barely an hour ago, Henry is in no position to demand such abject submission, and he must be made to understand that some humility will be required on his

164

part if his crown is to remain securely on his head. But he is not a man to take such advice — certainly not from a man of God such as I, nor his Grace of Canterbury, who has undertaken to mediate between them when they meet at Windsor.'

'And you see me as the person most likely to talk him round?' Simon stared in disbelief. 'I am not even one of his leading barons, and I only found myself at the head of the king's forces because there was no-one else. I, too, detest meaningless slaughter inspired by pride.'

The legate smiled. 'You are clearly a man of honour, and — if I judge you aright — a God-fearing man who also possesses a soldier's strong right arm. These attributes are rarely found together in the one man, and it may fall to you to ensure that England does not become a charnel house of high-born corpses.'

'How do you say I may further assist?'

'Henry clearly sees you as the leader of his army, as you have proved yourself to be. He will not agree to anything that detracts from his royal dignity for as long as he feels protected from the wrath of his leading barons. While the last thing I urge is that you join with them, it might be wise to leave him with the belief that your prowess on the field of battle is only available to those who deal righteously with the people he was crowned in order to protect.'

'That comes close to what I believe anyway,' Simon told him.

The legate nodded. 'It is as we thought.'

'We?'

'The Princess Eleanor and I. She has judged you well, I think.'

'Who rules the nation — Henry or Eleanor?' Simon asked.

'That is a question I frequently ask myself,' the legate answered.

Simon took his leave of the legate with a bow, after receiving a further blessing for which he was both gratified and relieved, and made his way down the hallway in search of some wine. He was intercepted by Fulk, who had obviously been awaiting him, and he sought urgent orders regarding the disposition of the armed force that was threatening to out-eat Chester.

'As for the men, see that they are given double payment for today. Tell them that they are free to return to their homes, but must be ready to return to our standard if called upon. But before that, invite them to dinner in the market square. Then enquire of those farmers who brought their beasts under our protection if they are prepared to sell two or three of them, and ask your wife to organise a massive roast that shall be free to all.'

'You are most generous,' Fulk said, 'except to the cook.'

'Henry is paying,' Simon reminded him, 'and it is the least he can do in return for remaining on his throne. I shall return briefly to Leicester; then, I believe, I am summoned to Windsor. '

XIX

On the two-day ride back, staying overnight at a Cistercian monastery where he gratefully heard Mass and confessed the sin of pride, Simon was deep in thought. It was just conceivable that he could prevent England descending into a lengthy war in which the only victors would be gravediggers, but he was still without the title he had first left France in order to claim. There could be no thought of returning to the land of his birth empty-handed, but the price of remaining in England seemed to be his adopting the role of peacemaker in a dispute that clearly went back many years. He would also need to persuade Henry to change the way he wore his crown. Or he could simply hide away in Leicester and play at being the lord of the manor.

As he crossed the Swarkestone Bridge that spanned the swollen and rapidly rising Trent, he was accosted by an old man driving several goats ahead of him.

'Don't tek the Donington Road, if ye're goin' ter Ashby,' the old man told him through his worn-down gums. 'The fields've flooded onter the track. Best head south terwards Leicester, then tek the road back north.'

Simon thanked him for what seemed like an attempt to warn him about the state of the road ahead, although he hadn't understood all of it, given his lack of English and the man's strange way of speaking. But he had caught the name 'Ashby', and an idea was forming in his head. If he was to have any hope of understanding what was at stake in the negotiations that lay ahead, then he needed to take a history lesson, and he knew the very man to ask.

Eustache de la Zouche was delighted to welcome Simon back into his spacious hall, if only because he was a man who appreciated his wine collection, and could help him drink it. Simon sat politely through a vast supper, then waited patiently for Imelda de la Zouche to retire for the night, before suggesting that he and Eustache withdraw to the chairs in front of the fireplace to talk about the past.

'How long have you been in England?' Eustache asked suspiciously. 'What interest do *you* have in the past? Has Henry sent you to ascertain my loyalty?'

'No,' Simon reassured him, 'you have my word on that. But I shall shortly be attending Court, where King Henry has agreed to meet with Richard Marshal in order to resolve their differences.'

'I hope they've set aside at least a month,' Eustache replied sarcastically. 'Even then, a month is hardly long enough to heal fifty years of open wounds.'

'It is those upon which I seek your counsel,' Simon urged him.

Eustache dismissed the serving boy who had been attending them, helped himself to more wine, refilled Simon's mug, and sat back in his chair. Then he raised his eyes to the roof beams and began to reminisce. 'It began in the days of the old king, Richard. I was a young man, and was only saved from my own impetuous plans to go on Crusade with him by my father, who very wisely refused me the money. While Richard was away, he left his younger brother John in charge of the nation, and a thoroughly bad job he made of it, strictly between you and I. We felt his jealous wrath and naked ambition most severely here in Leicestershire, since John seemed to take a fancy to the castle in Nottingham. He imposed taxes that we couldn't pay, enforced old forestry laws that we had believed to be obsolete, and hung anyone who protested.'

'He seems to have bequeathed his arrogant disregard of the law to his son,' Simon observed, mainly to encourage Eustache in his candour.

Eustache nodded vigorously. 'When John became king, we knew what to expect. And we were not disabused. The taxes he imposed were usurious, and had no legal justification that we could identify. He appointed his friends to positions of power and influence, and he turned his greedy eyes to former family possessions in your own country. Not only did this bleed the Treasury dry — thereby invoking demands for even more taxes — but he made a fool of himself, and a mockery of England, by losing what few possessions he might still have laid claim to.'

'My own father assisted him in that,' Simon replied with a rueful smile, 'which is why I still seek the Earldom of Leicester that was formerly held by Ranulf of Chester. John usurped it.'

'He usurped far more besides,' Eustache insisted as he spat into the fire. 'The leading barons decided to take a stand. They raised an army and all but besieged John in his castle at Windsor. He was only allowed out a few miles to travel to Runnymede Meadow, where he was forced to sign the "Great Charter" in return for his life and continued reign.'

'And what was in this "Great Charter"?' Simon asked.

Eustache allowed himself a hollow laugh. 'Freedom for all nobles from taxes that they had not agreed to in advance, an end to royal favourites and French influence at Court, no further attainders and executions without just cause, and the establishment of a *Curia Magna* that would govern the nation's affairs, in effect curbing John's freedom to do as he wished.'

'Then why is the nation in its present state, if that be the law?' Simon asked.

'Because John ignored it,' Eustache replied with another mouthful of mucus aimed at the fire. 'It was as if nothing had been agreed, and within another year the barons were in open rebellion, and only came to heel when Louis of France invaded because he saw England in turmoil as an easy target. This forced the barons to rally around the throne, if only to preserve the nation. Then John died on his way north, leaving the current King Henry at the mercy of the Marshals, who were among the leading barons, along with de Burgh and des Roches. They began fighting among themselves, and Henry somehow survived it all.'

'And is this "Great Charter" still the law of the land?'

'Officially, yes. Henry ratified it on the advice of William Marshal. The father, that is, not his goat of a son. It was at about that time that the Princess Eleanor was fed to the son like swill to a pig. But since then, Henry continues to behave as if his power were absolute, and as if the Great Charter were simply in the imagination.'

'And the leading nobles?' Simon asked. 'Why do they not insist on the law being upheld?'

Eustache looked Simon solemnly in the eye. 'I do not seek in any way to insult either you or the land of your birth, Simon, but if you wish the truth from me, then you must know that "the leading nobles" are not English anymore, but Frenchmen whom Henry regards as part of his extended family. They are easily manipulated. Henry forswears to take advice from Englishmen because he does not like the colour of their advice, which is always the colour of the Great Charter.'

Simon sighed and sank back in his chair. 'So the last person he will wish to negotiate with is Richard Marshal?'

'You have the situation well summarised. Of course, you are French, and he may be prepared to negotiate with you.'

'But I am no threat to him,' Simon objected.

'You are if you withdraw your support and side with the English nobles,' Eustache reminded him. 'Is it true that you held Chester Castle against Marshal and the Welsh?'

Simon's eyes opened wide in surprise. 'The news travels faster than I do, it would seem.'

Eustache smiled. 'You forget that some of your men were also mine, and two of them returned only this morning, singing your praises. I would guess that before too many more sunsets, Henry will also be advised of your triumph, and will see you as his ace card against the English barons.'

'But we only survived Marshal's onslaught due to the intervention of the Pope's legate,' Simon told him with a frown. 'Had they attacked, we would have been reduced to pig food. That same legate also persuaded Richard Marshal to attend Windsor and parley with Henry. I am not officially summoned to that meeting — think you that I should attend nevertheless?'

Eustache grimaced. 'Come over to the table with me, and I will show you what will happen if you do. Bring your wine with you.'

Simon did as requested, and Eustache took Simon's mug and placed it on the table.

'That is Henry, let us say.' Then he took his own mug and placed it next to Simon's. 'This is Richard Marshal.' He then took a slice of leftover lamb from the earlier supper, placed it between the two mugs and squeezed them together until blood began to seep from the tender flesh. 'And *that*, my friend, will be you, if you are fool enough to journey to Windsor.'

XX

Simon took the road to Leicester the following morning, even less sure of what he should do. He felt sure that Henry would be seeking his reassurance that, if called upon, Simon would re-raise a royal army of sorts to defend his throne. If he were prepared to journey south to Windsor with that promise, then he would no doubt be welcome. But was he prepared to guarantee that undertaking? The alternative was to forget that the meeting would be taking place at Windsor, and simply go about life as normal, always waiting for the summons to attend Court.

A third possibility was to pretend that he had somehow misunderstood, and had believed himself summoned to Windsor for reasons of which he was not aware. At least, by this means, he would learn how matters lay, and could perhaps position himself for whatever might be demanded of him. There was also the possibility that Henry, in his vulnerable state, would finally grant him the Earldom of Leicester. But did that not make him as bad as the foreign royal favourites of whom Marshal and the other barons were complaining?

It was with a troubled mind that Simon rode into the courtyard at Leicester, dismounted, handed his horse to the groom, and looked around for Merle. He frowned — every other time he had ridden home, she had been the first out of the door, racing towards him with open arms and prayers of thanks for his continued survival. Instead there was just an empty courtyard, with the sound of voices raised in heavenly supplication. Suddenly he feared the worst and called over to the groom, who was heading for the stables.

'Where is the Lady Merle?'

'In the chapel, my lord.'

'The what?'

The groom seemed to come to his senses and walked back, still holding the horse by its bridle. 'Sorry, my lord, I was forgetting how long you had been away. The mistress has built a new chapel, at the end of the barn there.'

Simon looked where he indicated, and there was now another door to the old barn, which appeared to have been recently extended. He was still gazing at it in silent wonder when a priest emerged, his hands clutching his breviary, and behind him a much changed Merle. Her hair was shaved almost to her scalp, and she was dressed more like a nun than the mistress of the manor. She smiled fondly as she became aware of Simon's return, and after dismissing the priest with a few words, she walked over.

'Have you taken holy orders in my absence?' Simon joked. Or at least, he hoped he was joking. 'Fulk would not be surprised, but I am.'

Merle stood looking up at him with a radiant smile. 'You must forgive me, my lord, but we lacked a chapel here, so I had one built. The mason requires payment for that — as do many other local merchants, some of whom are refusing to supply further goods unless we settle their accounts.'

'They shall be paid in due course,' Simon promised, 'but why a chapel?'

'Do you not need to preserve your soul?'

'Of course I do, but there is the church at Hinckley.'

'Which is fine for you, and perhaps I, but what of the gentle souls who serve the house and lands daily? Must they journey three miles each day, in each direction, to receive the Lord's grace?'

'Probably not — and I do not seek to chide you for what you have done. I am simply wondering why you should have given it such priority. I came by the north entrance, and the wall would seem to require some attention from a stonemason who was presumably distracted into building your chapel.'

Merle's eyes sank to the ground between them. 'In truth, it was for me. When you last rode away, heading for what seemed like your doom, I gained great comfort from praying to God for your safe delivery. Then God told me — in a vision, I suppose you could say — that I would only suffer more anguish until I resigned myself to the fact that you would never be mine. That I would never be your wife. I cried for several days, then a beautiful calm descended upon me, and I saw other visions — of my early childhood at my parents' feet, and the awesome presence of God's holy grace among our humble community, as it then was. That was before your soldiers arrived, of course, but it reminded me that God can cure all wounds of the soul, and I decided to offer Him my anguish at the loss of you. Then He urged me to build the chapel, and I devote all of my otherwise idle time in worship and reflection on the bounteous riches of the Lord's grace. But have no fear — I still maintain the household.'

A tear came to Simon's eye as he realised how much Merle must have suffered for love of him, and how unfeeling he had been towards her devotion. Merle saw the first tear roll down his cheek, and she wiped it away with a loving gesture as her face appeared to be suffused with light.

'I am still your sister, dearest Simon, and I shall ever serve you, and pray for your safe deliverance from the world you have chosen to explore. So God bless you, and come and eat.'

It was perhaps Merle's self-sacrifice that finally tipped the scales, but the next morning Simon made the necessary preparations, and the following day he pointed his horse south towards Windsor. He was still uncertain about what sort of reception he would receive, and even less certain of what role he might play in what was to follow, but if Merle could devote herself to God's will, then so could he. He just hoped that God would show him the way as clearly as He had obviously shown Merle.

As he dismounted in the lower ward, a familiar figure came striding down through the archway that led to the upper ward. Peter de Rivaux smiled and bowed.

'In my capacity as Steward of the Royal Household, you are welcome back, Lord Simon, although in my more recent role as Treasurer I am not so sure if you will be gladly received. The accounts that we receive daily from Chester suggest that you have been busy there.'

'Has the news not travelled south?' Simon asked.

De Rivaux laughed lightly. 'Forgive my jest — of course it has. Thanks to you, we expect the arrival of Richard Marshal daily. But I was also privily instructed to expect you, and I have once again given you the lower chamber in the Curfew Tower.'

'Privily instructed by His Majesty?' Simon asked.

De Rivaux tapped his nose and grinned. 'A privy matter of State, my lord. And talking of privies, once you have made yourself comfortable in your chamber, you are summoned to an audience with His Majesty in his private chambers in the upper ward. You take the main entrance into the residence building, then you turn right and proceed down the corridor to the doorway with the armed attendants in front of it.'

'His Majesty is expecting me?'

'At some point, yes, but my instructions were to watch for your arrival and see that you were admitted without delay. You have missed dinner, unfortunately, but I shall have food and wine sent to the Curfew Tower.'

An hour later, Simon was relieved to find that only Princess Eleanor was in attendance on Henry as he knelt and kissed the proffered ring.

'Your incurred debts have already begun to trouble my Treasurer,' Henry said, 'but it was money well spent. You were clearly a match for Richard Marshal.'

'It was God who conquered him, Henry,' Simon reminded him. 'Or at least, the representative of God whom you sent to prevent the almost certain slaughter of your entire army.'

Henry looked quickly sideways at Eleanor, whose face was beaming. 'You got that right, at least,' he confirmed grudgingly.

Simon deemed the time appropriate to confirm something else that she had got right. 'I have to report that Marshal was clearly aware of your plan to send me over to France to give safe passage to your wife's family.'

'That doesn't mean it was Isabel,' Henry told Eleanor out of the corner of his mouth, before turning to address Simon again. 'And now you are here to support me in my negotiations with Marshal?'

'If you wish, I should be honoured to assist where I can,' Simon replied diplomatically, 'but the primary reason for my attendance is to give an account of how matters fared at Chester. In particular, of the need to both maintain and expand your permanent army.'

'These things cost money, Simon, and once we have brought Marshal to heel, not only will we not need to defend ourselves against him, but he will be required to bring his forces under our banner once again.'

Simon exchanged an uncomfortable glance with Eleanor, but said nothing.

'However,' Henry continued, 'there still remains the matter of my queen's long awaited reunion with her family, and her uncles most particularly. We require you to take a small company across to Rouen, and then journey south into Savoy before the weather becomes too inclement.'

Simon remembered Marshal's angry words at the bridge at Chester, and the doubt he felt regarding the wisdom of bringing yet more French nobles to the English Court showed in his face.

Henry inclined his head to look inquisitively at Simon. 'You are still fatigued after your efforts at Chester? Or are you concerned at the cost? If so, be advised that the cost will be met by the Treasury. You also have my blessing to journey south with the title of "Earl of Leicester". But do not depart the Court until we have kicked Marshal for his insolence.'

Simon was still uneasy about the role he was being called upon to play as he sat in his chambers after supper, praying for God's guidance. It was of little consolation to finally have the long-coveted title if it meant helping Henry to divide the nation in his arrogance regarding the strength of his grip on the throne. In his heart, Simon suspected that the nation would be much stronger if it were united under the principles contained within the Charter that Henry seemed determined to ignore, and he felt more in sympathy with Richard Marshal then he did with Henry Plantagenet. He sighed, and once again asked God for a sign.

The page answered the knock on the door and admitted Adele de Lusignan and Princess Eleanor. Adele was carrying a gourd of wine, which she handed to the page, while Eleanor walked across the chamber and graciously held out her hand for Simon to kiss. Her perfume was once again almost hypnotic, and she had obviously taken great care over her grooming. Her light auburn hair shone in the light from the candles hanging from the ceiling, and her rouged cheeks glowed as she took the chair she was offered while Adele stood faithfully behind her. Simon perched on the window ledge, rather than sitting on the bed in the corner.

'We may speak freely in Adele's company,' Eleanor assured him, 'since she and I have no secrets.'

'Speak freely of what, my lady?'

'Please call me Eleanor when we are alone. And we are as good as such, with only Adele here to overhear us, should you feel emboldened to dismiss your page.'

Simon nodded for the page to leave them, and no sooner was the door closed behind him than Eleanor came to the point.

'Forget that Henry is my brother, and rest assured that we speak privily, but what think you of his state of mind?'

Simon's jaw dropped. 'You believe him to be … to be … bereft of his wits?'

'How else could you explain the way in which he blunders towards the loss of his crown?' Eleanor replied sadly. 'He is his father's son, clearly, but there is more of our mother in me. She wasted her best years trying to make Father see that he was not God, and that his subjects would shower him with love and loyalty only if he treated them fairly in return. I seek to similarly persuade Henry, but he sees no value in a woman's counsel.'

Simon chose his words carefully. 'It is true that I cannot in all conscience counsel him to deal other than openly and fairly with Richard Marshal, for I fear that he speaks for a good many others.'

'He speaks for most of England,' Eleanor confirmed, 'and somehow Henry must be persuaded that he cannot maintain his grip on the throne using threats, forfeitures and brute force.'

'You believe me capable of so persuading your brother?'

'He respects you — indeed, I believe he fears you. But above all, he believes that you will support him in everything he does, in order to retain your coveted title.'

Simon sighed. 'Certainly, it was the desire to reclaim what was stolen from my father that first brought me here, but now that it seems that I have it, I feel no sense of achievement. It was clearly that which led me to England, but since I have been here, the feeling has grown that I was drawn here for some other purpose.'

Eleanor rose from her chair, walked over to the window alcove in which Simon was seated, reached out and took his hand in hers. It was cool to the touch, and her perfume all but overpowered him. 'I, too, believe that you were sent here by God to preserve the kingdom when it most needs it, which is why I prevailed upon Henry to send the legate Monferrato to save you from extinction. In return, I wish you to work with me to save Henry from the worst of his nature. He is my brother, and I love him, despite that dreadful matter of his trading me to William Marshal in return for what he perceived to be his best advantage.'

'Can you not prevail upon Richard Marshal not to provoke him, perhaps by sending a warning through his sister, who is clearly in communication with him without Henry's knowledge?'

'That is something else,' Eleanor sighed. 'He refuses to believe that his brother's wife could be other than grovelingly grateful for her privileged position so close to the throne. This is how Henry thinks about everyone — even you, regrettably.

"Give them a bone and they will perform whatever trick you command" seems to be his entire life's philosophy.'

'And by accepting my title, I have unwittingly taken his bone?' Simon asked sadly.

Eleanor nodded. 'But he trusts you. I simply ask that you have the courage to argue with him on the matter of Marshal's undoubted demand that he honour the Great Charter.'

'You think that will be Marshal's price?'

'It is certainly the price of peace within the realm.'

'If he likes not my advice, he will simply cast me from Court, perhaps to the Tower.'

'I will ensure that he does not,' Eleanor assured him. 'Even if it means that I have to renounce a holy vow. But now we must take our leave. I shall return when I can, in order to bolster your courage. Make no other plans for the time following supper each evening.'

The following day there was a great flutter in the lower ward as the Archbishop of Canterbury, Edmund Rich, and his retinue arrived. It was rumoured that during the very first Mass that he'd conducted before the altar in the Lady Chapel, he'd broken off to remind Henry sternly of the need to observe the solemn vow he had taken at his coronation to uphold the laws of the land, and he'd even gone so far as to remind him of the ultimate fate of his father when he had forgotten to honour his pledges. No-one was prepared to confirm the story, but Henry was seen to be in a foul mood when news was brought to him that Richard Marshal had arrived, and was being accommodated in the Salisbury Tower, while the archbishop and his retinue had the entire Garter Tower to themselves.

Back in the Curfew Tower, Simon began to look forward to the nightly visits from Eleanor and Adele, and the superior wine that they always brought with them. The first of the renewed visits occurred at the end of the first day that Richard Marshal had been closeted with the archbishop, and the prelate gave word that he wished to meet with Henry the following morning.

'I fear that the archbishop will support Marshal's demand for the Great Charter to be honoured,' Eleanor confided to Simon while Adele looked on from behind her chair. 'If he does, Henry will dismiss him immediately from the Court, unless he can be persuaded to take time to consider the alternatives, rather than rejecting the demand outright.'

'What alternatives *are* there?' Simon asked.

Eleanor frowned. 'Perhaps his agreement to consult with the leading barons in some sort of council? It could be made to look like one of the Charter undertakings, although I doubt that Henry would pay much attention to anything with which he did not agree anyway.'

'I fear you may be correct. But from my brief conversation with Marshal at the bridge at Chester — as we prepared to launch armed men at each other — he seemed to resent the presence of so many foreigners at Court, Frenchmen in particular. Perhaps Henry might be persuaded to part with one or two of them?'

'Such as yourself?' Eleanor said.

'A very good point,' Simon conceded, 'but it can hardly be good that he intends to bring others over to England — members of the queen's family.'

'We may have to humour him in that,' Eleanor observed, 'if we wish to keep him compliant on more important matters.'

The following morning, in the Audience Chamber in the upper ward, a grim-faced Archbishop Rich sat where indicated at the long table, and raised an eyebrow at Simon sitting alongside Henry.

'He is my main advisor in this matter,' Henry informed him. 'You may speak freely in his presence.'

Rich cleared his throat, and if he felt uncomfortable with the news that he had to impart, it didn't show in his face. 'As I myself had occasion to remind Your Majesty during Mass, the nation has reached the point at which the Great Charter should be dusted off and implemented.'

'And that is Marshal's price for surrender, is it?' Henry demanded, the colour rising in his cheeks.

'It is hardly surrender,' Rich reminded him. 'But it is what he most earnestly seeks, if the nation is to be restored to tranquillity.'

'If the nation is to be restored to tranquillity,' Henry thundered, 'then men such as Richard Marshal should honour their oaths to *me*, as their lawfully appointed king! You may so inform him.'

Rich looked down at the table. 'Might I offer him *some* reassurance that there will be changes, Your Majesty?'

'You may reassure him,' Henry fired back haughtily, 'that there will shortly be a change in the identity of the Earl Marshal of England. I am far from impressed by the way he conducts his office.'

'Nothing else?' Rich asked.

'Perhaps a new incumbent at Canterbury?' Henry replied maliciously.

Rich rose from his chair with considerably more dignity than Henry was displaying, and made to leave. 'I will convey your current sentiments to the Earl Marshal, Your Majesty. But perhaps before I return, you might consider *something* that will have made his lengthy journey worthwhile.'

With that, he bowed from the presence, leaving Henry chuckling quietly to himself. After a short while, he turned to Simon. '*That* was telling him, was it not?'

'Indeed it was, Henry,' Simon replied with his head bowed, 'but Marshal is a proud man, and will not depart without *some* concession. Perhaps the dismissal of one of those from across the Channel who currently occupy positions here at Court? From my brief encounter with Richard Marshal, I am aware that some of these have been the cause of resentment among English nobles.'

'It is only from those you mention that I can be sure of any loyalty, Simon, yourself included. I have restored you to your title, and now you seek the removal of other favourites whom you see as rivals? Is this how you repay my generosity?'

'I do not seek further preferment, Henry,' Simon assured him, 'and if it makes you easier in your mind, then take back my title. I am here only out of loyalty to you, and the love I bear for this land that has adopted me. I would not see it reduced to nothing in a war among those who should be promoting its welfare.'

Henry sat deep in thought, then lifted his suspicious eyes back to Simon. 'If I were to dismiss one of my Court — de Rivaux, perhaps, since I cannot possibly do without des Roches — would that be sufficient for Marshal, say you?'

'Perhaps, Henry, but if I might suggest that you restore the practice of summoning the *Curia Regis* on important matters of State? That would be halfway towards honouring your father's Charter, which you yourself confirmed some years ago.'

'On what occasions would they be summoned?' Henry demanded, far from convinced.

'That would be a matter for future negotiation, clearly. But Marshal will depart in the belief that he has gained something in exchange for standing down his army, and we may all return to a peaceful life.'

'And of whom would this reconvened *Curia* consist?'

'Entirely a matter for you, clearly. But equally clearly, they must be both men that you trust, and men who are acceptable to the remaining nobles.'

'Men such as yourself, you mean?'

Simon shook his head vigorously. 'You have already rewarded me amply, Henry.'

'But if I were to ask you to take the head of the table at this new *Curia*, you would not refuse?'

'As a loyal subject, I could not refuse anything you command, Henry.'

The following day Marshal took his leave, with a final warning through the mouth of Archbishop Rich that if the promised changes did not occur very shortly, Henry could expect a large host to lay siege to Windsor. Henry then had the task of gently explaining to Peter de Rivaux that his days as both Treasurer of England and Steward of the Royal Household were at an end, but that he would receive a generous royal pension. But the strain on Henry of being forced to part with a Court favourite was obvious as he shut himself off from all but close family members, and refused to consider matters of State for an entire week. Simon was politely reminded that he should be making plans to cross the Channel to bring back more favourites, and when Eleanor sought admission to his withdrawing chamber to argue against it, Henry took out his anger and frustration on her.

'I might have expected you to seek to keep the man at Court, or at least in Leicester! Despite your vow of chastity, it is obvious that you lust after him, and he no doubt basks in your adoration of him. I shall delay proclaiming his new title, just to remind him of who rules the nation. I suspect his motives in all this — how am I to be assured that he does not tilt for the throne himself? He seemed willing to take the head of the table in any new Council of State — how can I be assured of his loyalty?'

Eleanor swallowed hard and remained silent. But she now knew what she must do.

The evening before Simon was due to set off for France with a small band of soldiers in the lion couchant livery of England, he received another visit from Eleanor and Adele. There was more wine, and Eleanor poured two goblets as she congratulated Simon on his success in restraining the worst of Henry's excesses. Then Adele screamed as she claimed to have seen a rat scuttling across her feet and out of the open chamber door. The page was sent to investigate, and upon his return was informed by Simon that his attendance was no longer required.

During all the excitement, Eleanor had extracted a small wrap of vellum from the placket of her gown, and tipped its contents into Simon's wine. Then she dismissed Adele from the chamber, and when Simon protested, she smiled.

'My brother need have no suspicions, since I took a solemn vow of chastity some years ago, and it has thus far preserved me from any temptation I might experience in the presence of men. Even handsome men such as yourself. In truth, if every man is like my former husband, then I would rather be a nun. So drink your wine, my Lord of Leicester, and let us raise a toast to your safe passage across the Channel.'

Simon took a deep draught, and they sat for almost half an hour, discussing his intended journey and his plans to be reunited with the older brother he had not seen for over ten years, until Simon's eyes began to droop. Eleanor kept up the conversation while watching the effect of the simple she had sent Adele to acquire from a compliant apothecary in the town. At the very last moment, she gently took the goblet from Simon's hand and persuaded him to lie back on the bed to rest his eyes.

The next morning, Simon awoke with a start. His last memory was of talking quietly with Princess Eleanor. He was now naked but alone under the covers, and while racking his brains as to how he could have ended up there he noticed several long, light hairs on the bolster beside his head. He leaned over and inhaled.

The perfume was unmistakable, and he feared that he had been a party to the breaking of a holy vow.

XXI

Amaury rushed forward and embraced Simon with an eagerness he had never before displayed.

'When they told me that the Earl of Leicester was seeking admission accompanied by soldiers wearing the livery of the King of England, I took it to be a jest. But here you are! You have clearly accomplished your mission — or do you come in fulfilment of another? You recall that I am now Constable of France, presumably?'

'Of course,' Simon confirmed as he stepped back to take a good look at the man who had been his boyhood hero. The hair under his fashionable bonnet was short, grey and grizzled, while the age spots on his face reminded Simon that the man would now be well over forty years of age. While he was taking all this in he heard a child whimpering, and looked behind Amaury to where a pleasantly plump woman was holding an infant in an attempt to quieten it. Behind her were two other small children. Amaury followed Simon's gaze, and his smile grew even wider.

'My children, and your nephew and nieces. Jean, the boy on the left, is now five, the girl standing next to him is Laure, aged three, and the baby is Marguerite, born seven months ago. The lady with them is their mother, and my wife, Beatrix, who is from Viennois.'

Simon bowed silently, and the infant burst into tears. Both men laughed, and Amaury led Simon down the hall to where a steward served them wine. Simon smiled with pleasure as he recalled the entrancing flavour of the local *vin de pays*, and gazed up at the ornate ceiling, with many carvings that had not been there when he had been staggering around the hall, nursing his battle wound.

'You will find that much has changed in your absence, which has been far too long,' Amaury told him as he placed one arm over his shoulder. 'Hopefully you will be staying for long enough to walk with me again around the lake, just like old times. Or does your royal commission demand that you make all haste? And where are you bound? Please do not say Paris, for I could not guarantee your safety there. Here, you are simply an emissary of King Henry, for whom chivalry demands safe passage through my lands. Lands that you rescued for me, before Fulk de Sevres had the opportunity to remove the head of Gaston de Nanterre. How is Fulk? Still in this world?'

'Currently in Chester, seeking to instil martial skills into the parcel of raw recruits that passes for a royal army. But please do not tell your king that. Fulk is married to the castle cook, but is otherwise the fierce old battle-axe that he always was.'

'And you, Simon? You are married?'

'I am not, and have no immediate plans to be. Before you ask, the woman Merle — the one you gifted to me at Carcassonne — has devoted her life to God.'

'She has become a nun?'

'As good as,' Simon said before lowering his voice to add, 'and no — I *never* had her.'

'I hope you will not reject further gifts from me with such ingratitude,' Amaury replied, 'since I hope to feed you to bursting for at least a month, and to drown you in this year's grape harvest, which has been plentiful, and of good quality. I may even let you play in the nursery with your nephew and nieces.'

'A few days only, then we journey on to Savoy, where I am to escort several close family members of England's queen back to Windsor. Whether they ever return in the opposite direction is a moot matter.'

'It is known here in the Île that Henry annoys his English barons by granting preferment at his Court to Frenchmen such as yourself.'

'Why do you not return with me?' Simon asked.

Amaury looked genuinely surprised at the suggestion. 'I fear that matters are not so friendly between our two crowns that Henry of England would welcome the Constable of France on his shores. You will be aware that their treaty regarding Brittany will expire in only a few weeks? Then I think you will find that it will be a case of English warriors once again crossing to the north of here on their way west — please ensure that you are not amongst them, else I may be called upon to kill you.'

'I am little safer in England, if the truth be known,' Simon admitted with a frown. 'Brother against brother is by no means unknown in that Godforsaken land.'

'Yet you choose to remain there? Why not join me in the Crusade to the Holy Land that Pope Benedict has proclaimed? King Louis is anxious that I should fly his banner in Jerusalem, mainly because he fears to risk his own neck in the enterprise, but seeks the ongoing goodwill of Rome. Hopefully I will be well south of here by the time that your King Henry chooses to make a fool of himself once again this side of la Manche.'

Simon laughed. 'The last Crusade that you and I were engaged in lasted for the first twenty years of my life, and is still ongoing. I now have estates in Leicester that must take priority. As must my progress south to Savoy, despite the distractions of Montfort-l'Amaury.'

Ten days later, he was presenting himself to Countess Beatrice of Savoy, assuring her that her daughter Eleanor,

Queen of England, was dearly missing her mother, and politely enquiring whether the royal uncles, Boniface, Peter and William, still wished to sample the hospitality of the English Court. He was surprised to learn that Boniface was a bishop, and that he seemed content to surround himself with an aura of holiness that did not actually require him to conduct any holy office, leaving others to perform those tasks on his behalf. He also declined King Henry's invitation to visit his niece, seemingly more interested in guiding the footsteps of her younger sister Beatrice. Peter and William were less parochially inclined, however, and eagerly accepted Simon's offer of a swift and safe passage north.

XXII

Back in Windsor, it was with a strong sense of achievement that Simon remained a few yards behind the two royal uncles as Queen Eleanor rushed, childlike, from the throne dais to embrace them with shrieks of delight. Then Simon caught the warning look on the face of the Princess Eleanor, and he froze when Henry glared at him and pointed a shaking finger in his direction.

'You — traitor — you are to remain outside until summoned! Do not attempt to remove yourself from the confines of the castle. If you do, the guards have my direct instruction to have you conveyed to the Tower of London. Now, get out of my sight!'

Simon backed out from the presence with as much speed as was consistent with dignity, and walked up and down the hallway outside with his ears ringing from Henry's outburst. He racked his brains for any action on his part that could have been mistaken for treason, and could only conclude that his brief stay as the feted guest of his own brother, the Constable of France, had been misconstrued and perhaps misreported. He finally sat down on a padded bench a few yards from the chamber door, where the armed men who permanently guarded it gazed at him in puzzlement mixed with what he hoped was righteous sympathy. Then the chamber doors were opened to allow the exit of the king's brother, Richard of Cornwall, who smiled palely as he beckoned for Simon to rise, placed an arm on his shoulder, and steered him out into the upper ward, where they came to a halt before Richard turned to speak.

'You must forgive my brother for his intemperance, and I am here to offer you my sincere apology that my wife should have been the cause of it. I hope it was unwitting, since she and the princess are close.'

Simon shook his head, attempting to make sense of all this meaningless information, and Richard smiled.

'Do not attempt to deny it, Simon. You were the cause of Eleanor breaking her vow of chastity. A holy vow, what is more, and it will be necessary to send to Rome for her absolution. God alone knows what the penance will be, and Henry fears that he will lose the friendly support of Pope Benedict for his ambitions in Poitou and Gascony.'

Simon was speechless, and Richard seemed anxious — eager, almost — to supply the detail.

'It is known that Eleanor was in the habit of visiting your chamber in the Curfew Tower after supper every evening. Nought ill was construed regarding this, given her vow of chastity and the fact that the Lady Adele was always in her company. But Adele was forced to admit, when my wife grew suspicious, that the night before you left for Savoy, she was dismissed from Eleanor's presence, and that the two of you spent the night together in your chamber. Eleanor did not return to her own bedchamber until cock crow, and her maidservant swore on her oath that her bed had not been slept in. *Your* bed, on the other hand, when examined more closely…'

'I was drunk!' Simon protested, not that he believed it would make his offence any less grave. 'Or at least, I was asleep. I believe I was, anyway!'

'The Princess Eleanor was in your bed, and you *slept?*' Richard asked, his face a picture of disbelief.

'On my oath before God,' Simon spluttered, 'if there was connection, I have no memory of it!'

'Then you are doubly cursed,' Richard said. 'Not only have you incurred the wrath of the King of England by having connection with his sister in violation of her vow, but you do not even have the pleasant memory of it to accompany you to the Tower.' He saw the distress on Simon's face and took pity on him. 'If it is of any consolation, Eleanor has made no complaint that she was taken against her will. If anything, when confronted with the accusation, she seemed pleased. But our brother was red-faced with rage, and accused you of plotting against his crown.'

'How can that be?' Simon asked, nonplussed.

'Who can tell, the way Henry's mind works? Perhaps he imagines that you intend to follow the example of the Marshals, and gain closer proximity to the throne by virtue of being related to him by marriage.'

'Marriage?' Simon echoed, aghast. 'Such a thought never entered my head, my word on it.'

'I am prepared to believe you, but you would not be the first to marry by royal command. As much as he may deny it, he was content enough when I was talked into further closeness with the Marshals by marrying their spare sister. Whatever the outcome, you must face Henry's wrath at some stage later today. You might wish to clean up before you do, since you resemble a man who has ridden from Savoy without breaking the journey overnight. As you will know, we no longer have a steward here at Windsor since poor old Peter de Rivaux was put out to grass, but I will give instruction that you be accommodated in your old chamber in the Curfew Tower. Unless it brings back unhappy memories, of course.'

'In truth, it brings back no memories at all,' Simon confessed, 'but thank you for your courtesy.'

An hour later he was lying on his bed and staring at the ceiling, wondering what dark secrets the chamber held, when Lady Adele was admitted. He sat up and gestured her to the vacant chair before looking meaningfully behind her to see if she was accompanied.

'Have a care, lady,' he said sourly. 'If we are alone together, my character will be further blackened in the mind of King Henry. And your reputation will be forever lost.'

Adele's gaze dropped to the floor. 'I am here to beg your forgiveness for my part in that, and to convey my mistress's congratulations on your safe return.'

'It would not seem to be so safe,' Simon grunted, 'given the king's mood towards me. But what do you mean by "your part" in what allegedly transpired?'

'Forgive me, my lord, but it was I who acquired the potion from the apothecary, and I who created the diversion while my mistress placed it in your wine.'

'I was poisoned, say you?'

'A sleeping draught only, my lord, but sufficient for my mistress to place you in your bed then climb in beside you, to set the tongue of the Countess of Cornwall wagging.'

'To what purpose, pray you? Does your mistress seek my downfall?'

'I cannot say, my lord, but from the way she talks constantly of you, I doubt if that was her motivation.'

'She talks freely of me, does she? Did she by any chance advise you whether she and I had connection while I was under the influence of your potion?'

'She did not, my lord, but it is obviously believed by His Majesty that you did, and my lady has said nothing to gainsay that. And — if I might make so bold, my lord — if you had been in *my* bed, I know what would have transpired.'

'Enough!' Simon admonished her, although he could not keep the self-satisfied grin from his face. 'Do you know when the king will next summon me, to explain myself?'

'He is currently with my lady in his withdrawing chamber, and she is feigning tears of regret and begging his forgiveness. She also claims to have been unable to withhold her passion when you made advances to her, and is imploring His Majesty not to punish you for her weakness.'

'Why do I feel such guilt for something I do not remember?' Simon muttered, almost to himself.

Adele felt sorry for him. 'If it eases your conscience, my lord, the apothecary warned me that the simple he handed me would ensure your total lack of awareness of your surroundings within an hour of your consuming it.'

'It may ease my conscience, but it does not improve my memory. Perhaps Princess Eleanor can in due course assist in that. You may leave me to ponder my fate.'

It was late in the afternoon before Simon found himself standing before Henry, with Eleanor at his side, a broad grin on her face whenever her brother was not looking directly at her. At least Henry's countenance seemed to have lightened somewhat since their last confrontation.

'The fact that your head is still on your shoulders is due to two things, Lord Simon,' Henry announced grimly. 'The first is that what you did with my sister was, she assures me, with her consent. The second is that you may be of further service to me in your new role.'

'What role might that be, Your Majesty?'

'*Henry!*' he yelled back. 'It is "Henry" when we are alone, and it would seem that we are destined to be in that position many more times in the future, as brothers-in-law.'

Simon took a few seconds to register what was being mooted, and his eyes flew to Eleanor, who gave him an adoring look as she nodded her head. Henry turned to follow Simon's gaze, and caught her gleeful expression.

'As you can see for yourself, she freely consents without your even asking. And you need not go through the motions of seeking *my* permission, since I command it.'

'You wish me to wed your sister?' Simon asked, open-mouthed.

'No, Simon, I *command* it, as I just said. I will not demean myself to ask Canterbury to perform the service, nor will it be at Westminster. It shall be here at Windsor, in the Lady Chapel, as soon as des Roches returns and dons his mitre.'

'I shall do my very best to prove worthy of the honour,' was all that Simon could mutter.

'And I will make sure that you do,' Henry insisted, before he pointed to the vacant chair to his right. 'Join us in a celebratory cup of wine, and assure me that you will show nothing but loyalty and fealty to us *both*.'

XXIII

Never had a royal wedding been celebrated in such apparent secrecy since the days of Henry's grandfather and his furtive nuptial ceremony with Eleanor of Aquitaine. The only witnesses were Henry and his brother Richard, and des Roches raced through the order of service as if ashamed, or apprehensive, of what he was about. Simon could barely believe what was happening, and only Eleanor appeared to be enjoying what was taking place, as she gripped Simon's hand and shed a silent but smiling tear. Once it was over, they went back to the upper ward to a supper that seemed no different from normal, and after having eaten virtually nothing, Eleanor took Simon blushingly by the hand and led him to her usual bedchamber.

The following morning, Simon looked admiringly at the long, slim body of his wife as she washed her face in the bowl left earlier by a silent attendant, and he decided that the time was right to seek further information.

'I think we shall be well suited, but you were not to know that when you laid your clever scheme. Why did you engage in such a ruse? I would have married you anyway, had I but known what awaited me.'

'But you did not, did you? And if I had chosen to show you, that night in the Curfew Tower, you would have accounted me a cheap whore. As far as I was aware, you'd known enough of those in your past.'

'So why?'

'For England,' Eleanor murmured as she sat back on the side of the bed and ruffled Simon's chest hair playfully. 'And for myself, of course — chastity is a dreadful condition for a young woman of my appetites.'

'How for England?' Simon persisted.

'Henry needs you constantly at his side, although he is too proud to admit it. This way you will be there naturally, and between us we can steer him towards policies that will ensure peace throughout the realm. He does not believe me capable of understanding affairs of State, but if it comes from your mouth my advice will be all the more accepted.'

'So I have become your mouthpiece, as well as your husband? You chose me in order to rule the nation from behind the throne?'

'Many a queen has done that, my own grandmother and namesake in particular,' Eleanor reminded him. 'Without Eleanor of Aquitaine, Henry Plantagenet would have remained merely Count of Anjou. But you and I share opinions as to how England may best be governed, and when you speak for yourself, you will also be speaking for me. But were it just me saying such things, Henry would not listen.'

'And if we disagree, as surely must happen from time to time?'

'Then your will shall prevail — unless I can persuade you otherwise with my body.'

'For your body I would become a Mohammedan, foreswearing the faith in which I was raised.'

'That is as it should be,' Eleanor said as she reached under the bedcovers. 'The serving girl will not return until summoned — would you care to be persuaded that Henry must place you at the head of his new Council?'

The first difficulty beset them at the end of their first week as man and wife. As they sat at dinner with Henry one day, the only others at board being Queen Eleanor, Richard and Isabel, Henry suddenly gave a loud chuckle.

'Your marriage has achieved one good thing, at least. It would seem that we have scandalised Canterbury with your wanton behaviour, sister dear. But there's no fool like an old fool, as the saying goes, and Rich is so doddery these days that hopefully the shock will prove fatal. Then we might find a role for your other uncle, my dearest,' he added as he squeezed his wife's hand.

'The archbishop is complaining that I broke my vow of chastity?' Eleanor said mischievously. 'Did you tell him that I did it for England?'

'I have told him nothing, nor do I intend to,' Henry replied with a smirk, 'but he has placed poor old des Roches under threat of excommunication, once the Pope can be persuaded. Fortunately, His Holiness is even now seeking to tweak my interest in his pet Crusade, so I may have to send Simon on my behalf, by way of penance.'

'Your chance to become a Mohammedan, as you offered,' Eleanor grinned as she reached forward and kissed Simon on the cheek, making a rude gesture at Isabel of Cornwall behind Henry's back.

'Should I not journey to Rome myself, and seek His Holiness's pardon?' Simon asked.

'It was not your sin, Simon,' Henry reminded him. 'And in any case, you and Eleanor must make urgent plans to travel to your new home.'

'We shall not be living here at Windsor?' Simon asked.

Henry shook his head. 'You have already seen my castle at Kenilworth, I believe, when you robbed its guardhouse of men who were needed more urgently in Chester. What thought you of it?'

'A fine enough house, but not much of a fortress,' Simon admitted.

'My father built the Great Mere in order to improve its defences,' Henry insisted.

'A pity he did not reinforce the walls inside it, and, while he was about it, create more accommodation for a greater number of fighting men,' Simon countered. 'When I called to collect men for Chester, they were all eager to come with me when I told them they would be sleeping in beds, and not on straw in the stables.'

'You will be able to remedy those oversights in my name when you take up occupation,' Henry told him, 'since it is my wish that you make it your home, as well as a base from which to repel any possible Welsh invasions. I am advised that we have not heard the last of Richard Marshal.'

'Then the sooner you summon your Council, the better,' Richard chimed in before Henry could say anything rude about his wife's brother.

Henry's face displayed a flicker of annoyance as he turned to Simon. 'You will recall that it was a condition of our truce with Marshal that I convene a Council of State from time to time, to advise me on matters for which I feel I *require* advice. Richard here has graciously agreed to be its convener, and he has suggested that you should be one of its founder members, Simon. By this means, two of the seats around the table will be held within the immediate family.'

'I would, of course, be honoured,' Simon replied with a slight bow of his head, 'but who else did you have in mind?'

'That is yet to be decided, but they should perhaps be those who claim to speak for the remaining barons who express discontent with the current governance of the realm. Had you anyone in mind?'

'Not at present, no,' Simon admitted. 'Perhaps once we are settled in Kenilworth, I can give that more thought. When do we depart?'

'As soon as you are able. I shall not be able to accompany you, since I must give attention to matters in Brittany, where our truce with Louis of the Franks expires within days, or so my clerks tell me. Our faithful ally Duke Peter will be under threat again, no doubt, and I wish to send him an army to show Louis the merchants' exit when that happens.'

Simon's memory of Kenilworth had not played him false. Most of the men at arms had drifted back after the aborted encounter with Marshal's forces at Chester, and were reinstalled in their stable block accommodation. The main tower had been hastily made ready after word was sent west that it was required for the accommodation of the earl and countess. Even so, there was obvious mildew on some ceilings following a lengthy wet season, and the Great Mere was floating with vegetation that smelled rank as they rode past it with their noses averted.

Simon took one look at the state of the men who were notionally responsible for their safe-keeping and sent a messenger north with an urgent dispatch for Fulk. He made a formal inspection of the outer walls in the company of the Captain of the Guard, who never once ceased complaining about the lack of finance that he had been granted for its upkeep. Meanwhile, Eleanor listened distractedly to the steward's litany of excuses for the state of the kitchens, the cobwebs on the faded tapestries, the lack of serving staff and the mediocre, almost flavourless, meals that were served twice a day.

They had endured a miserable month learning the extent of the lamentable conditions at Kenilworth, and ordering urgent improvements at royal expense, when they sat, late one evening, in their private chambers on the second level of the Great Tower. There was a loud commotion in the hallway outside, and the sound of a man arguing with someone in broken English. The steward stepped in deferentially, closing the heavy oak door firmly behind him.

'My lord — my lady — there is a *person* outside — a very rough and rude person — who demands entry, but who refuses to give his name. Instead, he demands that I advise you that he has brought with him the finest cook in England.'

Simon gave a yell of delight and leaped to his feet, walking swiftly towards the door. 'Have him admitted immediately!' he ordered.

Just then the door flew open, and there stood Fulk de Sevres. The two men embraced like long lost brothers, dancing up and down with delight, until Simon remembered his manners. He led Fulk eagerly by the arm to where Eleanor was seated, viewing the performance with raised eyebrows and a bemused smile.

'I don't believe you've met the Countess of Leicester since she was merely the Princess Eleanor,' Simon joked, as Fulk gave a sweeping bow.

'I hope you've been looking after the finest soldier I ever trained,' Fulk said to her with a mock severe look on his face.

Eleanor smiled warmly back at him. 'Indeed I have, and I hope that your arrival means that the meals here will improve. God knows there is a need for it.'

'May I present your new cook, Your Ladyship?' Fulk asked. When Eleanor nodded, and Simon clapped his hands in delight, Fulk yelled, 'Matilda — we are allowed in!'

A middle-aged lady who obviously sampled all her dishes personally poked her head around the chamber door, then sheepishly took Fulk's hand as he led her into the chamber and introduced her. Matilda curtsied awkwardly in front of Eleanor, and she indicated for her to rise.

'There is no need for that — just ensure that our future meals are better than the limp apologies we have been receiving of late. The kitchens are yours.'

'And the gatehouse is yours, Fulk, my friend,' Simon added. 'Some of the men here were in your host at Chester, so they know what to expect. You begin their superior training whenever you have recovered from your journey.'

Three months later, Kenilworth Castle was playing host to the finest company of men at arms that England could boast, while a physician was in daily attendance on the countess, who was with child. Simon was beside himself with joy at the prospect of becoming a father, and news had been sent to the Court at Windsor. A company of soldiers had been sent in response, carrying and guarding a box of jewels as a present to the mother-to-be. They also brought a lengthy letter from Henry to Eleanor and Simon, advising them that Eleanor would shortly become an aunt, and inviting Simon to be the godfather of the child that was due early the following year, within months of Eleanor's expected confinement.

The letter also contained the unsettling news that the Archbishop of Canterbury was not the only one displeased with the recent marriage. Richard Marshal had condemned the union, not because it had been necessitated by Eleanor's breach of her vow of chastity, but because of the secrecy with which it had been conducted, and the fact that the leading barons had not been consulted. He was threatening another uprising, and a siege of Kenilworth.

'Leave him to me, my lord,' Fulk requested. 'But give me leave to take as many men from here as I require, plus more that I will summon from Chester, and I will rid you of this thorn in your flesh.'

'What about your Leicester men? Did they come home?'

Fulk frowned. 'I had almost forgotten them. Since you are now officially the Earl of Leicester, does the estate become yours?'

'I believe so, since it would be strange indeed if the Earl of Leicester were resident in Kenilworth, but infeft of nothing in Leicestershire itself. There is also Merle to think about. It has been some time since I was last there, and I would like to know how she fares. Please journey over there without delay, collect what additional men you can, and advise Merle to spend whatever she needs to render the place fit for a royal princess. The accounts may be sent to Westminster.'

Fulk returned with news that Merle was still alive, apparently happy and well, and making plans to open a house for orphaned children. 'She even *looks* like the abbess of a convent,' Fulk said, 'which makes it all the more strange that she asked me to convey her fondest love to you, and to congratulate you on losing your virginity at long last.'

Simon chuckled to himself — he could not wish for a more devoted sister.

His and Eleanor's first child was a boy, and they named him Henry, after the uncle who had made their happiness together possible. News was sent to Westminster, and the messenger returned with advanced tidings that there was now a royal prince called Edward, named for the Confessor of blessed memory whose example so obsessed Henry's devotions. The nation would celebrate with a public holiday, and two christening robes had been commissioned from the royal seamstress. They were identical, and the second was conveyed in the pannier of the same messenger, as a gift for the newly born Henry de Montfort.

The Kenilworth birth had been an easy one, and the physician who attended it expressed his view that Eleanor's womb had clearly been intended for child-bearing. His professional opinion was confirmed only months later when he was able to advise that another de Montfort was on its way, and it was instantly agreed that if it was a boy, he was to be called Simon the Younger. As if proud to bear such a title, the second boy appeared just as the last of the snows melted from the castle walls, and the parents held a special Mass to celebrate his birth.

The only cloud on this blissful horizon was the declining health of the cook, Fulk's wife Matilda, who had developed a canker in her stomach that no amount of physic would shift. Fulk delayed his planned departure to Pembroke to put Richard Marshal in his place, and could be seen in daily attendance on his ailing wife. In the early hours of a windy autumn morning, he was led away from her deathbed weeping, with Simon's arm around him. The next day he was back out beside the Great Mere, yelling at his men as he forced them to run up and down its near bank, holding swords and shields above their heads. He also threatened to cut out Simon's innards if he ever told a living soul that he had seen the fierce old warrior in tears.

XXIV

Into the fourth year of Simon and Eleanor's blissful marriage, with no sign of any Great Council being convened, Simon sent word to Prince Richard, Earl of Cornwall, requesting that he use his best efforts with his older brother to honour the undertaking. One day, the news was brought to him that Richard Marshal had been killed in battle with Fulk's forces just east of Carmarthen, and that the Leicester forces were on their triumphant way home.

Three days later, as the column of dust approached from the south-west, Simon walked out to the Kenilworth gatehouse to welcome home his old friend. His heart missed a beat as he recognised the man at the head of the column as Geoffrey of Flint. Behind him was a horse pulling a small cart that was covered in canvas. By the time that Simon was formally advised that Fulk was dead, he was already on his knees, blending his tears with prayers for the soul of the man who had taught him so much.

They observed an entire week of official mourning, at the end of which Geoffrey humbly accepted the role of Captain of the Kenilworth Guard, and swore a lifetime's allegiance to his new commander in chief. They also sent news to both Leicester and Westminster that Fulk was dead, while Henry was advised that he no longer needed to concern himself about Richard Marshal, but that he required a new Earl Marshal of England. Simon indicated that he would be proud to accept this post, were it offered.

When Richard of Cornwall was admitted to the withdrawing chamber at Kenilworth a month later, Simon stepped forward with a smile, anticipating that he'd brought confirmation of his new appointment. But Richard's face was a mask of solemnity as he first embraced his sister, then turned to Simon with an outstretched hand of friendship.

'I am here with sad news, Simon. I will not embrace you with a Judas kiss, since I have orders for your arrest and imprisonment on charges of treason.'

Eleanor screamed, her hand to her mouth, while Simon stood dumbfounded.

'What on earth have I done wrong?' he asked meekly.

Richard inclined his head from side to side, in a gesture of uncertainty. 'It was a combination of things, I believe. First, it seems that you have pledged Henry's name in settlement of debts for land in Leicestershire, when you were only given authority to do so here in Kenilworth. But, more seriously, you brought about the death of Richard Marshal.'

'He was an ongoing threat to the Crown!' Simon protested.

'He was also my wife's brother,' Richard reminded him, 'and Isabel took it badly. She has ever been unkindly disposed towards Eleanor, because she resents her beauty, but of late she has ever been in Henry's ear regarding what she claims was a cowardly act against an innocent man.'

'It was open warfare against the man who posed the greatest threat of uprising against the throne!' Simon argued. 'I did what I did in Henry's best interests — can he not see that?'

'Be that as it may,' Richard told him, 'Marshal was also the figurehead for those who wish to see greater changes in the running of the nation. They now complain that if he can be murdered on Henry's orders, then no-one is safe, and we are back to the tyranny of King John. Given Henry's unease regarding the possibility of armed rebellion, he sees the safest policy in making an example of you, in order that those ill-disposed towards peace in the realm may be assured that justice is still available. It would seem that you are regarded by the rebel barons as a traitor to their cause, and Henry has chosen to hold you out as a traitor to England.'

'What are we to do?' Eleanor wailed. 'If Henry is so obsessed with giving the barons their revenge, is there no hope of reconciliation?'

'As yet, no,' Richard replied, 'but there is hope for the future.'

'*What* future?' Simon demanded hollowly. 'I, at least, will be dead within the week, although not even Henry would be prepared to execute his own sister, surely?'

'If Henry had seriously intended that I take you into custody,' Richard pointed out, 'then I would be accompanied by a contingent from the Tower Guard. Instead, he agreed to send only me, knowing that I would warn you and give you time to flee the country. I shall return to Oxford, and there bide for several days before returning with armed men. In that time you must journey back to France, to the safety of your own family there. As for myself, Henry has demanded that I answer the Pope's call for a Crusade to protect Christian possessions in the Holy Land, where the treaty with the Mohammedans has recently expired. I will meet you in Montfort-l'Amaury, and you may perhaps find favour once more with Henry by joining me under the Pope's banner with your brother. By the time we return, Henry's mind may well have been changed yet again, when he realises how uneasily his crown sits on his head without you in England to defend him.'

'What about the children?' Eleanor asked weakly.

'It will be for you to arrange for their wellbeing,' Richard replied. 'I doubt that you would wish to take them on Crusade, but they must be quietly hidden away where not even the barons are aware of their existence. That is your concern, dear sister. I have done the best I can, as your brother and loyal friend, and now I must ride back to Oxford.'

'Stay and eat something, at least,' Simon invited him.

Richard shook his head. 'I have delayed long enough, if my first visit here is to remain secret. Good luck — until we meet again in France.'

As he bowed out, Eleanor sank down heavily onto her chair and looked blankly up at Simon.

'Where on earth can we leave Henry and Simon for such a length of time, hidden away from the world? And what if we never return — who will look after them, as orphans?' She stared in disbelief at Simon's sudden smile. 'Do you find all this amusing?' she demanded, incensed.

'No, forgive me, my sweet, but your allusion to orphans has just given me inspiration. Go and begin the packing, while I select a small escort.'

Two days later, an hour before sunset, Simon and Eleanor, with their infant sons in a wagon guarded by a handful of men at arms who rode behind them, entered a fine courtyard that lay in front of a magnificent three-storey dwelling. A stable hand wandered across from the left, while two men at arms appeared from the other side, demanding to know their business. Then one of them recognised former colleagues from Chester, and amid the noise of reunion Simon asked the stable boy where Mistress Merle might be located at this time of day.

The boy nodded silently towards the front entrance to the house, where a woman in a white gown down to the ground, with a white wimple on her head, stood surveying them, squinting into the late afternoon sun as if her eyesight was failing. Simon dismounted, walked over to her, grasped both her hands in his and kissed her on the cheek.

Merle smiled. 'That kiss was real enough. I am not dreaming this visitation?'

'Indeed you are not. Did I just kiss a nun?'

'No, you kissed your sister under God. I will not become a bride of Christ until such time as I can be of no further service to you here in Leicester.'

'Dearest Merle, you can now be of greater service to me than you could possibly have imagined. In that wagon are my two sons — I would have you treat them as orphans, and hide them away from King Henry.'

Merle squinted out into the courtyard. 'And the lady is your wife? The Princess Eleanor? The one with the long hair whom I insulted all those years ago? She wishes *me* to preserve her children from her own brother?'

'I am accused of treason, for reasons that we need not discuss, but I am innocent. We must flee to France like common criminals, and it seems that I must once more don the Crusaders' surcoat. But that would be no place for children, and there can be no knowing when — or if — we will return. Will you take care of our children, as an act of mercy and charity?'

Merle smiled sweetly, and Simon felt like crushing her frail body to him. 'I was well taught in mercy and charity, my lord, by a young knight who had me at his mercy in a rough soldier's tent near Carcassonne. He could have done with me whatever he wished, but like the true man of God that he is, when not playing the warrior, he took pity on me and gave me cause to love him for the rest of my life. How could I *not* take in your children? But if they have already acquired the sin of pride, be warned that they will be raised among outcast village waifs, and will receive no special favour.'

'I would ask for nothing else, dearest Merle. Come and meet the Countess of Leicester, but you may no more insult her than you could the Princess Eleanor.'

The following morning they said their tearful farewells to their two infant sons and rode hard to Hastings in search of a Channel crossing. Dover would be well patrolled, and it was just possible that Henry had already learned of their flight, and had guessed that Simon would head for the land of his birth. After a stormy night crossing, during which Eleanor spent the entire time on her knees in prayer, they made the French coast at Rouen. Five days later, they were admitted into the Great Hall at Montfort-l'Amaury, where they were met by an anxious-looking Richard of Cornwall.

'Do not look for your brother, Simon, since our Crusade has turned into a rescue mission for another Crusader. It seems that Amaury and a group of other knights from the host of Theobald of Champagne grew tired of sitting in Jaffa with no sign of the enemy and unwisely laid siege to Gaza, where Amaury became a prisoner of an Egyptian potentate. He seeks to ransom him for a sum that King Louis is not prepared to pay. But he wants his constable back, and we are commissioned to travel to Cairo, where Amaury is currently held in a foul dungeon, to negotiate better terms for his release.'

'Such as?'

'If Theobald has Mohammedan soldiers in his custody at Jaffa, we may be able to conduct an exchange. But we must lose no time — it seems that a dreadful disease has overtaken those held in Cairo, and several of them still suffer terrible wounds.'

'Amaury?' Simon asked, his heart in his mouth.

'At present we know not, but your sister-in-law Beatrix is beside herself with worry, and the children keep asking for their father. Will you accompany me to Cairo?'

'Of course,' Simon assured him, 'since he is my brother, and it is my Christian duty to come to the aid of a fellow Crusader. But what of Eleanor?'

'She must remain here, to comfort Beatrix, while you and I take ship from Marseilles in a week's time.'

Simon and Richard eventually reached Acre, where they began urgent negotiations with the current ruling warlord among the Muslim hordes, An-Nasir Dawud. He agreed to the release of Amaury in exchange for a prince of the royal house of Jordan, whose custody he could use to his own political advantage in the squabbles and intrigues among the heathen tribes. As the prisoners were brought up from the depths of the Cairo stronghold in which they had been held, Simon raced over to a litter that was being carried by two former Crusader foot soldiers from Amaury's own household guard. He then looked down, aghast, at the once mighty warrior.

Amaury's face was yellow like old parchment, and his bony frame seemed to have shrunk. He was clad only in a dirty sheet, and he smelled revolting. At first he did not seem to comprehend what was happening, then finally his hollow eyes showed a flicker of recognition and he reached out a bony arm to grasp Simon's eager hand.

'You have never been so welcome, brother. I hope you brought some wine from the estate.'

They took the shortest sea crossing available, in the hope of finding some sort of physician in Italy, but by the time that they carefully lifted Amaury's litter onto the quayside at Otranto, they were unloading a corpse. A heartbroken Simon arranged for a local priest to perform the necessary service, and then spent the night kneeling before the altar of a local *chiesa*, praying for the soul of his dead brother and for the courage to carry the news back to his family.

He was very relieved, when he did so, to discover that there was a priest already in attendance. He had apparently arrived a week beforehand, seeking Simon, and he had occupied his time by conducting daily Masses for the safety of the now dead Amaury. As if seeking atonement for his failure to keep the man alive, he offered consolatory Masses that the entire extended family attended. Simon eventually remembered what he had been told by the family's steward when he'd first returned to find the priest in residence.

'I believe that you first came here in search of me?' he asked the middle-aged man whose face he had been trying to place for several days. He remained shrouded in the anonymity of a plain black soutane with a matching bonnet surmounted by a pompom, like any French parish *curé*.

The priest smiled back at him indulgently. 'You don't remember me, do you? From your brief journey to Savoy?'

Then Simon remembered. 'Forgive me, Father, but your humble vestments do not do you justice. Aren't you a bishop or something?'

'I *was*, and still am, Bishop of Belley, in my home country of Savoy. But I am shortly to become, or so I am led to believe, the Archbishop of Canterbury. The old one died, and King Henry, my niece's husband, has offered me the office. He also extends a pardon to you in return for your safe escort across to England, together with your wife. She has been absolved of her sin by His Holiness, at my supplication. There will be no penance, in view of your participation in the Crusade.'

'This is good news indeed,' Simon enthused. 'When are you expected at Court?'

'At Canterbury, rather. Henry has asked me to send a messenger to him when I have my safe escort organised, and the Court will progress south to Canterbury for my installation ceremony.'

'You may send that messenger now, Archbishop, and I would deem it an honour if you would allow one of my men to discharge that duty.'

Boniface agreed, and the man at arms was sent ahead to announce the imminent arrival on English soil of its new *primus inter pares* among the senior ranks of the Church of Rome in England. The same soldier was also privately instructed to locate a suitable vessel, not only for the sea crossing of an archbishop, but also the Earl and Countess of Leicester, in which the countess might make the return to England lying below decks, in view of her delicate condition. He would then need to deliver his joyous tidings to the Court, wherever it might be found, and ride back to Leicester and Kenilworth to announce the impending safe return of the Master.

A royal party awaited them on the quayside at Dover, and there was much rejoicing, embracing, hand-clasping and tears. This was mainly on the part of the queen and her uncle, although Henry did take a moment to welcome back his sister. He assured her that the royal physician would be on hand as soon as they reached Windsor, to ensure that the child in her womb was none the worse for its recent enforced travels in Europe. Simon and Eleanor had already agreed that if it was another boy, it would be named Amaury, after his dead uncle.

They had hoped to be allowed to slip away from Windsor after only a few days, particularly since Boniface, having been installed at Canterbury, immediately declared his intention of taking the next suitable vessel back across the Channel. But Henry insisted that Simon and Eleanor remain with the Court, and on the first evening after their return to Windsor they were summoned to a private supper with only the king and queen and Prince Richard in attendance. Eleanor immediately queried the absence of Isabel of Cornwall, and a somewhat sheepish Richard explained that she was out of royal favour.

'And the reason for that,' Henry boomed, 'is that she spread false rumour about you, Simon. She had me convinced that you meant my downfall in the rebellion that would follow the death of Richard Marshal. As it transpires, you did the nation a great service, and Pembroke now lies peacefully under the husbandry of yet another brother, Gilbert. I am free to appoint a new Earl Marshal, but you must forgive me if it is not you, Simon. I have a greater service in mind for you, and it suits my purpose to appoint another to the position — one who you will meet in two days' time, at the first meeting of our new Grand Council.'

'Is there to be no formal apology from Isabel for the anguish that we suffered as the result of her falsehood?' Eleanor demanded. Simon shot her a warning look, but Henry was ready with his reply.

'That cannot be, since she is married to a royal prince.'

'And Simon is married to a royal princess,' Eleanor reminded him. 'Does that count for nothing?'

'You must forgive my wife, Henry,' Simon said hastily. 'She was concerned only for my safety, and the future of our two precious sons. And of course she is now in a delicate condition once again.'

Once she and Simon had retired for the night, Eleanor gave vent to her anger. 'You failed me when I most needed your support, and offered my woman's weakness as your excuse! I expected better than that from you, and it would seem that, even to you, I am a mere woman, whose opinions count for naught.'

'Not so, my sweet. We must tread carefully where Isabel is concerned, since she will still have Henry's ear, once his brief displeasure with her fades as quickly as did his displeasure with us. She is a Marshal, and for all we know she plots revenge for the death of a second brother. We must still be circumspect whenever we are in conversation with Henry.'

Eleanor allowed her stony look to melt somewhat, but still seemed far from happy with the situation. 'I will of course be guided by you in these matters, but I can never relax fully when my own brother so easily condemned the chosen man in my life.'

'Your brother is a man in need of wise counsel and soft advice,' Simon replied as he extended his hand in an invitation to join him in bed. 'Let us hope that the Council he has finally got around to summoning can serve that function.'

XXV

It was with considerable foreboding that two mornings later Simon entered the Great Hall to meet those who were already assembled around the long table. Only one of them was known to him personally apart from Richard of Cornwall, who was talking to King Henry in muted tones until he spotted Simon and waved him in with a warm smile. Henry did not seem quite so welcoming, and his overall manner was of one who wished he were elsewhere as he left Richard to make the introductions.

'As you know, Simon, Henry has graciously asked me to be the convenor of this historic Council of State, which will henceforth guide the king in matters pertaining to the welfare of the nation where he feels he would benefit from wise counsel. I hope that the other members will feel no slight if I introduce them in the order in which they are grouped around the table, rather than on the basis of the seniority of their titles. First, the brothers Roger and Hugh Bigod, the sons of the late Hugh Bigod, Third Earl of Norfolk. He was one of those present as a surety when our father, the late King John, signed the Great Charter at Runnymede, and it is fitting that they serve on the Council in order to remind us of that significant event. Roger currently holds the family title, as the older son and the Fourth Earl.

'Next to them is the Earl of Hereford, Sir Humphrey de Bohun, who currently serves the crown as Constable of England. He was once married to Maud of Lusignan, which of course makes him an indirect relative, since our mother is now married to Hugh de Lusignan, our dear ally in Poitou. Passing to another relative, you will of course remember William of

Savoy, the queen's uncle, who will shortly assume the newly created role of Chancellor of England. Finally, to his left, my own stepson, Richard de Clare, Sixth Earl of Hertford, my dear wife's son by her first marriage.

'To complete this intimate gathering, may I introduce to you all Lord Simon de Montfort, Earl of Leicester, and husband of my sister, the Princess Eleanor.'

There were nods all round, and Simon took his seat next to Roger Bigod as Henry cleared his throat and addressed the small assembly.

'It is my hope that in due course there will be more of us, but at present we would seem to be a fair and representative sample of the leading nobles in the realm. I have undertaken to consult with you all when I feel that I need your counsel, and your agreement to the levying of taxes for urgent matters that threaten the safety of our nation. The greatest such threat is of course from King Louis of the Franks, who would be the king of the whole of France. He recently overran the estates of our dear friend and ally Duke Peter of Brittany, mainly because we could only afford a small army to send to his assistance. If Louis is to be opposed in his south-western conquests, we must commit a much larger force to the support of those who come under further threat. We are fortunate in having Simon here among us, since he spent his early life in the area of France they call the Languedoc.'

'I did so as part of a Holy Crusade against the Cathars,' Simon reminded Henry, 'and I acted in the name of King Louis' great-grandfather.'

There were mutters around the table at this revelation, and Henry scowled at Simon as he sought to retrieve the message he had hoped to impart.

'Be that as it may, Simon has great knowledge of that part of the world. Since he is now happily wedded to our gracious sister, the Princess Eleanor, there can be no doubt of his loyalty to us.'

There was a titter from across the table, and it was Simon's turn to glare, this time at Richard de Clare. Henry continued as if there had been no interruption.

'The latest threat is much closer to home, and to our extended families across the Channel. Louis is attempting to enforce the installation of his brother Alphonse as Count of Poitou, despite the hopes of our dear mother, the wife of the Count of La Marche, Hugh de Lusignan, that the title would go to our brother Richard. After all, the whole of Aquitaine was once ruled by our grandmother, Eleanor. If Poitou is to one day become part of our French estates through our family links, then it will be necessary to send a large force across the sea in support of Duke Hugh, who is now being threatened by Louis' army assembled at Chinon. For that we will require finance, and that will mean taxation.'

'How much this time?' Roger Bigod demanded suspiciously, as the low rumble of discontent could be heard around the table.

'One can never tell in advance, of course, how these ventures will proceed,' Henry replied as his eyes ranged nervously around those present, 'but the Treasury is all but empty. If we are to remain a powerful force across the Channel, then Louis' threats must be met with force whenever they are raised.'

'Louis no doubt has more in his war chest than we do,' Humphrey de Bohun pointed out sourly. 'He certainly did in the days when I was related by marriage to Poitou.'

'That was surely during the reign of his grandfather,' Simon argued. 'We know not how much money the present Louis now has available, and half his nobility were stuck in the Holy Land when I was lately there.'

'A good time to send our own forces over,' Henry enthused.

Simon frowned. 'I was not suggesting that we invade France, Your Majesty — I was merely observing that Louis may not be in a superior position to ours.'

'As I said, all the more reason to finance our own venture, to preserve our lands in Poitou.'

'Duke Hugh's lands in Poitou,' de Bohun corrected him sourly.

'You have not yet advised us how much such a venture would cost,' Roger Bigod reminded him.

Henry screwed up his face in annoyance. 'I have already advised you that we cannot tell, in advance of venturing south. But it is a cost to be borne, if we are to prevent Louis becoming too bold. Our failure to intervene on Duke Hugh's behalf will be taken as a sign of weakness. You presumably do not suggest that this be allowed to happen?'

'Of course not,' Bigod conceded. 'We must ever guard our own realm against foreign invasion.'

'Good, then that is agreed,' Henry said. 'Since that was the only purpose for which this Council was summoned, I thank you all for your attendance and wish you all a safe return to your estates. Lord Simon, I wish you to remain for a moment longer.'

As the remaining Council members shuffled out, some shaking their heads, Henry called for more wine. He was in the process of studying the ceiling carvings with a smug smile when Simon voiced his uncertainty.

'What did we just agree, Henry?'

'The imposition of a new tax to finance the largest force England has ever sent in opposition to Louis' territorial ambitions.'

'I did not clearly take that from our discussions,' Simon mused out loud, before turning back to Henry.

'I take it that my Leicester force will be required to muster under your banner?'

'The banner of England, certainly, but *you* will be the most important person beneath it, Simon. Apart, of course, from myself. You will recall that I referred yesterday to some great service I had in mind for you? When I ride out at the head of the English army, you will be there with me, as Commander in Chief of the massed armed host of Henry of England.'

Simon was stunned by the command, and Eleanor was outraged when he recounted it as they dressed ahead of dinner that day.

'We're only just back from that dreadful Crusade that killed your brother, and might well have taken you from me, were it not for my prayers,' she objected. 'And what about our sons, not to mention the child in my belly? Does Henry have no regard for any family other than his wife's?'

'No-one is suggesting that you come with me,' Simon reminded her. 'In fact, should I go, I will forbid you to accompany me. A battlefield is no place for a woman, believe me, and you must remain to see to the rearing of the children.'

'So I am reduced to the woman's role so early in our marriage? Is that what you are telling me?' Eleanor yelled back, her hands defiantly on her hips. 'I thought we had agreed that my views would be added to yours when you spoke with Henry, and it was certainly not my wish that you risk your head in his service so regularly. He is an indifferent leader of armies, or so it is voiced abroad.'

'All the more reason why he needs me,' Simon argued, 'although I have yet to decide whether or not to accept the commission.'

'You speak as if you had a choice, Simon. We have only just been pardoned for transgressions that we had not committed in the first place, and it will go ill with us if we defy Henry while he still has Isabel of Cornwall's poison in his ear.'

'So we are agreed on one thing at least,' Simon replied. 'That I have no choice.'

'You have no choice but to accept the commission,' Eleanor conceded as her lower lip began to tremble, 'but please God that Henry changes his mind, or the weather proves inclement, or the Pope steps in to forbid it, or…'

As the tears reduced her next words to gargles, Simon folded her in his arms.

'Let us look to happier matters for the time being. Tomorrow we may journey back to Leicester, to be reunited with our sons. Then there is perhaps another son to add to the nursery at Kenilworth in a few months' time. All that will transpire long before I am summoned to travel to Poitou.'

Four days later, they sat staring at the small group of children being led on a walk around the lake by a nun-like Merle. She smiled and waved as she saw them on their horses on the slight ridge above the water, then gave a short command to the children. They immediately sat down in a gesture of obedience, and Merle walked over to Simon and Eleanor.

'Where are our sons?' Eleanor demanded sharply.

Merle waved her hand towards the group by the water's edge. 'Henry and Simon are the two at the left hand, sitting together as usual. You have raised them to be affectionate brothers.'

'Where are Henry's long brown locks?' Simon demanded.

'On the floor in the barn, unless Beatrice has already swept them up. The children are shorn every week by Thomas the shepherd, in order that they do not acquire lice. I saw no reason to treat your children any differently from the others, and in truth they are learning much from the village orphans.'

'I dread to think *what*,' Eleanor retorted in a tone of pure vinegar. 'May we take them back to Kenilworth?'

'Of course,' Merle replied, 'since they are not prisoners. Although I shall miss young Simon — he is a beautiful child, with such a generous nature.'

'He is half de Montfort,' Simon said.

'And the other half is Plantagenet,' Eleanor reminded him as she turned her horse's head. 'Come, Simon, we must reach Kenilworth before nightfall.'

As she urged her horse back towards their escort, Simon smiled down at Merle.

'Thank you for taking such good care of them, Merle.'

'They are yours, Simon, so I had the temporary pleasure of pretending that they were also mine. I shall confess myself guilty of pride before I eat this evening.'

Back at Kenilworth, while Eleanor busied herself with leaving the household staff in no doubt of her opinion of the state of the rooms, Simon walked to the gatehouse and sought out Geoffrey of Flint. As his Captain of the Guard rose hastily from his chair and began to bow, Simon restrained him by raising his hand.

'Be seated, Geoffrey, and give me your honest counsel. If a man approaching his fortieth birthday, with no actual combat experience for the past twenty years, came to you and asked to join your force, what would be your reply?'

'It would depend on how fit he now was, my lord, and what sort of combat he had previously engaged in. Then, if satisfied on both counts, I would start him back on basic weapons training to establish if he still retained any skills.'

'And how would you first test his fitness?'

Geoffrey looked out into the yard and nodded. 'Perhaps twenty times around the keep. Then, if he still had any breath left in him, a few turns around the Great Mere with a sword above his head. Did you have someone in mind, my lord?'

'Indeed I did, Geoffrey, indeed I did,' Simon replied. Geoffrey's jaw dropped as Simon added, 'Twenty times, you said? Start counting, Geoffrey.'

XXVI

Simon cursed for the tenth time as he looked up at the massive rock fortress of Château de Taillebourg. In the immediate foreground was the strategic bridge crossing the Charente River, which they were obliged to take if they were to have any chance of moving any further north into Poitou. Behind them lay Saintes, Bordeaux and Aquitaine, and Simon asked himself yet again how he had been foolish enough to allow himself to be talked into this madcap venture. It seemed to be nothing more significant than a spiteful show of force between two powerful monarchs who had never quite grown up.

For as long as Henry and Louis continued to behave with this childish petulance, like two stags with their heads lowered ahead of locking antlers in a rut, Simon was destined to be separated from Eleanor and their three boys. The most recently born, Amaury, was still recovering from a cot fever that had almost proved fatal. Eleanor had pleaded with him not to answer Henry's summons, and her angry words of recrimination had echoed in his memory when he'd disembarked his men at Royan to discover that he was not the overall commander of Henry's army, as promised, but merely the leader of one wing of it.

Prince Richard of Cornwall had recently become a widower, the fork-tongued Isabel having died giving birth to her tenth child, which had also died. In his search for a new bride, Richard had turned his eyes to France, and made a great show of honouring his mother's wish that he claim Poitou. Henry's reaction had been to encourage him by granting him command of those who had flocked to the royal banner when the word went out that there was plunder and royal preferment to be had in the Saintonge region.

Simon now bitterly resented the two years he had spent humbly subjecting himself to the tutelage of Geoffrey of Flint. He had proved his ongoing basic fitness during months of arduous repetitive exercise that evoked memories of running back and forth to a river in the Crusader camp, carrying an anvil over his head. However, he had been warned that the wound he had incurred during the retaking of Montfort-l'Amaury had left him vulnerable in the matter of speed and agility. He was therefore his own liability if he sought to fight younger men on foot, and should restrict his fighting to wielding sword and shield on horseback. Since the force he now commanded was largely one of younger sons of minor nobles seeking advancement on horses drawn from the stables of humble estates, this was fitting, but it still rankled with him.

Simon had been sent with an advance party to survey the terrain around the river bridge, and, while he was about it, to try to assess the strength of the French forces holed up in the château on the other side. Henry and Richard were still in the safety of Saintes, entertaining the various minor nobles who had joined Hugh de Lusignan in his resistance to the Capetian claim to Poitou. Some of these were Henry's distant relations due to his mother's remarriage, and her birthright in Angoulême. They had brought few fighting men, and even less money, to the campaign, but Henry was feting them with an enthusiasm that sickened Simon, until he reminded himself that he was where he was now thanks to Henry's generosity towards French adventurers with hollow titles and little else.

Simon turned to Allen de Broches, lord of the manor of some insignificant estate in Wiltshire. He was his second in command by virtue of the fact that he had once defeated, on horseback, a marauding mob of Welshmen who fought on foot with bows and arrows. He was not Simon's choice, but Henry's, and Simon suspected that this was because Henry owed him money, although this didn't distinguish him from half the nobles in England.

'What do you think is their likely strength?' Simon asked.

Allen gazed up at the crenulated château walls with a frown. 'Hard to tell, really. Unless they have massive stables, the cavalry must be light in number, and their main strength will lie in their ability to withstand a siege with bowmen and foot soldiers.'

'Could we cross the river somewhere further north, thereby skirting the château and slipping past them?' Simon asked.

'Possibly, particularly if we do so silently, by night.'

'Have you ever heard the sound of five thousand soldiers on the move?' Simon asked testily, wondering again what madness had led to Henry assigning this fool as his second in command.

There was a heavy grinding of bolts as the massive front gates to the château opened. A force of some sixty or seventy heavily armed French knights on destriers draped in defensive metalwork thundered out of the château grounds and down the slope towards them. Allen turned his horse and yelled for the English to retreat, leaving Simon with no option unless he was to take them all on single-handed. Cursing loudly he galloped all the way back to Saintes, handed his horse to a groom with a mouthful of oaths and demanded an immediate audience with Henry.

He was admitted to the sound of laughter, the rattling of dice and the clinking of goblets. At least a dozen of Henry's Poitevin sycophants were seated around him, urging him to roll again in the hope that his fortunes would change. Simon stormed in front of Henry's padded chair.

'Louis sent a small force of cavalry out against us. We were all but slaughtered!' he yelled.

'So I heard,' Henry replied distractedly, as he watched another useless combination of numbers roll onto the low table in front of him. 'So what do you suggest?'

'What I suggest, Your Majesty,' Simon spat, 'is that we search for another river crossing well away from Taillebourg.'

'I am reliably advised, by my kinsmen here,' Henry said languidly, 'that the next nearest crossing is a ford well to the south of here. Do you propose that I defeat Louis with wet feet?'

'I am gratified to have it confirmed that you will be partaking in the actual fighting,' Simon retorted with heavy sarcasm, 'but my advice is that unless we can somehow skirt the château at Taillebourg, then we cannot progress any further into Poitou.'

'That is unfortunate, since Richard wishes to lay siege to it,' Henry said triumphantly. 'My order is that we set up camp somewhere across the river from this château, then decide what is best to do next. Your throw, Henri.'

As Henry concentrated once more on the dice, Simon gave the mere suggestion of a bow and stormed back outside to give the necessary order.

Two days later, he was back in a meadow, in a camp not unlike the ones he had grown up in, except that it was larger and contained a massive army clad in the lion livery of England. They glared across the Charente at a château whose main tower defiantly flew the lilies of France.

Despite all his efforts to give wise advice based on experience, intelligent strategy and pure common sense, Simon was ordered to take his cavalry to the bridge in an advance guard. With their protection, Richard's ground troops would advance with their ballistas, mangonels and siege towers in order to pen the French in behind their fortress walls. Once the château was under full siege, the remainder of Henry's army would, under Henry's personal command, cross the bridge, skirt the château walls and occupy the land to the north.

At daybreak, amid the sounds of swords being sharpened, horses being harnessed, and men nervously wishing each other well, Simon angrily sought out Prince Richard, who had command of all but the cavalry.

'We have only one hope of surviving this madness of Henry's creation,' he told Richard. 'I will take my horsemen to the near side of the bridge, provoking the French to send out their mounted force against mine. Once they are close, we will part in the middle, leaving them to foolishly charge over the bridge to attack. If you have your bowmen in the front lines, the French can be shot from their mounts, and we will then race across and finish them off. Then, and only then, will it be safe for you to advance your siege engines on the château.'

'Has Henry approved this?' Richard asked suspiciously.

Simon snorted. 'You might wish to journey back to Saintes, wake him up, and ask him.'

Richard nodded sadly and walked back to organise his front ranks, while Simon moved his horse troops out of camp and onto the narrow track that led from the village of Saint-James to the river bridge. They sat on the near side and looked nervously behind as the bowmen moved into position and knelt on the dewy ground, their spare shafts in front of them, and their taut bowstrings ready to loose the first salvo. Then the massive château gates opened noisily to the sound of a battle fanfare, and the full might of the French cavalry thundered down towards them.

Simon's men parted on his yelled command, and half the French cavalry clattered over the bridge into the face of a blizzard of English arrows, at which point the fatal flaw in Simon's battle strategy became horribly obvious. Richard's archers lacked recent practice, and half the deadly rain intended for the enemy began dropping on their own horse-born comrades on the near side of the bridge. Simon yelled for them to spur their horses in order to finish off the French wounded, and the few that still remained in their saddles. This achieved, they turned again on Simon's command, to form a heaving, sweating wall against which the remainder of the French *chevaliers* threw themselves and their destriers as they completed their charge across the bridge.

The line held for long enough for Richard to order his men to retreat. Once the English were in full flight, Simon ordered his own mounted troops to follow behind, turning from time to time to cut down any eager French horseman who sought to pursue them. A few minutes later, those in command on the French side must have realised the futility of the pursuit, and called it off. Simon took one backward glance at the château that they had hoped to place under siege, and gave the final order to retreat at will, being the last man through Saint-James and the safety of the wooded land beyond.

It was a despondent Simon who dismounted back at Saintes, and asked where Henry might be found. He was told that Prince Richard wished to parley with him, and he found the royal brother half drunk in the main hall of the fortified château that had previously been the English battle headquarters. Richard eyed him accusingly.

'Your strategy failed us, Simon. You failed to hold them back, and we were forced into retreat.'

'You needed little encouragement,' Simon snarled back. 'And if your archers had been trained to the bow rather than the citole, they might not have unhorsed so many of their own men. Should you wish to accuse me of incompetence, I will counter with an allegation of cowardice on your part. Where *is* Henry — back playing dice?'

'He is heading back to Bordeaux,' Richard admitted sheepishly, 'but he has left me in full command of our resources. We must delay Louis until Henry has time to take ship back across the Channel.'

Simon pulled off his heavy gauntlet and hurled it down to the floor with a flood of curses. Richard stepped back in alarm as Simon glared down at him from his full height.

'I don't know how many men we lost in that apology for a battle, but I'd wager that Henry's first task back in the safety of England will *not* be to make arrangements for the welfare of the families they left behind!'

'He left us behind also, Simon, to ensure that he makes it safely back to Bordeaux. I intend to seek peace terms with Louis for long enough for you to organise a rearguard defence west of here.'

Simon's eyes opened wide in disbelief, and he began yelling at the top of his voice. 'Henry flees like a rat from a grain mill fire, and *you* intend to dishonour the nation even further by pretending to parley with Louis while I perform the only meaningful fighting function, thereby placing *more* of my men in peril! At what point may I count on your support for a further strategic withdrawal of our *own* remaining men?'

'I leave that to you, Simon — you are in command of the troops.'

'As I recall, we were *both* in command — or has Henry finally seen sense and left these matters to me?'

'He did not remain for long enough to issue further commands, to be honest with you,' Richard admitted. 'But as his royal brother, I am making a military decision in his absence.'

'There is perhaps *another* decision you should make, as a royal brother,' Simon yelled back. 'Have the stupid oaf locked safely away in the Tower, for the good of the nation!'

He stormed out, leaving Richard with the sensation of having recently emerged from a tempest.

Four days later, Richard returned from Taillebourg with the news that Louis of France had offered safe passage to Marseilles for any remaining English troops, if they would join the Crusade that he was anxious to engage in, and provided that they were led by Simon de Montfort.

'I can only hope that you refused,' Simon said, glaring.

'I did indeed, but Louis countered by threatening that until Henry acknowledges the Capetian title to Poitou, we are still at war. You will need to block the route to Bordeaux as originally planned.'

'And what does Hugh de Lusignan have to say, given that it was he who began this nonsense?'

Richard's eyes fell to the floor as he braced himself for another storm. 'He surrendered to Louis two days ago, and has renounced his claim to Poitou.'

'So we came here for nothing, as it transpires!' Simon all but screamed. 'Except it will *not* have been for nothing, since apart from the unforgiveable loss of life, it must have drained the Treasury of every last groat. The nation will be in uproar!'

'That will be Henry's task to resolve,' Richard reminded him. 'Your task is to hold back Louis and his force until Henry, at least, has left Bordeaux.'

'I hope that, at the very least, you will commission enough vessels to take back what is left of our army!' Simon yelled as he stormed out.

Three days later, somewhere between Saintes and Bordeaux, on the border of Aquitaine with Gascony, Simon gave the order to his remaining troops to hold firm, as the glittering armour of the French cavalry shimmered in the hot morning sun on the far hill. There was only a broad valley of vineyards between them and the retreating English. When there was no movement from the enemy after a full hour, Simon urged his horse down the hill on the English side, and was gratified to see another horseman doing the same on the northern slope. Simon halted in the middle of the wine plantation as the French horseman drew close enough for him to recognise the golden crown above the fleur-de-lis livery. He nodded in recognition as King Louis smiled and came alongside him.

'You will not come on Crusade with me?'

'The last one was the death of my brother, sire.'

Louis nodded sadly. 'He was a brave man, and a fine choice as Constable of France. You would be welcome to take his place in that role should you wish, since you also are a brave man, although you are led by an idiot.'

'Idiot or not, he is my king, and my brother-in-law. I count myself an Englishman now.'

'And that is a great loss to France. But I respect your honesty as well as your bravery. Since I imagine that your king is by now somewhere on the sea, soiling his hose at his narrow escape, I may confidently return to Paris. You and your men are free to leave France without any further hostility from my army. And so I wish you Godspeed.'

The warmth and goodwill that were soothing Simon's thoughts as he rode towards Bordeaux turned to ice when he arrived there and learned that his men would be required to wait at least a month for an ocean crossing. The reason for this was that all the available vessels had recently set sail full of minor Poitevin nobles who had been invited by Henry to journey to England. There they were assured of pensions for life and modest estates — estates that rightly belonged to loyal English subjects who would no doubt be turned off them to make way for the favoured incomers.

Simon's burning dislike of the Poitevins was deepened when he learned that the disastrous campaign had cost the nation some eighty thousand pounds. It would have to be reimbursed to the depleted Treasury by way of further taxation, since Henry had run out of those from whom he could borrow simply on his word as king. It only made matters worse when those being taxed could see for themselves the lavish expenditure, not only on Windsor Castle, but also the creation of a new royal complex at Westminster. This included a completely refurbished palace, an abbey, and an extended Tower of London for those who displeased him.

XXVII

Eleanor was concerned to find Simon so ill-disposed towards her brother upon his return to Kenilworth, where he immediately launched himself into a daily routine of arms practice and physical exercise. When she finally cornered him and demanded that he explain to her what had recently come over him, he gave her a bitter account of how Henry had arrogantly bungled the Poitou campaign, then fled for his own safety, leaving the common soldiery at the mercy of Louis' army. He also added, for good measure, that the nation was being bled dry by a tyrant who was no better than their father had been, and would probably come to the same sticky end.

Simon's temper did not improve when he received information about Henry's latest actions by way of friends he had at Court. The king was driving his sheriffs and justices to exact as much money as possible from alleged transgressors of the law, whether they had actually transgressed or not. He was enforcing legislation that was intended to vilify the Jewish community, who had refused to advance him any more money, on the not unreasonable grounds that he had received it all already. The final straw came with the appointment of a Poitevin half-brother, Aymer, as Bishop of Winchester.

It was probably in Henry's best interests that Simon refused to attend Court, even when summoned to Council meetings, not that they occurred with any frequency. In the meantime he continued with his daily arms practice, where he was frequently watched, first from an upper window, and then from the side wall of the keep, by his oldest son Henry. He was now seven years old and curious about the strange behaviour of his father as he slashed and thrust at a heavily padded Geoffrey of Flint.

When not seeking to maintain his battle readiness in the belief that one day he would need to employ it in the best interests of his adopted country, Simon made frequent trips across to his Leicester estate, where a visibly ageing Merle now ran a thriving orphanage. She never asked for any more money than the modest revenue that came in from the local tenant farmers, and she was always happy to see him, and to eagerly show how his benevolence was preserving young children from starvation and abuse.

Eleanor made no secret of her unease when Simon made these four-day journeys, remembering the elfin girl who had been his travelling companion when he'd first arrived in England. She suspected she had been his mistress at that time, despite Simon's denials. However, there was no reduction in their own sexual activity, and just over a year after Simon's return from Poitou Eleanor gave birth to their fourth son, Guy, with the same ease that the first three had been delivered.

For several years, Simon barely travelled beyond his estates, and the summonses to Court became more and more imperious. Henry had dug himself into a variety of holes, financial, diplomatic and domestic. He and Queen Eleanor still enjoyed a harmonious relationship, as the birth of their two daughters Margaret and Beatrice demonstrated to the entire nation, but Henry was under constant pressure from his Savoyard spouse to promote the interests of her constantly arriving relatives. Every pension or estate that Henry gifted to a Savoyard was deeply resented by English-born nobles who were thereby either further impoverished or denied preferment of their own. There were also a considerable number of Henry's own Poitevin step-family enjoying royal preferment, and they were despised not only by native English nobles, but by the Savoyard faction with whom they quarrelled and occasionally came to blows.

Henry eventually arrived at Kenilworth with only the minimum of notice, for what was heralded in advance as a family visit. But once installed, he left no one in any doubt of his real agenda as they sat at supper on the first evening.

'Why have you not been attending Council meetings, Simon?' he asked pleasantly.

'I see little point, since so far as I can deduce from the reports I receive, the interests of the nation are not well served by those foreigners who now dominate it,' Simon replied gruffly.

Queen Eleanor bristled. 'You refer to my relatives from Savoy?'

'Partly, but there is a worse faction.'

'Poitevins?' Henry asked with a frown.

'Poitevins,' Simon confirmed. 'You cannot allow the honest barons of England to continue to believe that their fortunes and aspirations are held hostage to foreign influence. The Council must be seen to represent the views and wishes of ordinary Englishmen.'

'Such as yourself?' Henry retorted sarcastically. 'If I had not been prepared, some years ago now, to support the ambitions of one particular landless wanderer from France, you would still be tilting at Albigensians.'

'Since that time, I have become a loyal Englishman,' Simon replied as calmly as he could, 'and what is more, I have married into the royal house of England, to which all my future endeavours are committed.'

'We are delighted to hear that, Simon,' Henry said with an expression only normally seen when he was winning at cards or dice, 'since we have two important gifts to bestow upon you in return for that loyalty.'

'Do tell!' his sister enthused, while Simon looked hard into Henry's face for the trickery that he had learned to anticipate.

'First of all, this estate here in Kenilworth. Until now, you have held it on my behalf, and not in your own right. As of this evening, it is yours as a gift, along with the title that you already have.'

'And Leicester?' Simon asked suspiciously.

'Yours also,' Henry beamed back.

'Are these the two gifts, or is there something more?' Simon probed.

Henry smiled even more broadly in the hope of making it sound like an act of great generosity. 'I wish you to accept the office of Seneschal of Gascony.'

Eleanor of Leicester clapped her hands in delight, but was somewhat nonplussed at her husband's seeming indifference to the great honour that was being bestowed upon him. 'Simon, at least have the decency to thank Henry for his generosity.'

'I haven't accepted the position yet,' Simon replied quietly, his eyes still searching Henry's face for evidence of duplicity. 'There are certain questions to which I require answers before I swallow a poisoned chalice.'

Before they retired for the night, Simon had reluctantly accepted the new role, largely at the joyous encouragement of his eager wife. But he had not done so without a full explanation by Henry of where he perceived the main difficulties to lie in the governance of the province, and a firm assurance that Simon would be given a free hand in his new duties, with no interference from Henry or anyone else back in England. Simon also negotiated for a seven-year term of office, two thousand marks a year and the service of fifty knights of the royal entourage to be hand-picked by him.

They were installed in the ancient castle in Bordeaux six months later, where Simon set about dealing with the serious problems that had led to his being chosen for a mission that might result in his death or dishonour. Simon had been warned in advance that the unrest in Gascony was largely the result of the activities of two of its leading noble brigands, Gaston of Bearn and the Viscount of Gramont. Given that Gaston was distantly related to Queen Eleanor, Simon tactfully negotiated a non-aggression pact with him before imprisoning the viscount without trial. While a stunned minor nobility looked on with apprehension, Simon then summoned a third troublemaker, the Viscount of Soule, who learned his lesson the hard way after declining to answer the summons. He was fined ten thousand *molas* when eventually apprehended and dragged to court. Gascony suddenly fell silent, and Simon allowed himself a determined grin before reporting this to Henry.

Simon's next challenge was under his very nose. Bordeaux was due to elect a new mayor, and the two rival parties, the Solers and the Columbines, took to fighting in the narrow streets late one evening. Summoned grumpily from his early night, Simon consigned the Solers' leader to the local gaol, where he died shortly afterwards, having received the sad tidings that his opponents had won the election, and he was no longer Mayor of Bordeaux. Both sides sent their representatives to England with tales of Simon's allegedly brutal interference with the democratic process in Bordeaux, and Henry made a note for future use.

While Simon was distracted by diplomatic duties in Paris, he received word of the threat of widespread revolution about to break out in Gascony in his absence. On his return, he put all further question of rebellion beyond doubt with a bloody encounter that left all the leading malcontents dead on the field. He then moved back to Kenilworth with his wife and family, resigned his commission, and asked only that he be reimbursed the money he had expended from his own purse in preserving English authority in Gascony.

Henry — who did not have the money to give to Simon anyway — refused to accept his resignation, and ordered him back to Gascony for the remainder of his original seven-year term, the expense of which he was to bear personally. Even Queen Eleanor attempted to argue the injustice of this, but Henry seemed to be a man beyond control. All that Simon could do in his own defence was to demand a formal hearing into his management of Gascony, with a view to exposing the treachery of which Henry was capable, even to family members who were doing their best to fulfil his wishes.

The trial was scheduled to take place before a group of commissioners who were sent to Gascony in order to ascertain for themselves what had been happening during Simon's time as seneschal. When the commissioners returned a unanimous verdict in Simon's favour, Henry responded by ordering Simon back to Gascony in order to secure peace among the warring nobles, hand back any properties he had confiscated, and ensure that the province was safe for the reception of Henry himself. He clearly intended to demonstrate that he could be a more effective Seneschal of Gascony than Simon.

Simon returned to discover that in his absence Gaston of Bearn had dishonoured their earlier truce, and had gathered together a force that Simon was obliged to defeat in battle twice before a commissioner sent by Henry ordered Simon to observe the truce. When Simon made the not unreasonable retort that he was not the one who had broken it in the first place, the same commissioner handed him an obviously pre-prepared second order removing him from office. Simon blankly refused to remove himself, and Henry walked into a trap of his own making when he sought the sanction of the Council for the dismissal of his obdurate seneschal. The Council refused, in effect siding with Simon, and Henry was obliged to bribe Simon out of office by promising to repay all that he had expended of his own money in suppressing Gascony, plus a further seven thousand marks by way of compensation. Simon took the money and departed for Paris.

XXVIII

Simon stood watching his oldest son attempting to kill the heir to the English throne. But the blades were guarded, the two young men were heavily padded, and Geoffrey of Flint was carefully supervising their every thrust and parry in the keep of Kenilworth Castle, where they were receiving weapons training. Of the two boys, Henry was the older by a few months, but Prince Edward had the height advantage, standing at slightly over six feet tall, an impressive size for a boy of nineteen.

Then again, Edward had seemingly achieved every milestone in life at a precocious age. He had become a pawn in the royal marriage game at fourteen, when his father Henry had bought off the Gascon ambitions of King Alfonso of Castille by arranging for Edward to marry Alfonso's strikingly beautiful young sister — yet another Eleanor to add to the family collection. They had now been married for four years, but had only one stillborn child to show for the union, which according to the rumours was a passionate one.

But Edward also had his wild side. While his parents were basking in the sun of Gascony — where King Henry continued to demonstrate his superior peace-keeping abilities over those whom Simon had effectively silenced for him — the young heir apparent had fallen under the baleful influence of his mother's family. They were collectively known as 'the Savoyards' by the English-born barons who resented the privileges afforded them by Henry.

One of them in particular, Count Peter, who was Edward's great-uncle, was in the process of building a fine palace on land granted to him on the north bank of the Thames. From there he would ride out, terrorising the local populace as his massive war horse threatened to trample them in its anxiety to avoid its master's spurs. He galloped from one disreputable alehouse to another, running up bills that were never paid, physically abusing those who worked there, and never ceasing to remind them of who he was, and the fact that his niece was the Queen of England. The pale, lanky young man who accompanied him on many of these occasions was sometimes loudly introduced as their next king. However, this didn't prevent complaints and petitions for redress being sent down the road to Westminster, where an increasingly desperate and frustrated Richard of Cornwall sought in vain to curb his nephew's excesses while governing the nation's day-to-day affairs during the extended absence of King Henry.

It was Richard who had pleaded with Simon to do what he could with the wayward young man who clearly had energy to burn. Simon had chosen weapons training as the best way to exhaust Edward, as it had exhausted him at that age. His oldest son Henry had always shown an interest in martial matters, so Simon included him in his tutelage. The two boys hacked and slashed with wild abandon, watched from the side wall of the inner keep by Henry of Almain, Richard's own son by the late Isabel, and a close childhood companion of the long-limbed heir to the throne.

This arrangement had been in place for less than six months when Richard visited Kenilworth, ostensibly in order to take his son and his nephew back to Westminster. But he had a far more important agenda, which he revealed to Simon as they sat having a private supper with Eleanor.

'Simon, you have withdrawn yourself from the nation's affairs for too long, and we now have urgent need of you.'

'We?' Simon asked with a cynical sneer. 'Please do not pretend that your brother has finally come to realise that his best counsel comes from men whose hearts are devoted to England.'

As Eleanor placed a restraining hand on Simon's sleeve, Richard looked down mournfully at his trencher.

'Henry is driven by pride, Simon, as you yourself have had cause to learn, sadly to your cost. But once you get beneath that pride, he is a man in urgent need of wise and unbiased counsel — not the weasel words of relatives who seek only their own preferment.'

'The Savoyards, you mean?' Simon grimaced back at him. 'Hopefully the young Prince Edward is no longer in thrall to them, thanks to our generosity in taking him off your hands and burning up his youthful impetuosity.'

'The Savoyards, certainly,' Richard conceded, 'but now it seems that the Lusignan family are determined to bring Henry down. Not deliberately, of course, but what they are now urging upon him will bankrupt the nation and lead to rebellion. I speak primarily of Guillaume de Lusignan, who now styles himself William de Valence since Henry made him Earl of Pembroke. He is obviously our half-brother, along with his brothers Guy and Aymer, and between them they are filling Henry's head with all sorts of nonsense regarding the latest Crusade and the crown of Sicily.'

'I dearly hope that our brother does not expect my darling Simon to go on Crusade,' Eleanor interposed as she drew closer to her husband and put a protective arm across his shoulder. 'He will be fifty years old later this year, and his fighting days must surely be over.'

'Simon's true value to the nation lies not in the strength of his sword arm, but in his quiet, unbiased wisdom,' Richard replied. 'And — on this occasion — his proven ability to stand up to Henry.'

'Your meaning?' Simon demanded as he poured himself more wine.

Richard sighed deeply. 'What I have to impart — and in particular what I have to ask — must remain entirely privy to the three of us. Were word of it to leak out, I would be risking my head, given Henry's taste for finding traitors under every bed. But I am here to ask that Simon attend the next meeting of the Council, and persuade the barons to deny Henry's latest request for finance.'

It fell uneasily silent, until Simon sought further information. 'What is he planning this time? The conquest of Rome?'

'Almost as foolhardy,' Richard admitted. 'He seeks the crown of Sicily for Prince Edmund.'

'That is part of the Holy Roman Empire, is it not?' Simon asked.

Richard nodded. 'Indeed it is, and in recent years it's been ruled by Germany. But Emperor Frederick died some years ago, and his son Manfred has displeased Pope Innocent. His Holiness has offered to meet part of the expense, should Henry invade Sicily and claim it for England.'

'And the cost to England?'

'Apart from more humiliation, when we are soundly thrashed by the massed armies of Germany?' Richard replied sadly. 'Who knows the financial cost, but — to be honest with you, Simon — there is not enough left in the Treasury to invade even the Isle of Thanet. Added to which it is rumoured that the Welsh are planning a revolt against English rule while they see England so weakened, and we have doubts regarding the loyalty of William de Valence. He may be stirring Henry into this foolhardy Sicilian venture in order to further the Welsh ambitions, so that he might become king in Henry's stead.'

'So you wish me to persuade the Council members to deny Henry his requested finance?' Simon asked. 'Or is it your wish that I gather an army to fight the Welsh?'

'Pray God it will not come to that,' Richard replied with a shiver, 'but while you are about the task of denying Henry his money, you might sound out the loyalty of the barons.'

'To Henry, or to England?' Simon demanded sharply. 'It seems to me that they are not the same thing.'

'I cannot be heard to urge rebellion, Simon, but equally clearly we must somehow prevent the nation becoming further weakened by lack of finance to defend ourselves.'

Simon remained deep in thought for a long minute, while both Eleanor and Richard sat nervously looking down at the board. When Simon looked up from his reverie, he turned to Eleanor. 'What say you, dearest? He is *your* brother also.'

Eleanor smiled sadly. 'I agree with Richard — we cannot allow Henry to squander much-needed riches on an idle tilt for an Italian island for which England has no use anyway. And if it is true that the Welsh are ready to invade, then you must rally the barons into supplying England with an army with which to repulse them.'

'Is Henry currently still in Gascony?' Simon asked Richard.

'At present, yes — but in his latest dispatch to me, he wrote of his intention to return to Westminster in order to urge his suit.'

'Then we must lose no time. Could you summon the Council for, say, one month hence?'

'Of course, but can it not be made sooner? Preferably before Henry sails back across the Channel?'

Simon smiled unpleasantly as he rose from the board. 'It seems that even you fear his wrath, yet you expect me to place my head in the noose once more? I shall accede to your request for the love of my country, and to prevent its loss to foreign adventurers, of which I was once one. But your dear sister has made me an Englishman, and one who does not fear to stand in the way of even its own king, if it be in the best interests of the common people.'

Four days later, as Simon sat deep in thought in the private chamber he shared with Eleanor, who was distractedly working at her latest needlepoint, a messenger was granted entry.

'I come, my lord, from my own lord, Eustache de la Zouche. I had the honour of serving with you on the walls of Chester, and he bids me summon you to his estate without delay.'

'He has more of that excellent wine that he needs my assistance in consuming?' Simon asked jauntily.

'He is at death's door, my lord, and wishes counsel with you before God takes him from us.'

Simon rode east at daylight the following morning, after warning Eleanor that he might not be back before the summoning of the Great Council to Westminster. She clung to him, weeping quietly, and begging him not to place his life in unnecessary danger.

'I shall pray day and night to the merciful God that he guides your words and actions,' she said between sobs.

'You might also offer the same prayer on behalf of your brother,' Simon suggested as he pulled gently away and swung into the saddle.

He broke his journey overnight at his Leicester estate, where a grey-haired and gaunt-looking Merle welcomed him with a warm sisterly kiss. She asked after his family, particularly the two boys who had been under her care while Simon had been in hiding.

'The boys are thriving, thanks partly to you,' Simon replied. 'Henry and Simon have grown to manhood, and Henry in particular seems destined to bear arms under the de Montfort standard that Fulk once held aloft so proudly, God rest his soul. God has also blessed our union with Amaury, who is now sixteen, and shows none of the brutality of his uncle, God be praised. Guy is fourteen and is just discovering that there are women in this world as well as men. Richard is a lively six, charging around the nursery on a make-believe horse, while little Eleanor, our only surviving daughter, is still at her mother's breast, when not being competed for by wet-nurses.'

Merle poured him more wine. 'God has definitely blessed your union, as He has blessed this happy house that you founded all those years ago. Here, His children who have been abandoned by fate may receive His loving bounty.'

Simon chuckled. 'You really *have* become "Saint Merle", as Fulk predicted. But have you no man of your own?'

'Not in body, no. But ever in my heart is the *real* saint who brought me to this place, for whose safety I pray at least twice a day. The man who, if I judge aright, is determined to bring peace to this beautiful land that we found together. God bless you, Simon, and God bless whatever venture it is that has brought you back among us, for in truth you never visit except to dwell briefly on your way to somewhere more important.'

Simon gazed, shame-faced, down at the simple bench upon which his supper had been served to him by Merle, and nodded sadly. 'It is to my eternal shame that I do not visit more often, Merle, but it is also to your credit that I do not need to, safe in the knowledge that my Leicester lands are so well administered.'

It was Merle's turn to look sad as she gently took his hand and gazed searchingly into his eyes. 'It is also in order to keep peace with your gracious wife, is it not? She fears that I may ensnare you into my bed, as she has suspected that I often used to do, in our early days together?'

Simon was unable to meet her eyes as he nodded. 'Something of that also, I grant. But this time I am merely an overnight guest, as I journey to visit Eustache on his deathbed.'

'I am surprised to learn that he is still alive,' Merle replied. 'Was it the pox that laid him low — or perhaps his love of food and wine?'

'Merely the ravages of time, I suspect. He must be fifteen years or more my senior, which only serves to remind me that I have not so many years left to me, even assuming that I do not die on the field of battle.'

'Those days are over, surely?' Merle asked with a brief look of alarm.

Simon shook his head. 'I had so hoped, but it seems that the nation will soon be plunged into a civil war of the king's own making, unless wiser men than those in Henry's Council can be prevailed upon to parley with honest and open hearts. And so I must bid you a good night, that I may be fully rested for what lies in store — whether in Ashby on the morrow, or in Westminster in the days to come.'

'God be with you, on both missions,' Merle whispered as she raised his hand from the trestle table and kissed it, before taking her leave.

XXIX

Early the following evening, Simon was seated by Eustache's bed in his privy chamber. His weeping lady was on the other side, bathing his sweating forehead with scented damp cloths that did nothing to mask the odour of impending death all around him. Eustache managed a weak smile as he reached out for Simon's hand.

'Fear not — it is nothing more contagious than old age, my good friend. It will present *you* with its account in a few more years, which is why it is so important that you act now, while you still have both the bodily strength and that iron will that has brought you thus far in your life.'

'What would you have me do?' Simon asked.

Eustache gave a great sigh. 'Restore the nation to its former greatness, Simon. The days before the noble King Richard was tempted to play the Crusader. As you will know, the harvest has failed yet again, and the people are hard-pressed to put food on their families' tables. They look to King Henry to ease their suffering, and he looks only to the country for more money to hazard his pride across the sea. He does so by forcing his officials, on pain of dismissal from office or worse, to find that money for him wherever it may be located and diverted — lawfully or otherwise.'

'Of what do you speak?'

Eustache gave another frustrated sigh. 'In recent months I have received, here in my hall, supplications from many worthies — sheriffs of counties, justices of the peace, even abbots of holy houses that collect revenues due to the Crown — all of whom seek my protection for doing their job.'

'How may that be?' Simon asked, wondering whether the old man was beginning to ramble in his last hours.

'They receive orders indirectly from Henry — handed down through minor royal functionaries, given the want of any justiciar these past years — that they must seek every possible means of extracting coinage for the Treasury, even if it means stretching their lawful authority like a bowman at his bowstring. They do not shrink from that, since they thereby maintain their offices. However, their fear is that should the king be held to account for what is happening, they will be led to the scaffold as symbolic lambs to the slaughter, while Henry publicly washes his hands of any wrongdoing.'

'That is indeed disconcerting to hear, my old friend,' Simon agreed, 'but how do you believe that I may prevent such abuses?'

'By forcing Henry either to abide by the law that he was sworn to uphold, and implement policies that will relieve people's burdens, or hand over the reins of office to those who are prepared to do both.'

Simon laughed hollowly. 'You know the Court as well as I, Eustache. Those who have his ear most constantly are his distant family — the Poitevins and Savoyards — and their interests are not those of England. They have even begun to infect our next king — the Prince Edward — with their coarse manners and unruly ways, and it is doubtful that there will be any improvement in the state of the nation until their influence is removed. But Henry would not be likely to listen to anything of that nature, I feel certain.'

'Then you must set yourself the task of improving his hearing, Simon. You will not be alone, for there are many on the Council who think as we do. But Henry must be separated from those leeches who see England simply as a pot into which they may piss with impunity.'

'I thank you for your wise counsel, Eustache, and I will do my utmost to...'

The rest of what he intended to say was drowned by a shriek from Imelda de la Zouche, and he looked to where she was staring in horror. Eustache lay motionless, the colour drained from his face, and his rasping had ceased. The physician who had been temporarily dismissed while the two men spoke was hastily summoned back in, and he took one look at the prostrate form and shook his head. Simon led Imelda out, and gave instructions to the steward to organise a funeral.

It was a week before Simon felt the time to be right to slip away from the communal mourning and make his reluctant way down to London, where he learned that Edward had been banished from his father's presence on his recent return. This was due to a persistent rumour that while Henry had been away, Edward had been plotting to usurp the throne. Prince Richard was doing his inadequate best to heal the rift, and risking his own safety by gently suggesting that the instability that had gripped the nation during Henry's lengthy absence in Gascony had been largely caused by petty outbreaks of hostility between the Savoyards and the Poitevins, or 'Lusignans' as they were now more commonly called.

Richard wished to delay no longer in summoning the Council, and Simon was anxious to return to Kenilworth, so the messengers were sent on their various routes. Several days later, the first Council members began to fill the available accommodation within the greatly expanded Palace of Westminster that had been another of Henry's early extravagances. Several key members were still unaccounted for as Henry let it be known that he would wait no longer for the assembly of a group of barons whose only task would be to agree to the obvious need for more royal finance. It was therefore a very apprehensive Simon who took his seat shortly before Henry breezed into the Council Chamber with a goblet of wine in one hand and a chicken leg in the other. He threw himself grumpily into his throne seat, and then glared when he saw Simon among the assembly.

'I take it that my sister is well?' he asked with heavy sarcasm.

'Very well, thank you, Your Majesty,' Simon replied with exaggerated politeness. 'She sends you her love.'

'She also sends me *you*,' Henry responded disdainfully, 'which is the best measure of how much love she feels for me. It is so long since you attended the Council that I am surprised you could still find your way to Westminster.'

'It has, in truth, been so long since the Council was summoned,' Simon countered, 'but at least I remained in England.'

'Only because your face would not have been welcome in Gascony,' was Henry's final jibe before he clapped his hands in annoyance. It fell totally silent as he surveyed the company down the long table. 'Members of Council,' he announced with his usual haughty stare, 'I do not intend to delay you long, since the matter upon which we are met is a simple one. You are here to approve an additional tax to finance the God-given opportunity to add Sicily to our many overseas possessions.'

In the silence that followed, all eyes turned to Simon. He took a deep breath, said a silent prayer, and voiced what everyone else was thinking.

'It would indeed be a simple matter, if the people upon whom this tax would be levied had the wherewithal to pay it. For the past five years there has been one tax after another, and what do we have to show for it? As for "our many overseas possessions", the last time I was across the Channel we held only Gascony, plus a future claim in Castile through the prince's opportune marriage.'

'We only hold Gascony thanks to me,' Henry spat back. 'As for the matter of whether or not the barons can afford it, the ones I can see down the table look sleek enough to me, so are obviously not starving. No less a person than the Pope blesses our initiative in Sicily.'

'The *former* Pope,' Simon pointed out. 'I am advised that the new Pope, Alexander, has sent his delegate over here to excommunicate you for non-payment of money already expended in your cause against the Germans, who still hold Sicily. We are, it would seem, being asked to approve a tax to preserve your immortal soul. And if this latest venture has the blessing of the Pope, why has God blighted the last three harvests?'

There were angry shouts of agreement down the table, and Henry grew red-faced with anger. He glared at Simon and pointed a finger at him that was shaking with rage.

'I *knew* it was a mistake to admit you into the royal company, but I did so only for the happiness of my sister, who you cruelly seduced in order to gain favour and advancement here in England. When first you refused to kneel before me, you were a landless wanderer from France, seeking a fortune in a land that was not yours by birth. You have repaid my generosity very poorly!'

'Not as poorly as *other* foreign adventurers who have been granted estates and heiresses in this country that you have sworn to rule with justice and equality!' Simon thundered back, all caution thrown to the wind. Encouraged by the supportive growls and oaths by which he was surrounded down the Council table, he let fly another volley. 'As for landless adventurers, you were handed your throne on the death of your father John, who was known behind his back as "John Lackland". He usurped the throne while his brother was embarked on a *real* Crusade, and not a greedy land-grab to feed yet another royal mouth. Your father was obliged to come to terms with the barons in the matter of how he ruled the nation in a series of undertakings that were dishonoured, first by him, and now by you. Your claim to rule this land is no better than his, and you have, if anything, proved yourself *less* worthy than him!'

Henry rose to his feet, crimson in the face. 'You speak treason!' he yelled.

'He speaks it fluently, Henry,' came a loud voice from the doorway, 'but unfortunately for you, so do we!'

All eyes turned to the entrance, where a group of knights led by Roger and Hugh Bigod stood with drawn swords. From behind them, Richard de Clare and Peter of Savoy advanced with drawn weapons onto the throne dais towards Henry. He sank back, the colour gone from his face as he stared at the blades.

'Am I to be seized and dragged from my own Court?' he stammered.

Hugh Bigod stepped between Henry and the Council seated slightly below him, and addressed the company. 'Would any noble here seek to intervene were we to take this allegedly royal personage from hence and remove his head in yon courtyard outside?'

In the stunned silence that followed, it was Simon who spoke. 'Cutting off the head would not prevent the young limbs from working,' he observed sagely. 'There are royal princes who would seek vengeance, and the nation would be plunged into civil war. Better that we have a king who rules through a wise new Council. Unless I misjudge this assembly, we have here the makings of such a Council, were His Majesty to give an undertaking to be governed by its edicts.'

Hugh Bigod lowered his sword and grinned back at Henry. 'It may be that your choice of a brother-in-law was a wiser one than you have thus far conceded. Were such a new Council to be appointed, would you agree to be bound by its rulings?'

Henry's throat was by now so dry that he could barely form the words, but his vigorous nods confirmed that ruling through a Council was preferable to having his head removed. 'Willingly,' he croaked, 'but unless anarchy is to govern the nation, we must be careful in those we select for such advice.'

'No Lusignans!' Peter of Savoy bellowed from behind Hugh Bigod.

'And no Savoyards!' came a responding yell from William de Valence down the table.

Simon stepped up onto the throne dais, then turned to address the entire assembly. 'This must be achieved carefully, but swiftly. We need a commission to be appointed — an assembly to represent *all* the interests of the people of England, common as well as noble — that shall, in turn, determine the composition of a new Council to advise His Majesty, without whose blessing the king must be powerless to act. But be under no illusion — should this venture fail, and should King Henry one day regain the sole sovereign power, those who have embarked upon the creation of this new Council will be accounted traitors, and will be hanged in public view until their rotting corpses have fallen from their heads, which in turn shall be spiked on London Bridge. On that understanding, who among you is prepared to strike a blow for a new and better England?'

His challenging gaze swept across the nobles around the Council table, some of whom could not meet his eyes. Finally, a lone voice broke the silence.

'You among all of us possess the courage, my Lord of Leicester. It must be your choice.'

Simon shook his head. 'That would be to replace one tyrant with another. Henry, would you be prepared to choose twelve men whom you trust, to be joined by twelve of my choosing, in order to form a commission that shall report back to this assembly on the creation of a new Council to advise you in all matters?'

Henry made his choice of twelve in a voice still hoarse with fear and outrage.

Simon made his own selections, before announcing, 'We meet in Oxford one month from today.'

XXX

'They are saying that you saved Henry's life,' Eleanor told Simon as she threw her arms around him and hugged him close.

Simon grunted. 'You should not listen to kitchen gossip, my sweet. But it's true that if he hadn't agreed to the establishment of a new Council, the Bigods may have consigned him to the Tower to cool his heels and re-think his attitude.'

Eleanor's face fell. 'I know my own brother, and once he regains his position of strength he will be unforgiving, even towards his own sister's husband. You must tread carefully, Simon.'

'If I were given to treading carefully,' he replied, 'I would not have ventured this far. But now I am committed, and whatever else may befall the nation, I am a marked man in Henry's eyes. Either this new proposal meets with success, or you may visit my head on Tower Bridge.'

'What must you do next?'

'I must travel back to Oxford by the month's end, to devise a new form of government.'

'Alone?'

'I sincerely hope not, since there are over twenty others chosen to assist in the task.'

'I meant must you travel there alone?'

He looked down at her and smiled. 'Do you recall the first time we met? *That* was at Oxford, and I could not kneel to Henry. Not much has changed since, it would seem.'

Eleanor's mouth set in an expression of displeasure. 'Your woman at the time — the French girl with no hair — she was very rude to me.'

'She is now an Englishwoman with very little grey hair, but she was never *my* woman.'

'So you constantly assure me. But you do not answer my question.'

'Do I not? Well, you *shall* ride with me to Oxford. Bring Henry and Simon also, so that they may see for themselves how hazardous a business it is to be too close to the throne of England.'

All those who had been chosen as Commission members honoured their pledges to attend. Within days it had been agreed that the nation would henceforth have a fifteen-member Baronial Council to advise Henry in all matters, whether he considered that he needed such advice or not. The king could not act without the consent of Council, all members of which would swear oaths of allegiance, not only to him but to the people of England. The office of Justiciar would be reinstated, and the corruptible system of legal administration at a local level under sheriffs was to be replaced by a new justice network under which knights would enforce the king's peace in those lands that they held from him.

This bundle of reforms became known as 'The Provisions of Oxford', and Henry appeared to agree to them without demur when they were presented to him at Westminster. He and Simon then sat with Prince Richard in order to elect the members of this new Council. At Henry's personal request, Simon agreed to become a member, in return for Henry agreeing that it would contain no Lusignans. This meant the exclusion of the powerful William de Valance, who was still guarding the Welsh Marches in his capacity as Earl of

Pembroke, and he blamed Simon personally for his fall from preferment. However, the Savoyard faction was still represented by Peter of Savoy, at the queen's insistence.

Although Simon had succeeded in establishing the Council, it was soon obvious that his next battle would be to ensure unity within it, if it was to avoid Henry's immediately adopted tactic of seeking to undermine it by bribing selected members with new estates. It rapidly emerged that the newly created Baronial Council was far from unanimous in the matter of how far the reforms should go, with Simon urging towards greater representation of, and concern for, the 'common folk', while members of the old nobility such as Richard de Clare, Fifth Earl of Hertford, Sixth Earl of Gloucester, Second Lord of Glamorgan and Eighth Lord of Clare, were nervous of the incursions that had already been made into the status quo of power within the nation. He was the stepson of Prince Richard by the latter's first marriage to Isabel Marshal, and he had inherited the ambitions of his Marshal forebears.

Hugh Bigod, who was created Justiciar of England by virtue of the Provisions of Oxford, sat somewhere between these two extremes. He would sometimes be required to mediate between Simon and Richard de Clare, both of whom respected him for his bold initiative in forcing King Henry, at sword-point, to concede the need to rule by Council. Henry sensed that there would be insufficient unity among the rebels were he to renege on his undertaking, and he embarked on a series of secret discussions with Pope Urban. In return for a promise to commit an English army to the cause of Rome once he was free to do so, Henry was able to announce, to a muted and somewhat shamefaced Council, that he had received papal absolution from his sworn undertakings, and that the Council was dismissed.

Simon sat fuming behind the walls of Kenilworth Castle, as he learned daily of the systematic unstitching of all he had strived for. A further knife was twisted into the open wound by the defection of William de Clare to the royal camp, and Prince Edward's announcement that he would offer military support for his father, in which he would no doubt employ the skills he had learned while a guest of 'Uncle Simon'. In disgust, Simon took his entire family off to their relatives' estates in the Île-de-France, where the de Montfort cousins delighted in each other's renewed company until Simon received secret intelligence from England that raised his hopes of continuing what he had begun.

The Welsh had risen in rebellion under Llywelyn ap Gruffudd. The only powerful baron who could have offered any hope of resisting the Welsh, Richard de Clare, Earl of Pembroke, had recently died. This left his son and heir Gilbert in minority under the wardship of Sir Humphrey de Bohun, Earl of Hereford, another member of the original Council that King Henry was now ignoring. Realising that there was no hope of Henry being able to raise an army to halt the Welsh, Humphrey sent urgent messages to Simon in his self-imposed exile, promising the support of both Hereford and Glamorgan for any future political reforms that he might have in mind if he would return and defend England. Within the month, Simon and his family were back in Kenilworth, and the Welsh had withdrawn back into their hills, unwilling to take on an England that might become united once more.

Simon had finally accepted that Henry would never agree to being governed by a Council. Therefore, this time he summoned his *own* Council to Oxford, containing those barons he could most trust to rule the nation, defying Henry to do anything about it. For several months he was the *de facto* King of England, summoning a new assembly that was to contain two representatives from every shire as the first form of a true 'parliament of the people' that England had ever known. But he was reaching too far for most tastes, and even some of those formerly loyal to him began to question what he was about.

Henry, still in Paris, took the diplomatic route, by calling in King Louis IX of France as an arbitrator. Simon had been subtly side-stepped, since on the surface Henry's offer to submit to mediation seemed a reasonable alternative to civil war, and those barons who were still wavering urged Simon to accept the outcome of Louis' ruling. Simon suspected the worst, but was not to know that Henry had bribed Louis with an undertaking never to wage war again across the Channel in exchange for a ruling in his favour. Simon raged, hurled things at the wall and bellowed in disbelief when he learned that in the 'Mise of Amiens' Louis had come down firmly in favour of the right of every monarch to rule unopposed in the kingdom granted to him by God.

Simon, still in Kenilworth and finalising a list of items for the agenda of the next Council that he intended call, received urgent news that Prince Edward had, in the king's name, rallied many of the barons under his banner on the promise of future preferment. Among them was Gilbert of Glamorgan, whose forces had begun to mobilise to the west along with a large contingent supplied by England's constant enemy, and inveterate trouble-maker, Llywelyn of Wales, while Edward intended to complete the pincer movement by marching from his eastern strongholds.

A family meeting inside the walls of Kenilworth became a council of war, as Simon planned the deployment of the force he had available. It was agreed that the main army would march west into Wales, led by Simon, with his oldest son Henry alongside him. Simon the Younger was sent to Leicester, to rally what men at arms he could, then instructed to return by way of Kenilworth before joining his father wherever he might be found. They would then turn back north-east and take on the royal army under Prince Edward, which had last been heard of in Ludlow, where he had been joined by a consortium of barons who preferred to be ruled by a king rather than a foreign-born usurper. They now included not only the powerful Roger Mortimer of Wigmore, but also the treacherous Gilbert de Clare.

A wild plan came to Simon's mind as he called Simon the Younger into his chamber late on the night before he was due to head north-east for Leicester.

'Simon, I have in mind seeking out Llywelyn of Wales, and joining his force to mine before we strike back to Ludlow.'

'But he is an enemy of England, is he not?'

Simon laughed hollowly. 'And how do you think they describe *me*? But once Llywelyn has served his purpose, I will appoint him Lord of the Welsh Marches. He will have every reason to keep the peace in the name of England, and he will have no-one as powerful as himself to worry about.'

'And think you that he will agree?'

'That remains to be seen, but our own limited force would benefit greatly from being joined by his.'

'It is still a hazardous plan, and Llywelyn himself may seek a reward from Edward by handing you over.'

'That is the risk I must take. But when you reach Leicester, there is a favour I would ask of you. I would be obliged if you would say nought about it to your mother.'

'Ask, and it shall be done.'

'You remember the lady called Merle, who runs the orphanage there? You were there some time yourself, with your brother Henry.'

'The scrawny lady who looked like a nun and ordered us around like a captain at arms?'

'The very same,' Simon said. 'I wish you to say goodbye to her on my behalf. Tell her that I always loved her as a true sister, and ask that she offers prayers for my soul.'

'You fear you will be killed?'

'I do not have the confidence that this old body will withstand any long drawn-out challenge on the field of battle, and yet I must be seen in the vanguard of our men, if they are not to adjudge me a coward.'

'Pray God that your fears are groundless.'

'I do not fear for myself, but for England, should I fail in this final act. Should I do so, I consign your mother's welfare to your keeping.'

'That would surely be my brother Henry's privilege?'

'If I am to die, then I have no doubt that Henry will also die in the attempt to save me. He has my wild impetuosity, whereas you inherited your mother's ability to reflect before acting.'

'I also inherited her love for you,' Simon croaked as he flung himself at his father and began to sob.

Simon choked back his own tears as he broke the embrace and stepped backwards to look his second son sternly in the face. 'If you truly love me, do not fail to deliver my message to the Lady Merle.'

XXXI

Simon muttered a prayer in the chamber window alcove in which he stood, watching his second son crossing the Great Mere with his handful of men at arms, heading into the rising sun on his way to Leicester. He reached it shortly after the main meal of the day had been served at the orphanage, and as he dismounted Merle was waiting for him in front of its main entrance, wringing her hands.

'You bring me news of your father's death?' she whispered hoarsely, the pain deepening the lines in her face.

'No, my lady,' Simon said, 'although he is about to go into battle against the king's force, to defend what he believes to be best for England. I bring you a message from him, that he loves you like a sister, and he entreats you to offer prayers for his soul when he is gone.'

Merle nodded sadly. 'He must also have had the same sad dream as I. I saw him lying on the field of battle, his body broken into many pieces. It must be an ill omen for us both. But come in and eat.'

While Simon organised the feeding of his small force, and set about rounding up more volunteers to wear the de Montfort livery for more than show, Merle was making plans of her own. She took her assistant Elizabeth into her confidence, and obtained from her an assurance that she would look after the children as diligently as Merle had done. Then, while the entire company slept, she climbed into the back of a baggage wagon and hid under a mountain of tent canvas, smiling to herself the next morning as she was awoken by the jerking movement of the wagon. By the time she slipped out again, they were under the walls of Kenilworth, and the canvas was being put to good use.

In Simon the Younger's absence, his father had begun the march westward with the main rebel army, his older son Henry riding proudly alongside him. In consequence, when various local lords had begun to send their men to the de Montfort standard, there had been no-one in residence at Kenilworth to receive them. It fell to Simon the Younger to welcome them, and to take command of a considerably swollen force. Because the new arrivals had been allocated most of the barrack space within the castle walls, Simon opted to encamp his own original force on the land immediately in front of the castle, and in his over-confidence had mounted no guard.

They had been tracked by scouts sent out by Roger Mortimer, and as they lay under the canvas they were quickly routed. Many of them were killed in their night attire before they could seek shelter behind the castle walls, from where a group of defenders drove off Mortimer's men. Most significantly, the royal band had captured several de Montfort standards, which they were soon to put to good use. Merle had watched the skirmish from the safety of an old windmill. Once the enemy had ridden off — and while what was left of Simon's force was inside Kenilworth, being fed and having their wounds dressed — she was able to slip into one of the abandoned tents and equip herself with appropriate attire for someone who wished to march with an army without being recognised as a woman.

Over in Wales, Simon Senior had persuaded Llywelyn to augment the rebel army with his own fierce Welshmen. None of them — their leader included — needed any great encouragement to throw themselves at the hired help of the hated Plantagenet dynasty that had held them under conquest for so long. From his new Welsh ally Simon learned that the bulk of the royal force lay at Worcester, and he opted for a siege. In the early light of an August morning, with mist rising off the water beneath them, the main force formed narrow lines in order to cross the Avon using the somewhat frail Abbey Bridge. They would then form up again in the meadow to the south of Evesham.

Simon was expecting his son to come in from the east with his relieving force. As the sun began to heat the chainmail on the infantrymen, and the eager Welsh bowmen began swatting angrily at the flies that were beginning to annoy them, there came a call from an advance sentinel that an armed force was approaching from Evesham itself, and that they were flying de Montfort pennants. With a sigh of relief, Simon ordered his men to stand down, and stood up in his saddle in order to catch sight of the welcome younger Simon riding at the head of his relief force. He was joined by Llywelyn, who was more familiar with the livery of the local barons, and was suspicious of the oncoming ranks.

'Has Mortimer joined your son's retinue?' he asked anxiously.

'Of *course* not,' Simon replied dismissively. 'His is the mainstay of Edward's royal army.'

'Then we had better call the men to arms without delay, for I see his battle standard to the rear of this advancing force, which is gaining speed even as we dally. Call to horse!'

Simon turned his own mount and galloped back to where his men were beginning to pitch their tents in anticipation of an idle day. As they looked up at the sound of pounding hooves, he screamed them into action.

'A-horse! To arms! The enemy is hard upon us!'

They had been caught in a trap of their own making. Behind them was the River Avon, a huge obstacle to any heavily armed man seeking to retreat, and it was doubtful whether the tottering wooden bridge they had carefully crossed earlier would withstand the combined weight and motion of an entire army in hasty retreat. They could only stand and fight, with no prospect of falling back. The front ranks of the enemy were already dismounting, their swords raised in anticipation of an easy slaughter.

It was over quickly. The bowmen had not even been able to put shaft to bow when they were cut down in droves by heavily armed dismounted royal knights, who showed no mercy to the old enemy. Behind them, knots of Simon's men received the front ranks of Edward's force with stern resistance, trading blow for blow as they were inexorably pushed back towards the river.

Simon yelled across to his son Henry, and they stood shoulder to shoulder, taking on all comers. All around them, men from both sides were screaming in their death agonies as they fell on the muddy ground of the river bank, but father and son slashed and thrust in an effort to fight their way out. Then Henry's left arm weakened, and as he staggered sideways under the blow of a battle-axe on his shield, his head was split from crown to shoulder by a huge warrior's broadsword.

Simon saw his son fall, and a crimson rage misted his eyes as he cleaved the man's arm from his shoulders, then began hacking wildly in a fury at anything that came within his line of sight. He grinned to himself as he counted the eighth man falling to his sword, and realised that he had exceeded his own record all those years ago at the gates of Carcassonne. Then he sensed a blow coming from his right, and turned quickly, at which point his right leg gave way under the pressure placed on his old battle wound.

As he made efforts to correct his stagger, he received the first of several blows from a select group of Mortimer's men who had been commissioned to either bring back the traitor's body, or not return at all. The first cut through his neck, severing his head from his shoulders, while the second removed his left arm, and the third his left leg. The remaining limbs were hacked off with triumphant shouts, and it was left to William Maltravers to reach down and claim the testicles with a deft flick of his dagger. The head was lifted from the mud, still in its battle helm, and carried triumphantly back to Wigmore Castle as an object of amusement. The mutilated remains were kicked, urinated on, and generally abused while the remaining royal troops put paid to the remnant of the rebel army as they attempted to ford the Avon in their heavy chainmail, leaving the sluggish stream red with their blood.

This was Simon the Younger's first indication, as he rode in from the south, that all had not gone well for the main body of his father's army. This was confirmed by a man who had succeeded in crossing the river, and had evaded capture by the enemy, but who now lay in his own welter on the far bank, beyond any earthly assistance. Simon cantered his leading horsemen over the river bridge in time to scatter those of Edward's troops who had begun to rob the corpses of the dead, then turned his own mount back sadly in search of his father's remains. He found a badly mutilated body lying in the tattered remains of a de Montfort surcoat, minus its head, but confirmed that he was contemplating his father's corpse by reaching inside the chainmail for the cross that Simon always wore. It had been a present from his mother on their wedding day; a mother to whom the news had to be broken without delay.

Simon knelt by the body for long enough to bid a fond farewell to the man he had so idolised, and through his tears he offered a prayer for the salvation of his soul. Then he walked away to remount his horse, paying no attention to the slightly built man at arms who was staring at the scene from a few yards away. He would have been startled, had he remained, to see the same person throw off the chainmail hood covering their head, to reveal a thin thatch of white hair and the most intense dark eyes that flooded with tears. Merle threw herself over the remaining torso and cried herself to the point of exhaustion.

The crows were returning to their roosts late that afternoon as Merle — this time more appropriately dressed in a long black gown that had been hidden in Simon's personal baggage train — led two young monks from the nearby abbey down to the flyblown remains. She then begged them to carry it off the field and give it a decent burial in their grounds.

Almost a year to the day later, the elderly nun rose for the final time from the depression in the ground in which she had planted a cypress tree. She wiped her hands on the cloth she had brought with her, and through her tears Merle dedicated it to the remains of the man who was buried beneath it in the abbey gardens.

'They would not let you be buried in sacred English soil, so I have given you a tree from the land in which we first met. You always knew that my frail body was yours should you ever desire it — but did you know that you also commanded my very soul? You see me now, the bride of Christ that many predicted I would finally become, and I shall visit this spot on every one of the days that now remain to me, in order to honour your final wish that I pray daily for your soul.'

By the time that she made her final visit, supported on either arm by two young novitiates who revered the saintly old lady, Simon de Montfort, Sixth Earl of Leicester, had been dead for sixteen years.

A NOTE TO THE READER

Dear Reader,

Thank you for taking the time to read this final novel in a series of seven that between them cover the twelfth century, a period during which England was transformed beyond recognition. I hope that it lived up to your expectations. Once again, the basic plot line was written for me by the events that really happened during another of the many unsettled periods of that tumultuous age.

Most people have heard of Simon de Montfort. Some might even be able to tell you that he was 'the father of the first English Parliament.' But very few could tell you anything more about the man behind the name, myself included until I began researching his life. Very few facts remain on record of what seems to have been a life led in the pure spirit of medieval chivalry. He was a formidable warrior, certainly, but he also had something of the romantic troubadour about him. He was deeply pious, and lived a life of remarkable purity for a man of his era, while fighting fearlessly for what he believed to be right. In other circumstances, he might well have become one of those legendary armed monks who came down to us in the chronicles of those times as 'Knights Templar', but Destiny had other things in store for him.

He arrived in England a landless adventurer, seeking to reclaim the forfeited family Earldom of Leicester. He departed this world married to a royal princess, the brother-in-law of a tyrant whose refusal to honour either his coronation vows or the terms of the 'Great Charter' caused him to forfeit the allegiance of the one man who could have turned his reign into something more glorious. As it was, Henry III of England proved himself as unworthy of loyalty as his even more infamous father King John, and Simon de Montfort was fated to die in his attempts to make the English monarch more accountable to his people.

At Evesham, Simon paid the ultimate price for being a man ahead of his time, a God-fearing man of principle who would himself have made a worthy monarch in the tradition of the better side of Richard the Lionheart. As events transpired, he died grubbily on the field of battle, his corpse hacked limb from limb, and his memory as obscure as the location of his final resting place. What was left of his corpse after the trophy-hunters had left was originally interred under the altar of Evesham Abbey, only to be removed on the order of an indignant Henry III and reburied in obscurity under a tree. In filling in some of the blanks in his story, I have taken the liberty of attributing this reburial to a devoted friend.

I hope that you are sufficiently encouraged to acquire the other novels in the series, but whether you are or not, I'd love to get feedback from you on this one — or perhaps even a review of it on **Amazon** or **Goodreads**. Or, if you prefer, send your thoughts to me on my author website, **davidfieldauthor.com**.

David

Sapere Books is an exciting new publisher of brilliant fiction and popular history.

To find out more about our latest releases and our monthly bargain books visit our website:
saperebooks.com

Printed in Great Britain
by Amazon